SHOW

ALSO BY SHANE PEACOCK

The Great Farini (1995)
Unusual Heroes (2002)
The Artist and Me (2016)
The Book of Us (2022)

Dylan Maples Adventures
The Mystery of Ireland's Eye (1999)
The Secret of the Silver Mines (2000)
Bone Beds of the Badlands (2001)
Monster in the Mountains (2003)
Phantom of Fire (2019)

The Dark Missions of Edgar Brim Trilogy
The Dark Missions of Edgar Brim (2016)
Monster (2018)
Demon (2019)

Seven series
Last Message (2012)
Double You (2014)
Separated (2016)

The Boy Sherlock Holmes series
Eye of the Crow (2007)
Death in the Air (2008)
Vanishing Girl (2009)
The Secret Fiend (2010)
The Dragon Turn (2011)
Becoming Holmes (2014)

The Northern Gothic Mysteries (for adult readers)
As We Forgive Others (2024)
A Place of Secrets (2025)

SHOW

SHANE
PEACOCK

We acknowledge financial support for our publishing activities: the Government of Canada, through the Canada Book Fund and The Canada Council for the Arts; the Government of Ontario, through the Ontario Arts Council, Ontario Creates, and the Ontario Book Publishing Tax Credit.

Library and Archives Canada Cataloguing in Publication

Title: Show / Shane Peacock.
Names: Peacock, Shane, author
Identifiers: Canadiana (print) 20240537947 | Canadiana (ebook) 20240537955 |
ISBN 9781770867963 (softcover) | ISBN 9781770867970 (EPUB)
Subjects: LCGFT: Novels.
Classification: LCC PS8581.E234 S56 2025 | DDC jC813/.54—dc23

United States Library of Congress Control Number: 2024951790

Cover and interior text design: Marijke Friesen
Manufactured by Friesens in Altona, Manitoba in April 2025.

MIX
Paper | Supporting responsible forestry
FSC® C016245
www.fsc.org

Printed using paper from a responsible and sustainable resource, including a mix of virgin fibres and recycled materials.

Printed and bound in Canada.

EU RP eucomply OÜ
Pärnu mnt 139b-14, 11317 Tallinn, Estonia
hello@eucompliancepartner.com, +3375690241

DCB Young Readers
An imprint of Cormorant Books Inc.
260 Ishpadinaa (Spadina) Avenue, Suite 502, Tkaronto (Toronto), ON M5T 2E4, Canada

Suite 110, 7068 Portal Way, Ferndale, WA 98248, USA

www.dcbyoungreaders.com
info@cormorantbooks.com / www.cormorantbooks.com

"All the world's a stage,
And all the men and women merely players."
William Shakespeare

For Canada

CHAPTER ONE
APPROACH AND DIVERSION

Long ago, or perhaps it was yesterday, passenger balloons were floating like bubbles in the sky as Solomon Hunt neared the city of York. He gazed up at them, feeling anxious, a country kid bearing just the clothes on his back and a few adventures in his satchel. York was a big place, at least for North Britain. Solomon's family could hear it rumbling from their farm. But while his father was alive, he had forbidden them from coming here and the boy had never disobeyed him, until now. "Evil lurks in its streets," the late Jacob Hunt had told them. Solomon didn't care about that anymore. Today, the world was wide open to him.

His stomach was growling by the time he was among the big buildings, but he'd brought no money to buy food. It had seemed wrong to take even a single dollar bill from the jar that was kept high on a shelf in the kitchen — the jar his father had pointed at as he lay writhing on the floor, clutching at his chest. The boy had left it all for his poor mother, for his little brother and sister — what there was of it. He would get them more and soon. He had to. That would be his first mission here in the great unknown.

He moved along the black and white avenues, taken aback by the noise, the smells, the grime, trying to calm himself and think clearly. A dirigible, cigar-shaped and gleaming, hung directly above in the smoke-filled air. Solomon was mesmerized by it — it was hard to believe that such things existed. He mounted a plank sidewalk and saw someone sitting in the flow of pedestrians, begging, holding out his hand for food, and a woman leaning against a wall as if she were unable to stand. He noticed how many First Inhabitants were walking the streets too, dressed half in their native garb and half in clothes like his, poverty stricken. And yet, as he neared the lower part of the city at the lake, palatial buildings, made for folks with a great deal of money, stood so tall they seemed to be going up to the skies. They glittered when the sun came through the smog, looking down on the unfortunate as if gloating.

Solomon had always dreamed of an extraordinary life, imagined what he could do and be as he read the thrilling tales in his books, but he had to be wide awake now. "Find something for them," he told himself. "My fortune will come later."

This city would pale next to a metropolis in the American Empire, where diversions were everywhere, but York certainly had its entertainments, and to Solomon, everything seemed thrilling. There *must* be opportunities here. America could wait a few weeks, and he needed money to get there anyway. A motorized vehicle roared past, weaving through the carriages with a cloud of stink behind it and a klaxon horn honking. It made the boy jump.

He had read in the red pages sections of news dailies he had found discarded on the country roads that if you went farther toward the lake in York on an artery called Yonge, there would be theaters, and he knew that in those halls, actors, high-rope performers, and acrobats from exotic countries like the Kingdom of England and the European Empire were often on display. He knew too that that was where the so-called freaks were — people whom folks gave their hard-earned cash to stare at, even here in North Britain. Amusements paid well and Solomon figured there was employment in one of those theaters, even if just sweeping the floors. What a place to begin to make his way, to start to be someone!

In most of his adventure books, the hero left home and entered upon exploits and grew rich without setbacks. But Solomon's hands shook as he stood staring at the brass-handled doors of the Grand Opera House at the corner of Yonge and Adelaide streets. Then one opened and a showwoman came out, rushing past him, her face colorful and powdered, giving him a smile his father would have said he deplored. Solomon blushed and stepped back.

At that moment, another entrance opened across the street and the music that spilled out was unlike anything he had ever heard — hypnotic notes from some sort of flute. "*SPRINGER'S DIME MUSEUM*" read a sign above the windowless door. "SNAKE BOY TODAY!" shouted a sandwich board nearby. Solomon couldn't look away.

"Step right up! See the Snake Boy bite the heads off living creatures! See him drink their blood!" cried a short man in an American accent. Solomon had never seen anyone dressed like him. He wore a bowler hat and a red suit with a yellow waistcoat and gold chain. He had a big belly and there were scars on his face.

The man noticed Solomon through the passing traffic. He paused, licked his fingers, and smoothed his eyebrows.

Solomon crossed the street toward him and was almost struck by a man on a nag and then a fancy vehicle a driver could barely control. The showman's eyes widened as the boy approached, glaring at his rough trousers and boots and his soiled work shirt.

"Clear off, you little rat!" he shouted.

Solomon Hunt backed away, all the way to Yonge Street again and around the corner so the man couldn't see him in the crowds walking south. But his fear quickly turned to curiosity. *The Snake Boy?*

He turned and glanced along Adelaide Street once more. The man was still there, shouting out his spiel, facing the other direction now, trying to draw folks into the dime museum theater. Most pedestrians looked away, but a few poorer people stopped and heard him out. One or two gave him coins and entered.

Solomon moved down Yonge, but an alleyway soon appeared, leading toward the back of the building where the snake child was performing his gruesome act. He knew he shouldn't — that everyone should leave such things alone, but Solomon turned into the alleyway — walking toward the sound of the strange flute as it slithered out an opening in a rear door.

CHAPTER TWO
THE SNAKE BOY

The alley was dark and damp. It smelled of urine. About ten strides in, behind the boy, something landed on a trash can and knocked the lid to the ground. It crashed and rattled on the stones. He turned around to face his assailant, his heart pounding. But all he saw was a black cat scurrying away. Up ahead, the music was growing louder. Solomon figured this was his last chance to leave but he couldn't turn back, not when he was so close. He kept imagining what was inside those walls. As he neared the building, he could see that it indeed had a back door.

It wasn't open, not all the way. A crack of bright light, about three or four inches across, sent a red bar out into the alley. There was a padlock on the door, attached to a big chain that stopped the door from opening any farther. He moved up to the crack and peered in.

There was the Snake Boy, right there, in a tiny room that smelled of animals and their refuse. The red light lit the windowless space with a dim glow. It seemed like a prison. The performer wasn't facing the alleyway or the crack in the door. What Solomon saw was his profile, and it was obvious that others, beyond the sightline out here in the alley, were staring at the act. A few hens bobbed back and forth on the little stage, caged behind a wire fence with the snake child who sat on a hard floor, dressed in leopard skin like Tarzan of the Apes, barefooted. Several big snakes slithered near him, one twisting around his leg. The hens kept their distance. A deep voice, sounding like a cross between God and the Devil, began booming in the room.

"Ladies and gentleman, for your viewing pleasure this day, we have *the Snake Boy*! Raised in the jungles of Siam, he eats nothing but raw meat and loves the taste of blood. He drinks it as his liquid sustenance. He subsists on nothing else. Our scientists and medical experts alike have studied this phenomenon, but none truly understand him. We bring him to you today as an exclusive presentation of Sunshine Entertainments, originating in Florida, U.S. of the A.E. I might add that all around him, you see displayed the pickled remains of human babies, the likes of which can be seen nowhere else on earth! But watch closely now as *the Snake Boy* places the head of the unsuspecting chicken in his mouth and viciously bites it off! Then he will happily drink its life blood! Observe in silence but listen for the sounds of the habit of a creature unknown to our civilized world."

The man's terrible words made Solomon shiver. But he couldn't resist seeing more. Who could? He *had* to get closer. He doubted that anyone would be able to spot him since he was off to the side of the stage and couldn't see the audience, just the crude setting, the snakes, chickens, and the poor boy presented as a freak. The crack in the door was narrow, but Solomon Hunt was slim and double-jointed. He could twist and turn all his limbs in disgusting ways. In fact, he often did it as a trick … to impress friends and disturb girls.

But as he started trying to get through, squeezing the crack a little wider, the Snake Boy noticed him. Solomon had gotten one arm in and was holding his breath to make his chest thin. It seemed like he wouldn't make it. The little performer had turned to seize a chicken and happened to glance toward the door. Their eyes met. Solomon jerked back, pulled himself out, and ducked down. The chain rattled. He waited for the Snake Boy to cry out or for a show employee to come running around the corner into the alley. But all Solomon heard was the sound of spectators gasping. The Snake Boy must have turned and done his terrible deed.

Solomon stood up and looked through the crack again. The little performer was regarding his audience now, blood trickling down his chin, the headless chicken lying motionless on the ground before him.

"Thank you, ladies and gentlemen. Come and see us again. There will be another show in fifteen minutes. Did I mention that at eight o'clock each evening our young phenomenon devours a live snake? It is our ultimate moment! Return then and bring your friends! We will be pleased to host yu'all … for a slightly increased admission. Good afternoon. Sunshine Entertainments brings one and all this continent's most extraordinary shows! Entertainment, my dear citizens, is everything!"

The audience moved out, murmuring as they went, then there was silence. The Snake Boy waited for a moment and then did something marvelous. He lifted the headless chicken to its feet, popped its head out from under its wing, and let it run off into another part of the enclosure. Then he stood up and walked toward Solomon Hunt!

Solomon turned to move away, but after just a few steps, he heard a grunt. Turning back, he could see the Snake Boy looking out through the crack, his face almost bulging through it. He was frantically motioning for his visitor to come toward him and moving the fingers on his other hand to mime the act of speaking.

"You want to talk with *me*?" asked Solomon.

The performer grunted again, loudly, like some sort of animal, and vigorously nodded his head. He was obviously mentally incompetent, probably deaf and mute, certainly illiterate.

Solomon walked back to the crack.

"Look, I have to be on my way. I can't stop here. I've got to —"

The Snake Boy stepped back and Solomon sensed a sort of aura about him, as if there were a light shining down upon him from above. It was a strange sensation to emanate from such a wretched little person. It made Solomon Hunt shiver. The Snake Boy grunted and motioned to him again, this time glancing toward the inner entrance to the room, as if afraid of something or someone.

"You want me to come in?"

The Snake Boy nodded, and a grin came over his face.

Solomon wondered if this creature's plan was to draw him in and then have those slimy owners attack, taking Solomon's clothes and money. Little did they know — the North Britain boy had no possessions at all, except his books.

But there was an expression on the Snake Boy's face — a terror that indicated he wasn't in cahoots with his owners, that he actually feared them.

There was something else about his face that was startling as he came more clearly into view. He wasn't a boy.

The Snake Boy was a man, at least a young man, maybe eighteen or nineteen years old. He stood about three feet tall, his skin an unusual bronze, his hair ragged and blond, his eyes violet. It was hard to tell what part of the world he came from. He was perfectly formed, nothing of the show-business-presented dwarf about him. In fact, he was handsome … but terrified.

"I can't come in," Solomon whispered to him, his heart racing, wondering why he found the Snake Boy hard to resist. "The crack, it's too narrow. I already tried. You saw me."

The little fellow shook his head vigorously and made a grunt that sounded like a "no." Then he started twisting his body, as if giving Solomon instructions, and pointed at his eyes and then back at his visitor.

He had seen Solomon getting most of the way in.

"You think I can make it?"

The Snake Boy gave a loud grunt and nodded, then placed his hand over his mouth and looked toward the inner doors. He put a finger to his lips, as if reminding both of them to keep quiet. He moved up to Solomon, turned sideways at the crack, and again imitated someone squeezing through. He pointed at himself and shook his head, then at his visitor again and nodded.

"You can't go through? You think I can? But I'm twice your size."

The performer pointed at Solomon again and nodded, twisting himself one more time.

Though the boy knew he should leave, the thought of actually being in that room next to this bizarre fellow was enticing. He shoved himself sideways into the crack, held his breath, and tried to get through.

But halfway there, he seemed stuck.

The Snake Boy made a motion as if he were trying to dislocate his shoulders.

Somehow, he knew his visitor could do what he was miming.

Solomon held his breath, popped one shoulder out of place, slipped by, then popped the other ... and fell into the room. The Snake Boy was jumping up and down, silently clapping his hands. The chickens clucked loudly. The snakes had stopped moving. In fact, Solomon could see now that they weren't real. There were black strings attached to them that emerged from tiny holes in the wall and ran into the dim room — others could pull on them from the other side and make them wriggle.

The Snake Boy didn't celebrate for long. He quickly pointed up on the wall next to the door Solomon had just come through. There, a little more than six feet high, was a key on a hook.

"Uh!!" he grunted.

Solomon wasn't particularly tall, less than a finger beyond five feet at the age of fifteen, but he could reach that key if he extended himself. The Snake Boy, at about three feet tall, had no means to get to it — there wasn't a single bit of furniture in the room to climb up on.

That's when Solomon Hunt realized what this was all about: the young performer wanted to escape.

As they stood looking at each other, their gazes locked, Solomon could see sadness in the little fellow's eyes, pleading with his new friend without making a sound. It reminded him of how he often felt back on the farm, he and his family victims of his father's violent ways.

Then a noise came from the other side of the inner door.

The Snake Boy's owners were coming back.

CHAPTER THREE
THE JAR

Solomon had to make a decision and make it fast. He knew what the smart move was, the safe one. Instead, he pushed up onto his tiptoes and grabbed the key. He and the Snake Boy turned and fled to the door. Solomon doubted they had time to unlock it. Jamming himself into the crack, he dislocated his shoulders and slipped through, then reached back to pull his new friend with him, hoping he had slightly dislodged the door. But the so-called freak wouldn't take his hand. Grunting and groaning, looking at his liberator with the most horrible expression of fear, he mimed the action of sticking the key into the lock and turning it.

"Snake Boy!" came a terrible shout from indoors. The owners had heard the commotion.

Many things that are easy to do when one has time become horribly difficult when rushed. Solomon seized the lock and bobbled it in his hands, then tried to insert the key. But he couldn't seem to get it into the hole. He was just too excited.

He could hear them coming through the inner door, slamming it open.

"Uh!" grunted the Snake Boy, looking even more terrified.

Solomon squinted his eyes, aimed, shoved hard, and the key went in. He turned it; the lock fell open; the chain dropped to the ground. He ripped the door wide.

But the Snake Boy didn't follow him. He hesitated, as if losing his nerve, turned and ran back toward his evil owners.

"What are you doing?!" Solomon cried.

But the young performer wasn't really going toward them — he was headed for the big jars of pickled babies. He smashed most of them to the floor in one sweeping gesture as if he hated them, paused, then seized one, and hightailed it back, struggling because of its size, the owners now rounding the corner and after him. Solomon held the door open and, once the Snake Boy leapt through it, slammed it shut, snapped the lock back into place, and fled down the alleyway with his accomplice, the key still in his hand.

The owners were cursing them, pounding on the door, slamming it with their fists and kicking it. Solomon glanced back. He could see two faces poking through the crack: the visage of that short showman he had seen on the street, the one dressed in the colorful clothes with the big belly and scars; and next to him, above him, his head a sort of floating skull without a body, he saw a face that stopped him in his tracks.

"UH!!" grunted the Snake Boy out in front of Solomon. He had sprinted down the alley at a pace that surprised his new friend, as if he had supernatural running ability. He was almost at Yonge Street.

By the height of the floating skull, Solomon could tell that the second man was very tall. His head was unnaturally wide and appeared to be about a foot across, even wider in the jaw than through the top of the skull. It was the size and width of a

Halloween pumpkin. The eyes were dark and dead-looking, the hair was black and slicked as if oiled, and mutton chops spread down the sides of the face, a vein rising on the forehead.

"UHH!!"

Solomon turned back to the Snake Boy. He was standing near the end of the alley, frantically waving at his savior to come. The men were still cursing and pounding on the door. The chain rattled and appeared ready to snap.

Solomon stirred himself and ran toward the Snake Boy, who was holding the big jar with the pickled baby. It looked heavy. A "punk" … that's what showmen called them. That too, he had learned from the red pages sections of the news dailies. Solomon could see the baby curled up inside the jar, floating in some sort of liquid. The jar was so big that the little man was having a difficult time holding it. It was the size of his entire torso.

The baby's eyes were closed in a grimace, as if he had been murdered before he was placed in that jar. It almost turned Solomon's stomach.

"You can't take that with you!"

"Uh!" He turned away from Solomon, clutching the jar.

"If you keep it, I leave. Make up your mind." The boy's voice cracked a little as he made his demand.

In the distance, the men were putting their full force behind their kicks. The chain was about to break.

The little "freak" was full of surprises. Now, he surprised again. He took the lid off the jar, poured the liquid out, and pulled the baby from the inside, gripping it in one hand like a child might hold a rubber doll. Solomon felt this morning's breakfast of stale biscuits and tea rising. The Snake Boy could see his revulsion. He smiled and shook his head, holding the baby up close to his new friend's face. Just before Solomon's stomach heaved, he realized that the punk wasn't real: it was indeed a rubber doll. The little man tossed it into a pile of rubble and the smell of formaldehyde began to fill the air. Then he ran out of the alleyway still clutching his jar.

It wasn't the pickled baby that he wanted to keep.

"Hey!"

Solomon raced after him, as fast as a motorized vehicle.

"We will find you!" the showman shouted. "We will kill you!"

As he fled the alley, the North Britain boy spotted the Snake Boy weaving through the crowd on Yonge Street, heading south. He darted after him and disappeared too.

"KILL YOU!!" cried a different voice: a deep growl, with much more volume than the showman's. Solomon could hear it all the way out to the street. It had come from the floating skull and there was conviction in the words. What he said sounded like more than a threat … it seemed like a promise.

CHAPTER FOUR
FIRST SHOW

Solomon couldn't believe how far the Snake Boy went, or that he followed him. The escapee kept moving at top speed, never once breaking into a run but still rushing forward in a lightning-paced walk that made him seem like he was powered by a new kind of electricity. He didn't look back until they were all the way to the foot of Yonge Street, down at the wharves on Great Lake Ontario. Even then, seemingly out of land and aware that his young liberator was following, he didn't stop; he turned and headed west along the waterfront. As the steamboats whistled on the lake, they passed factories, lawn bowling greens, and even the ball diamond where the minor league professional York Maple Leafs played rounders in a stadium that could hold almost ten thousand spectators. It was frozen in the winters so the highly paid hockeyists could play North Britain's violent game in front of even more rabid fanatics. The Snake Boy's legs kept churning on by these palaces of diversion. He wasn't hard to keep track of — a tiny man in a leopardskin parted the crowds like a miniature Moses at the Red Sea.

Solomon could tell that he was still afraid. It seemed like he couldn't put enough space between himself and those two men. "But why is this blood-drinking fellow so valuable to them?" the boy asked himself. "Surely, they could find many poor souls like him to do his terrible trick. But no: his owners don't just want him back — they would *kill* to retrieve him."

Solomon didn't want to run after him, to make a scene, so he simply kept him in sight, hoping that the fugitive would slow down soon. His stomach was beyond growling now — he felt like he might faint. After a while, he could see where the Snake Boy was going: toward the entrance to the North Britain National Exhibition grounds, that huge area near the lake in the southwestern part of the city where big crowds gathered every fall to see everything from horse and cattle shows to knock-about comedians, bloody bare-knuckle prizefights with deadly endings, and hot-air balloon ascensions. It would likely be jam-packed today. Perhaps the runaway performer was simply trying to find the biggest crowds he could to disappear into. But how did he know about the NBNE?

Solomon caught him at the King's Gate.

"Where are you going? What are you trying to do?" he asked.

"Uh!" said the Snake Boy, smiling up at Solomon, his face perspiring. He set his big jar down, glanced behind them, and then pulled something out of his leopardskin. It looked like a bundle of rags. Then he shook it out and started putting it on, right over the skin — a soiled shirt, once white, and a black pair of trousers with suspenders. He took out a flattened bowler hat too, popped it open, and set it on his head. He didn't have any shoes. He turned and pointed past the ticket taker and over the concrete gates with the statue of the King above it; he took his new friend's hand and squeezed it tightly, but Solomon shoved him away. The Snake Boy smiled again anyway.

"You have to pay to get in there. Do you have any money?"

He reached into his pocket and took out two dirty shillings, likely all he had in the world. Admission was half of that.

"Save it for food. I know it won't buy much, but it will help.... Say, would you mind lending a fellow a bit?"

But the Snake Boy had already turned his back to Solomon Hunt and was walking toward the ticket collector. He handed him both coins.

"No!" Solomon shouted.

The ticket man nearly thrashed the North Britain boy when he tried to retrieve the coins from the box.

"Hey, Mac, you and the wee fella have paid. You're in. Now, scram!"

The Snake Boy was already standing inside the fair, a good ten feet away, the jar on the ground in front of him. He was staring wide-eyed at everything around him and watching for signs of his pursuers in the rear. But the coast must have seemed clear, because he soon smiled again and waved Solomon toward him.

"Listen, I don't know who you are or how you got yourself into that disgusting show back there, or why they want to kill you for running away, but this has nothing to do with me. I have things I need to accomplish. You are on your own."

Solomon tried to turn away, but the Snake Boy was eyeing him, and as he did, he caressed his belly and raised his eyebrows in a questioning expression.

"Yes, yes, I'm hungry. In fact, I'm starving. I have to —"

The Snake Boy rubbed his fingers together, as if fingering money, then fondled his belly again and grinned.

Solomon had had just about enough of him. "Yes, of course, we need money to eat, you idiot. But you gave it all to —"

The Snake Boy offered a "come with me" wave and walked away.

Solomon was hungry enough that he followed, against his better judgment. There was a weird authority about his new acquaintance. They moved through the exhibition grounds, surrounded by a dream-like world. Lining the lanes were massive buildings displaying motorized auto cars or exhibiting food or livestock or presentations of muscle and technology. Their big doors were wide open, spectacular entrances in concrete buildings, wide enough to let dinosaurs through. People were streaming in. A passenger balloon, bigger than any Solomon had seen over the city, had settled above the grounds, patrons looking out the little windows down upon the crowds, advertisements for all sorts of products and elixirs painted on its sides. Ragged boys with dark complexions were holding news dailies and calling out the issues of the day, those red "Diversions, Entertainments, and Amusements" sections noticeable in their newspapers as the pages fluttered in the air. Showtalkers with American accents were shouting the attractions of their games of chance, men were throwing balls at targets for their sweethearts (none of the faces contestants threw at were white), cotton candy was being sold, peanuts and lemon drinks were making Solomon's mouth water. Not far away, they could hear and see the midway humming, Mr. Ferris's big sky-wheel, seen first at the Chicago World's Fair a few years ago, capable of carrying five hundred people, rising above all the other rides. The noise was almost deafening.

As enchanted as he was by his surroundings, the Snake Boy also seemed to have a plan. He clutched the big jar and moved through the crowd like an expert, muttering to himself. When he found a spot a little off to the side of a busy walkway where a patch of grass was surrounded by the mud and gravel of the busier areas, he stopped and set down his jar and took off his hat, shirt, and trousers. A lady in a long, elegant dress, her arm through her gentleman's, stopped and stared at the leopardskinned Snake Boy. Several pigeons roosted on a nearby fence, one of them entirely white. The little performer moved toward the birds and lunged. Solomon couldn't believe the speed at which his arm darted out. His reflexes were astonishing. In a split-second, he had the white pigeon in his hand. It struggled mightily to get free.

"OH!" screamed the lady. "Look at what that nasty dwarf did! John, make him put it down!"

The North Britain boy was startled by her aggressive tone.

"Look, fella," said her gentleman, "the lady is a bit squeamish about —"

But the Snake Boy held up his hand and the man, curiously, stopped talking. Solomon noticed several other pedestrians lingering, watching what they probably saw as a novelty: a strangely dressed miniature man with the beautiful white pigeon in his hand. He let it flap its wings violently but didn't let go, holding on tightly to its legs. Then, he made a graceful motion with his arm … and threw the pigeon violently to the ground, landing on top of it and then driving his fist against its little head.

"OH!! OH!!" cried the lady. And several other women shrieked too. Now there was a circle surrounding Solomon and the Snake Boy, moving in. Solomon backed away, searching for an escape route. The bird looked like its neck was broken, its head tucked under its wing.

The gentleman released his lady and stepped toward the Snake Boy, his right hand balled into a fist. But once again, the performer magically arrested him with the motion of his arm, holding his palm up flat in a mesmerizing gesture. The gentleman stopped in his tracks. The Snake Boy smiled at his spectators, picked up the bird … and brought it back to life!

The crowd gasped.

The white pigeon flew like a freed dove of peace into the gray York sky above the North Britain National Exhibition grounds.

Then the Snake Boy held out his hat.

Moments later, he and Solomon Hunt had thirteen shillings.

CHAPTER FIVE
DEBUT

It was probably the best meal Solomon had ever had. It started with cotton candy, lots of it. Then they moved on to other sweets, including mounds of chocolates, before finishing with five hot sausages on buns and gallons of sweetened lemon drinks. The Snake Boy, who had put his street clothes back on, ate with the joy of a ten-year-old. The two of them lay on that little stretch of grass, staring up at the darkening skies, their bellies distended, grins on their faces, saying nothing. Every now and then, the Snake Boy would bolt to his feet and look around, scanning the crowd, then he'd relax and lie back again. He kept the big jar close.

Solomon wanted to talk to him. He wanted to know about him. He was making them money and perhaps could make them more. Where did he come from? How did he get into the situation Solomon had found him in? And why, for God's sake, were those two wicked men pursuing him so desperately? Despite his size and unusual appearance, there was something remarkable about him beyond the skills he had exhibited. Solomon couldn't put his finger on it.

He sat up.

"My name is Solomon Hunt."

"Uh," said the Snake Boy, sitting up too and extending his hand, that lovely smile on his handsome face again.

"You can't speak at all? Not a word?"

His face fell but then lit up a little as he mimed the motion of writing on something.

"You can write?"

He shook his head sadly.

"You can't write? So, you can't read either?"

He shook his head sadly again but then mimed the motion of graceful movements with a pencil.

"You can draw?"

He stood up and nodded vigorously, his smile resplendent once more, taking Solomon's hand again and giving it a good shake.

"We'll have to get some paper and a pencil."

The Snake Boy frowned again, stuck his hands into his trouser pockets, and pulled out the empty linings. That was when Solomon realized that they had spent every last one of their thirteen shillings on food. It was incredible. How could two people spend that much on one meal?

"Yes, that is a problem, bigger than you think, actually. I kind of ran away from home today. And I did it to find a job, to raise money for my mother and little brother and sister because my father … he, uh, he died … just yesterday. I don't have a way to make a single shilling right now and neither do they. They just have the money my father left, which will run out soon, and I've never had a job, and don't really know how to go about getting one. If I can't earn something, make something of myself, my mother will lose our home, and my family will be sent to a poorhouse or worse. My father always said I was nigh on to useless, not helpful like I should be on the farm, reading books all the time, dreaming ..."

The Snake Boy looked like he might cry.

"Well, there's nothing for it. No use in moaning over it, is there?"

The fugitive nodded.

"We just have to make more money. How about another bird trick?"

The Snake Boy shook his head.

"No? Why not?"

He gave Solomon a sly smile.

"What?"

He pointed at the jar.

"The jar? I've been meaning to ask you about that. What —"

The young performer started taking off his clothes.

"Listen, I wish you wouldn't do that. It attracts attention."

The Snake Boy clapped his hands and nodded at his friend, as if he had given the correct answer to a question. Once he was back in his leopardskin and bowler hat, passing pedestrians began slowing to look at him again. But he didn't seem to mind, in fact he encouraged it. He put his fingers into his mouth and whistled. The sound was so loud Solomon thought it might arrest the attention of everyone in York. It shrieked above the swirling calliope music, the shouts of the showtalkers, and the buzz of pedestrians. Then the Snake Boy started acting like a fool ... of an uncivilized sort. He began running around on all fours, making ape sounds, howling and grunting, and letting drool drip from his mouth.

Now many people were lingering. In fact, a crowd had formed. The electric lights, some colored, were coming on up and down the walkways. They lit the exhibition in a glow: red and white and blue.

The Snake Boy ran at Solomon and leapt into his arms. The boy didn't know what to do, but he tried to play along. In a second, his companion was on his shoulders, first sitting on them, and then standing.

The crowd kept growing.

The Snake Boy jumped down, turning a somersault before landing on his feet.

Then, he pointed at the jar. Then, he pointed at Solomon Hunt.

"Uh!" he cried and nodded at his friend's boots, miming the action of taking them off. The North Britain boy did as he said, remembering the thirteen shillings they had made. Solomon pulled off his smelly socks too. Then, the Snake Boy pointed at his accomplice's shirt.

"No," said Solomon, "I'm not taking off my shirt." His father had taught him and his siblings that nudity was the Devil's idea and that clothes were meant to shield them from the sinful nature of their naked bodies.

"UH!!" demanded the Snake Boy. He didn't seem to care about any of that.

The two of them had nothing at the moment, a desperate predicament, and Solomon supposed it called for a desperate measure. He reluctantly unbuttoned his shirt and took it off, looking down at the ground. He noticed two girls about his age pretending to avert their gazes but glancing at his bare chest.

"Uh!" shouted The Snake Boy, pointing at Solomon's trousers ... and miming the motion of removing them too.

"Oh, no! No, no! NOT my trousers!"

Folks in the crowd looked uneasy, but no one moved away. In fact, the audience kept growing. The two girls stayed rooted to their spot.

"NO! I'm not taking them off!"

"Come on, do it lad!" came a shout. "Yes!" cried a girl and then covered her mouth. Solomon turned to see her in the crowd and while his attention was on finding her … the Snake Boy leapt at him!

He seemed to know something of wrestling, for he pinned his bigger friend quickly, had his arms under his back and his fingers on his fly in a flash. He appeared to have Herculean strength. In seconds, he had the trousers undone and had moved down Solomon's legs to the ragged cuffs. He seized them and pulled everything completely off in a graceful motion, like a fancy waiter pulling the tablecloth out from under a setting of dishes and glasses without disturbing them.

As Solomon felt his trousers come down, he prayed that he'd remembered to wear his underpants.

There was a gasp from the crowd. Solomon glanced down. Underpants on, yes, but his short ones, very short — his hands shot down to his crotch to cover himself.

The Snake Boy was smiling … and pointing at the jar again.

"What … what are you —" Solomon asked.

The Snake Boy spun the lid off the jar and gracefully set it on the ground. He pointed into the opening, then walked over and helped his partner to his feet. He shoved him toward the jar.

"What the —"

The Snake Boy began making the same motions he had made when he wanted Solomon to slip through the narrow crack in the door. He mimed not only the dislocation of shoulders, but other limbs, up and down the body, all the way to his hips, legs, and ankles.

"You want me to get into the jar?"

The crowd roared. Solomon Hunt glanced at them. Every spectator seemed filled with anticipation. They began rhythmically clapping. The Snake Boy looked into his friend's eyes: His face was glowing.

CHAPTER SIX
SUCCESS

The jar wasn't even as wide as Solomon's shoulders and not much longer than his torso. He was certain there was no way he could fit into it. But the Snake Boy kept nodding his head, smiling at his partner in crime, gesturing to the jar, then bowing to the crowd. Their rhythmical clapping grew louder, their numbers increased.

"All right," Solomon said, "let's give it a whirl."

The crowd cheered. The Snake Boy jumped up and down with delight and gave his friend the thumbs up.

As Solomon approached the jar, their audience went silent. In the distance, he could hear the hum of the rides, the whirligig music, others talking. The Snake Boy had set the jar down so it was directly in the glow of a light that emanated from a nearby Cracker Jack popcorn booth. It looked lit the way a lonely actor would be on a stage.

Solomon put one foot into the jar. This was impossible. He turned to the Snake Boy and whispered, "How am I going to do this?"

Never once taking off the pasted grin he aimed at the crowd, the young performer indicated how Solomon should place his feet tightly together on the bottom of the jar, then squat down, his rear end on the surface, between his feet.

Solomon did as instructed, dislocating his shoulders and folding them inward as he squatted. He squeezed down into the container. But he couldn't quite get his butt on the bottom. His head was still several inches above the top, in fact, his eyes looked out above it at the crowd. Then, he felt pressure on the top of his skull. The Snake Boy was forcing his head down! He couldn't resist him: his arms, with shoulders dislocated, were pinned against the sides of the jar. He felt an excruciating pain in his hips as they began to dislocate too. He actually heard them snap out of place as his rear end touched the bottom. There was a roar from the crowd … but it dulled for Solomon as the Snake Boy screwed the lid onto the jar.

Almost fainting from the medicinal smell of the formaldehyde and gasping for air, the boy looked out with alarm at the crowd. They peered back at him through the convex glass, their faces distorted, weird grins looking wide and ghoulish, their shouts and claps muted. Solomon realized that he must have appeared like just a head, a human head, with feet under its chin, blue eyes staring out in terror from a jar, his evident fear adding to the spectacle.

The Snake Boy *had* to let him out! He couldn't breathe!

The chicken-head-eating geek picked up the jar, with Solomon in it. The boy couldn't believe the little fellow was capable of it. He indeed had extraordinary strength. Then he began passing Solomon around to some of the bigger men. The crowd laughed and a few put their faces up to the glass, less than an inch from Solomon's, their features appearing bizarre to him, and their laughs like distant hyenas.

Inside, the boy was dying. His eyes began to roll up in their sockets. He started to black out. Outside, the Snake Boy had taken off his bowler hat and was passing it around. Folks were pouring in coins.

Everything faded for Solomon.

Then, suddenly, there was a rush of senses — sounds (calliope music, cheers, hips snapping back into place), smells (fresh air), and sights (the Snake Boy's hands, gripping his ears, pulling him up and out of the jar).

Solomon lay on a patch of grass for a long time afterward, the Snake Boy sitting nervously beside him. The formaldehyde had done something to his senses. As he looked up into the night sky, the stars moved about, the top of the Ferris wheel expanded and contracted, mosquitoes grew to great sizes and looked like flying rats. Finally, after what seemed like an hour or more, things began to focus, and he rolled over and glared at the Snake Boy.

"You shouldn't have put the lid on!"

"Uh," he said and sadly nodded. But then he smiled and offered Solomon his bowler hat. In it, the boy saw a big pile of coins — more than twice as many as they had made before. The young fugitive stood up and began clapping his hands at Solomon Hunt, then bowing as if in homage to a great artist.

"Yeah, well, leave the damn lid off next time."

The Snake Boy nodded his head vigorously.

"Let's get something to eat."

They didn't gorge themselves this time. And they tried to be smarter about what they ate: For this meal, they replaced the cotton candy with several bags of deep-fried potato slices. The Snake Boy was like an anxious little mammal, like a meerkat wary of attack as they dined on their grass patch. Every now and then he would stand up, drop his food, and scan the crowd, his head rotating 180 degrees, his fingers up to his mouth, tapping against his teeth, looking both pensive and frightened. Solomon knew who he was looking for.

After they had eaten, they tried some of the rides. The Snake Boy loved them all, even more than Solomon. It was as if he had never been allowed on one before. He grunted and screamed louder than any kid Solomon had ever seen as they swooped down the exhibition's roller coaster, and his face glowing like the Christ child's at Christmas as he gazed out over the newly electrically lit city of York from the top of the Ferris wheel. At one point, he stood up to scan the setting, looking for his pursuers. He seemed unafraid of falling. Solomon had to pull him down.

But after their fifth ride, they realized that their money was dwindling again.

They were growing tired too. The Snake Boy, his eyelids becoming heavy, got Solomon's attention and put his hands together as if praying, and laid the side of his head on them.

"Yes," said Solomon, "we should sleep. How about lying down right here on the grass?"

The fugitive shook his head violently, then turned and surveyed the crowd. He was right — their pursuers could pounce on them if they found the two of them asleep.

They had to stay somewhere private, out of sight.

The Snake Boy pointed in the direction of a big building at the far end of the midway. Solomon could see its electric sign from where they stood. "Showman's Hotel" it read. How did he know about that place? Had he stayed there before?

It turned out that they had enough money for a room for one night; and for two pencils and some pads of paper. The interior of the hotel had the most colorful innards of any building Solomon had ever seen. The lobby's walls were not only bright red and pink and purple, but there were colored electric light bulbs everywhere, marking out words and patterns, all with a show business theme. There were massive paintings throughout too, depicting acts in famous extravaganzas, from singers, dancers, and musicians, to exotic animals, carnivals, and sideshows. As the unusual duo ascended the stairs toward their ninth-floor room they came face-to-face with a big portrait at the top of the first landing. Solomon recognized the man immediately — the angular, lizard-like visage of the world's greatest showman, Leopold J. Coop, an amusements and diversions man so popular that he was planning a run for the presidency of the Empire of America.

His trademark white cowboy hat, encrusted with diamonds, was tipped back on his head, his long white hair cascaded down past his shoulders and over his buckskin coat. The Snake Boy gave a start, lowered his head, and ran past the portrait up to the next floor. It was a curious reaction.

But in the room, the young fugitive was delighted by the leopardskin bedspreads that matched his costume, and he caressed the covers and patted the bed in wonder as if he had never been in one before. But he soon set the jar down and was fast asleep right after his head touched his pillow. Solomon lay there across the room looking at him, wondering again who in the world he was and why those men were so angry at losing him. He was certainly a remarkable person, a sort of genius — the events of the day had shown that.

It was hard for Solomon to sleep. He kept thinking about his mother and sister and brother, feeling guilty that he hadn't taken some of the money they'd made and brought it to them. But he needed more money than that to help them. He looked back at the Snake Boy. They had made nearly fifty shillings in half a day. Could they do it again? And again? Was this mysterious person, sent to Solomon almost from God at the moment he needed him, going to be the answer to his problems? What other tricks did this fellow have up his sleeve? The boy wondered if he should head back into the city and seek a job or stay with this individual. The latter seemed to make more sense, at least for a while. He figured he should give it another day, then imagined what tomorrow would bring.

The next morning, hungry and anxious to get going, they didn't linger in the hotel. But as they reached the bottom steps of the gold and silver staircase, the Snake Boy froze. He was staring straight ahead, out the front doors and into the sunshine. When Solomon looked in that direction, he saw a head, high above other people entering — a wide one the size of a large pumpkin!

They bolted down the last steps and made a beeline for the biggest sofa in the lobby, the Snake Boy bobbling the jar as they ran, and barely got behind it as the two men came in. The short showman was still sporting that red suit with the yellow waistcoat and the big man was wearing a black trench coat that stretched almost to the floor, below which Solomon spotted two enormous black boots.

"Do you think the Seer would stay here?" asked the short one.

"He knows about it," answered the big man in his deep voice. "He knows about everything."

"We have to get him back."

"No kidding. You must be a genius."

"Maybe he's put a spell on us?"

"Maybe he's the son of God."

"Don't say that, boss. That ain't funny."

The Snake Boy was breathing heavily. His face, inches from Solomon's, was turning red, and the boy thought he might cry out. Solomon put his hand gently on one of his shoulders.

"Inquire at the desk, Mr. Pawn, ask if a dwarf and a boy were seen here. I'll scout out the lobby."

The big man stepped toward the desk. The showman paused for a second and then moved toward the seating area. Solomon and the Snake Boy were near the doors. The latter stood up and made for them. Alarmed, Solomon darted after him.

"Pawn!"

The showman had seen them!

The prey were down the steps and onto the grounds of the exhibition in a flash, into the late summer sunshine. Unfortunately, the crowds were still thin so they knew their pursuers would be able to see them. Though the Snake Boy ran again with incredible speed for his size (clutching the big jar as he went) and Solomon, a good sprinter in school athletics, matched him, they both understood that the legs of the man named Pawn were much longer than theirs. He would catch them in a minute!

The fugitive was grunting and groaning as he scooted along, and when Solomon glanced over, he could see tears rolling down his cheeks. He was absolutely terrified. *Why are they after him like this? What was that about him knowing everything? Being the son of God? But that was just a joke.*

Solomon could tell that the Snake Boy was trying to get away from the open spaces. He veered in different directions, like a target trying to avoid a hunter, seeking a crowd.

What would those two beasts do to him if they caught him, thought Solomon. *What would they do to me?*

Then the fleeing pair spotted a crowd: a large gathering of spectators who had obviously just entered the grounds. They were all women, perhaps a Society of some sort on a group excursion who had come to the NBNE together. They were dressed well in long flowing dresses, some daringly showing their legs just above the ankles, all with sun umbrellas in hand.

The Snake Boy gave a little shriek and pointed toward something not far from the group: two policemen in long, blue, buttoned coats, happily keeping an eye on the ladies.

Solomon couldn't believe what his companion did next: He slowed down! Pawn was almost upon them! The villain angled away from the excursionists, but the Snake Boy walked right into them. Pawn ignored Solomon and followed him, not slowing at all, his hands reaching out. The Snake Boy slowed again, so the big man could almost touch him, then he darted right up to two young women and abruptly veered to their side.

Pawn ran into them.

They screamed.

The policemen sprang into action. Rushing over, using

admirable muscle, impressing the female victims, they held on to Pawn as he struggled in their strong arms.

"Hold on here, chap. Come with us. We must have a little chat."

They doffed their caps to the ladies, gripping the protesting and struggling Pawn who glared back at the Snake Boy as he was pulled away.

The two friends walked for a while, trying to look inconspicuous. In fact, they kept moving slowly for some time, despite the fact that the showman continued following them from not far away, walking at a steady pace, his face held in an angry expression.

Finally, he caught up to them. They kept moving, not even glancing at him. The Snake Boy didn't seem to fear the showman as much as the other, perhaps feeling that the two of them could fight him off, or that he was too cowardly to take them on alone.

"I'll catch you, Seer!" he said as loudly as he dared, trying not to make a scene.

"Uh!" snapped the Snake Boy and shoved him away.

"I'll get Pawn out of this. And we'll catch you, and if you don't show us what you know, there will be dire consequences, believe me!"

The Seer started to run. He and Solomon were out of sight of the policemen now. They headed toward the King's Gate and back into the city of York. The short showman followed for a while, but soon stopped and yelled, his southern drawl slowly fading into the distance.

"We'll catch you! And when we do, it will go even worse for your friend!"

CHAPTER SEVEN
TO THE LAND OF DREAMS

The Snake Boy, or the Seer, or whatever in the world his name was, stopped talking (or grunting) for a long while after that. He simply walked at another brisk pace, his jaw set and his violet eyes fixed, as he made his way back along the route they'd followed near the waterfront, returning to the main part of the city.

"Where are we going?" Solomon asked, not sure he still wanted to stay with him. His companion might help him make more money, but at what cost? That showman had made it clear that Solomon had become his target too. It was likely best to part ways now.

The Snake Boy reached into a pocket and pulled out a pencil and one of the sheets of paper they'd bought at the hotel and began drawing without breaking stride. He pressed the paper against the big jar, somehow holding the latter with one hand, and threw himself into his work. It was amazing. He kept walking.

When he was done, he handed Solomon the paper and pointed south over Great Lake Ontario. His drawing was remarkable: a picture of a flag — the American flag, the Stars and Stripes and

Cross, the twinkles for all sixty-six states meticulously marked in the large X in the upper left corner, thirty-three going one way and thirty-three the other. It was beautifully conceived — the flag actually looked like it was rippling in a breeze.

Solomon could even see the word "Freedom" and the dollar signs that were known to be barely visible in the red stripes if you looked closely. But the boy thought he must be imagining that last part.

"The American Empire?" Solomon asked and swallowed.

"Uh!"

"That's where *I* was planning to go."

But by the time they reached Union Station, York's marvelous old steam train terminus, and entered the gorgeous, arched hall, its ceiling looking a mile high, Solomon wasn't so sure he wanted to go to America. He had never been beyond his countryside, let alone his homeland. North Britain was really a very small country; next to America, every country was — the great empire surrounded its neighbor in more ways than one. Solomon had left North Britain many times in his head and in books and yearned with his very soul to visit the giant to the south, but when it came time to actually do it, it frightened him to the bottoms of his boots.

It might be better to find work here, or better still, to go home, see what he could do there, perhaps even get a job as a hired man on another farm. But that wouldn't support his family. Shouldn't he be bolder, anyway?

"Uh!" said the little man, pulling the empty linings of his trouser pockets inside out again. His voice echoed in the cavernous hall. Up above, the names of the great cities to which the North Britain National Steam Railway went were marked. You could not only go just about everywhere in NB — in the two provinces of Ontario and Quebec — but you could travel to the east coast of America too, to Halifax, and the west coast to distant and dangerous Vancouver in the state of New Columbia. Someday, Solomon was sure, Americans would find a way to run a steam train all the way up to their Arctic lands. But if he had his way, he'd go south to New York or even further to San Francisco or even Mexico City, American urban areas where things were really happening. … Or would he?

"Uh!" said the Snake Boy, shaking his friend this time to get his attention.

"Yes, yes, we need money, I know."

He waved Solomon toward a washing room. Inside, he started removing his outer clothes again. Luckily, they were the only ones there.

"The jar trick again?"

He held his tiny hand out flat, palm down, and tipped his wrist back and forth.

"Yes and no? What do you mean?"

He pointed at the jar.

"Yes, the jar."

He unscrewed the lid and motioned for Solomon to get into it again.

"Now? But doesn't that ruin the trick?"

He shook his head.

Solomon didn't know why, but he got in.

"Don't put the lid on!"

The fugitive nodded and set the lid on the washing room sink counter. Then, he picked up the jar, of course. They headed out into the hallway. He set Solomon down and emitted another of his powerful whistles. A few pedestrians stopped.

The Snake Boy started tap dancing and grunting loudly. More pedestrians paused. Every time they slowed, he motioned toward the item he had set on the floor. Folks began realizing that a human being, or at least a human head and feet, were inside a jar, right there, in front of their eyes.

When a suitably large group had gathered — and still no policemen near — the Snake Boy gave a flourish with his arms and motioned in Solomon's direction, then walked right up to the jar and made an extravagant gesture that a magician might employ if he were trying to conjure something into rising up, something that was either dead, inanimate, or impossibly immobilized. He nodded at Solomon and winked. He wanted his partner to rise. Inside the glass, Solomon could see the spectators excitedly talking to each other, becoming aware of what they now hoped was about to happen.

But the boy couldn't get up — his arms and legs and hips ached when he tried, and he couldn't get any purchase on the bottom of the jar anyway. So … his dear little friend grabbed his ears again and began to pull upward. It appeared (and felt) as though he stretched them a foot, but it worked. In fact, it worked extremely well because the scream Solomon uttered seemed to please the audience and they were absolutely in awe when they saw the boy emerge, all five feet plus of him, out of his confines to stand before them in the hall.

That made enough for two tickets to Buffalo and a good hearty breakfast on the train, as well as a couple of round-meat sandwiches for afterward. They also exchanged their few remaining shillings for American money. Solomon stared at it. The coins with the presidents' faces, instead of the King's, looked strange, like play money. But it was exciting to think of what it might buy him ... in the Empire of America!

The trip took about three hours. They could finally relax — the Snake Boy had looked frightened until the moment they got onto the train, glancing behind as he carried his big jar, scanning the station for not only his pursuers, but also the York Police — it was doubtful they would look kindly upon performances in this public space. The time on the steam train gave the two new acquaintances a while to chat — or, at least, time for Solomon to talk at his unusual companion, and for him to draw.

"So, is your name Seer?" The short showman had pronounced it with two syllables: "See-er."

He shook his head at first, then nodded, a little sadly.

"Where are you from?"

He shrugged.

"I mean, where were you born?"

He shrugged again.

"You don't know where you were born? What about your parents, where are they?"

But the Seer had turned his head toward the window, pressing it to the glass, staring out as if he hoped to be where the train was going. He obviously didn't want to communicate. For a long time, Solomon said nothing to him, looking straight ahead, thinking again about how long he should stay with this wanted fellow: a day, maybe two. If things didn't go well, then he should take whatever they made and head home. He would, at least, have finally seen America.

Soon, the Seer turned back from the window and started to draw. He didn't seem to mind Solomon looking over his shoulder and the boy quickly became fascinated with what he was doing. This time, he didn't draw something simple like a flag. This was a scene, detailed and complicated, with human figures and buildings and carriages. And it was stunningly well done. He had a way of drawing that was dramatic in itself. He seemed to draw the least interesting aspects of a figure or a scene first, and then slowly bring out what was intriguing and individual in his subject. It was like a series of revelations. The boy sat there, staring down in astonishment.

It was the first drawing his friend ever created while Solomon Hunt watched, the first work of Seer art, and the boy was enthralled.

The scene depicted an extravaganza playing in the center of a busy city, the tent roof cut open so the viewer could look inside. Down in there, watched by an enormous crowd, the human cannonball act was being performed. Solomon had heard of this act but had never seen it. In fact, he had never seen an extravaganza at all — his father had not allowed him and his mother and siblings to view such "immoral and indecent shows." But Solomon had certainly imagined being the bullet in the cannon. He had thought of entering the mouth of the great weapon as the crowd roared and being shot halfway across a stadium, flying at lightning speed, performing a triple somersault before he landed in a net. The cheers were always deafening.

This remarkable trick was a new one in the extravaganzas and a showstopper. There was nothing like it. Solomon often wondered who had come up with such an idea, who had thought of actually putting a human being into a cannon … and shooting them out! Making a human being fly! No one *really* knew how to fly, not even in the American Empire. This was as close as it got. It was genius.

"Buffalo, American Empire!" a porter cried.

Solomon Hunt was about to enter the land of his dreams.

CHAPTER EIGHT
INTO THE EMPIRE

Solomon was right about America. Buffalo, though not much bigger than York, had everything North Britain had, but in spades. Everything was bigger and more colorful; people were louder and more aggressive. They even seemed to move faster. And diversions were everywhere.

Getting down from the steam train in the station, the first thing he saw above the packed crowd of pedestrians rushing to and fro in the massive granite hall was an American flag the size of a barn. The sixty-six stars seemed to twinkle. Behind the flag on a wall was a huge portrait of the president, John M. Self.

The Seer, still clutching his jar, smiled at his companion and mimicked closing a gaping mouth. They were just a step or two from the train. Solomon closed his lips and started walking. The crowd surged out into the main part of the hall, almost picking up the two friends and carrying them along. The boy was instantly concerned that the Seer, so small in stature, might get swallowed up. But not him. He seemed to enjoy the crowd and before long, his bigger sidekick was scrambling to keep up. The two of them made for the wide iron doors leading out into the streets. They must have been twenty feet high. The sounds of the steam trains and the buzz of the crowd echoed in the building, and all around them vendors shouted their wares — yard-long news dailies with more than half their pages bright red, magazines with tales of celebrity people, prepared food, and train tickets. Solomon couldn't believe how loudly they could shout. Above and all around them signs advertised for everything from churches to peep shows to Edison's Everlasting Elixirs. Entertainment, in all its forms, was everywhere in America.

The American military had a dominant presence too — men of all ages in the uniforms of the Army, Navy, and Balloon Force strode about in the station's crowds, citizens saluting when they noticed them, sometimes holding their hands over their hearts as well. It was all strange to Solomon Hunt. He couldn't remember the last time he'd seen a North Britain soldier. But America was often at war, always in other countries, looking out for their interests, fighting for "freedom," as they put it.

The Seer stopped in front of a long wall plastered with adverts for diversions. The boy glimpsed him up ahead, through the pedestrians, staring up. Then the Seer moved away again, with what seemed like a greater purpose. When Solomon neared, he glanced at what his companion had been looking at — a series of identical posters running up and down the wall, all with enormous red letters that stood out from everything else. "SHOW OF SHOWS!" they read. "SEE THE BLACK GIRL PERFORM THE WORLD'S MOST DANGEROUS FEAT!" Solomon looked down to the bottom of the broadsheets. "MOFFAT'S GROVE, NORTH OF THE CITY. WILL SELL OUT! DON'T BE DISAPPOINTED! GET YOUR TICKETS NOW!"

The boy wondered how that could mean anything to his friend. The Seer couldn't read. But had the posters somehow told him something? The fugitive was walking quickly again. He seemed to know where he wanted to go now and definitely appeared to know this place. Solomon caught up to him just outside the doors but then lost him. It was the North Britain boy's fault: the scene before him was staggering. Where there were a dozen big buildings in York, there were fifty here; where they were a dozen stories high back home, they were thirty here. The highest had a sign on its roof that read "Amusements Inc., COOP PRODUCTIONS." Brown and black and gray, mostly made of concrete and stone, the buildings scraped the sky above teeming streets that were filled with carriages and many motorized vehicles.

It was an explosion of sound. Up above them, docked with gigantic ropes to the tips of the roofs, were veritable fleets of cigar-shaped passenger balloons, and here and there Solomon could see people descending from staircases, down from the airships and into the upper floors. He had to shake his head, look back to earth, and pay attention. The Seer had vanished again.

But then he spotted him, more than twenty strides ahead, still darting through the crowds.

They walked for hours, it seemed, and the Seer wouldn't say anything. He had his attention fixed ahead, though every now and then he'd look back, his eyes gazing slightly above the heads in the crowds, obviously searching for a tall man on their trail. At those moments, Solomon could see fear flash across his face.

They moved north, just as the posters directed. Though they saw many wealthy people — men in velvet bowler hats, women in billowing silk dresses and carrying sun umbrellas — the endless number of poor people almost brought tears to Solomon's eyes. And the rich barely looked at them. Where were the folks who were neither poor nor wealthy? They seemed few and far between. And most of the poor were Black. The destitute at times even lay on the ground, some crying out for food or money, some, it seemed to Solomon, their faces sallow and skeletal, on the point of starvation. The whiter, wealthier folks kept pressing past. The North Britain boy stared at the scene — he had not known the great American Empire was filled with such sadness and inequality.

Soon the city grew less dense, and the unusual pair seemed to be approaching the countryside. But before they did, the street they were on ended in a big archway, beyond which Solomon could see a park and the top of a gigantic red-and-yellow striped tent. They could hear calliope music, hear the calls of men selling candy floss and Cracker Jack popcorn and all those wonderful foods.

Two men in straw hats and red-and-yellow striped coats stood at the entrance, selling tickets. The crowds hadn't gathered yet; it was obviously a long while before showtime. On the ironwork that ran across the top of the archway, Solomon read the words "Moffat's Grove" and just beyond it were big signs on makeshift pillars announcing the "SHOW OF SHOWS!"

"Seer!" Solomon cried, seizing him by the elbow. "How did you know this? How did you know to come here? You can't read."

The other looked up at his companion with a wry smile, tapped his index finger on his chin for a moment, then sat down on one of the big stones that lined the street just before the park entrance, pulled out his paper and pencil, and began to draw.

He drew another extravaganza scene. And he didn't skimp on detail this time either. There was the big-top show tent again, folks gathering around in a park outside it, the roof peeled back for his friend to view the action inside, and another human cannonball act, this time with the bullet flying out of the weapon and through the roof, coming right at them. The Seer giggled at his art. Then he penciled in the entrance to the park where the drawing was set. "Moffat's Grove" read the sign above his perfect archway. He looked at Solomon, smiled again, and tapped his temple.

"You've been here before, haven't you?"

The Seer glanced over at the sign on the archway again and drew the letters again, at the bottom of the sheet, copying them just as they appeared.

"But you can't read."

He nodded.

"You memorized the shape of the letters on the sign!"

He nodded again. And with that, leapt to his feet and approached the ticket seller, taking most of his share of their money out of his pocket and handing it over.

"Hey!" Solomon cried and ran forward. "Stop spending our money on shows! We can't just give up all that for amusements!"

But the money was already in the hand of the ticket seller, who pocketed it with alarming speed, then smiled at Solomon and handed the Seer two ducats.

"I wanted to send some of that home to my mother! Or use it for food!" Solomon growled as they made their way into the park, passing a man dressed in the red-white-and-blue of the American flag, wearing a white wig and a long beard, like Father Christmas though thinner, impossibly high above them on twenty-foot stilts, shouting out the attractions of the show on a megaphone. "Instead, you're wasting it on THIS?"

But the Seer ignored him, his mind far away, like a man with a plan.

They sat on the grass outside the tent for three hours, the big jar between the Seer's legs, waiting for the show to begin, their time interrupted only by the purchase and consumption of a meal: three bags of salted peanuts, two of chocolate raisins, and seven candied apples … for health.

The crowd grew. Soon, it seemed as if more than half of Buffalo was here, as if no one could possibly miss an extravaganza.

But they were first in line when the gates opened.

Once inside, the Seer raced to a seat in the middle of the tent, about five rows up, and planted himself there, his jar on the next seat to save it for Solomon. The boy arrived, panting with exertion — his friend had beaten everyone else to their seats though they had all hurried with everything they had. The Seer stared up and around at the interior of the tent, his eyes sparkling. Solomon had to admit, it was marvelous. Yes, they needed the money, but he had never seen anything like this and what was ahead promised to be fantastic. The tent had looked large from the outside, but from inside, it seemed immense. A huge pole went up the center and pushed the roof up so high that it looked like it was its own blue sky.

Other poles held that sky in place every twenty feet or so above and around the tent's oval shape — the shape of a racetrack, lined with newfangled electric lights.

There wasn't much electricity yet in North Britain, so Solomon Hunt stared at the glowing magic. When he gazed in either direction from their central location, it seemed as though he were looking for miles. On the sawdust grounds in front of them were five big circles, one-foot walls around their circumferences, together stretching the length of the tent, and in them were all sorts of contraptions — wires and poles and nets and stools and whips and cages. Solomon's imagination flew.

Then he remembered something he had read in the red pages one day — Leopold J. Coop had invented the five-ring extravaganza.

The boy could hardly wait for things to begin. His body tingled from his scalp to the soles of his feet. His palms became sweaty, his heart thumped. Beside him, the Seer remained absolutely silent, his eyes glowing down at what was before them.

And what a show it was! A masterful diversion!

They sat enthralled for two hours, shoving mouthful after mouthful of candy floss into their maws, staring out at all the color and dangerous action in front of them. The Seer shrieked with delight and pointed when the walkabout began, the "spec" that opened the show. A beautiful lady wearing a golden headdress that was woven into her hair and rose high above her head and dressed in a sparkling costume (that didn't cover much of her and made Solomon blush) rode astride the head of an elephant from the Realms of Asia, gripping its huge neck with her bare legs, and twirling around it as it lumbered by. He had never seen such a beast before, and its size and majesty took his breath away. When it trumpeted near them, a deafening jungle cry, he leapt to his feet. A cage of lions and tigers and camelopards followed, and then the performers dressed in exotic costumes: handsome men with bulging muscles, gorgeous women with long, naked limbs.

The parade was barely out of the tent when the action began. It was difficult to know where to look: in the center ring at the trapeze artists; to the left at the frightening animals roaring in cages as men taunted them and made them do tricks; to the right at the ladies descending upside down entangled in ropes from the roof; or at the cyclists on motorized bicycles racing directly at each other, only to swerve to the side at the last moment. A group of First Inhabitants, from the last known to exist as a community in the American Empire, were chased by bulls (dressed up to look like nearly extinct buffalos) around the oval, barely escaping being gored and killed right in front of the audience. The crowd went wild. A band played loudly, and drama was all about them: Death seemed imminent at every moment in every act.

But nothing matched the ending.

As the drummers thundered, a black cannon was wheeled out, appearing like a medieval weapon of war. The Seer cried out and slowly rose to his feet. The look in his eyes was different from any of the expressions that had been crossing his face throughout the show. This time he watched in awe ... and, curiously, with pride.

"LADIES AND GENTLEMEN AND CHILDREN OF ALL AGES, NOW APPROACHING THE GREATEST CANNON ON THIS EARTH, A WEAPON FOUND ON THE BATTLEFIELDS OF WATERLOO AFTER NAPOLEON WAS VANQUISHED BY GENERAL WELLINGTON AND ENHANCED AND ENLARGED BY OUR INGENIOUS INVENTORS, CAPABLE OF FIRING A CANNONBALL ONE HUNDRED TIMES THE SIZE OF A NORMAL BULLET, OF BLASTING A HOLE IN THE TALLEST BUILDING IN NEW YORK CITY AND BRINGING IT TO ITS KNEES ... IS CLEOPATRA, THE BEAUTIFUL BLACK GIRL."

Out from the performers' entrance came Cleopatra, dressed

in gold, looking more beautiful than any girl Solomon had ever seen. And she was indeed just a girl, perhaps a year older than him, frightened and unsure. Solomon's heart went out to her. He felt like rushing down onto the sawdust grounds and stopping this terrible act. The Seer noticed his reaction. He took the boy's arm and smiled.

"How can you smile?"

But he was absolutely glowing. He pointed at Cleopatra.

"THIS MEMBER OF THE SECOND RACE OF AMERICAN LIFE, HER GRANDPARENTS AFRICAN ROYALTY BROUGHT TO OUR EMPIRE'S SHORES A HALF CENTURY AGO TO WORK THE FIELDS OF OUR GLORIOUS SOUTH, WILL ENTER THE MOUTH OF THE CANNON ON MY COMMMAND … AND BE FIRED FROM IT … THE ENTIRE LENGTH OF THE AMPHITHEATER!"

Why, thought Solomon, *does your skin color matter so much in this country?* But the crowd roared. A huge net, erected by nearly naked muscular men turning a series of wheels with handles, was rising hundreds of yards away, five extravaganza rings distant from Cleopatra and the monster cannon! Solomon looked at the Seer, expecting to see the grin wiped from his face. How would he feel now? How would he react to the prospect of witnessing what could easily be the death of this young girl? But his smile had grown.

Down below, Cleopatra, her hands visibly shaking, jumped and grabbed the mouth of the cannon. She pulled herself up with great strength and slid most of the way in, leaving just her head sticking out.

"READY?" asked the booming voice.

"Ready," came Cleopatra's response, barely audible.

She slid down and disappeared into the cannon. Solomon looked around to see if there were any policemen present. Something should be done about this. This was taking things too far.

But suddenly there was a boom so loud that for a moment the boy thought he might never hear again. The concussion thundered in his ears and chest, a huge flame burst from somewhere near the horrible weapon … and Cleopatra, beautiful young Cleopatra, shot out of it. She flew into the air at a terrifying speed, over the first ring … the second … third … fourth … the …

CHAPTER NINE
CLEOPATRA

That was when Solomon Hunt saw the most terrifying thing he'd seen in his life. But it wasn't the finish of Cleopatra's act. As she shot out of the giant cannon, expertly holding her hands by her sides, then tucking her chin to her chest, bringing her arms down, pulling her legs to them, turning one, two, three, four, five somersaults, and landing like a dove in the net to a standing ovation … he saw a face across the extravaganza's tent the size of a pumpkin … glaring at him!

"Seer!" he cried in the din. But his friend didn't hear him. He was jumping up and down and cheering louder than anyone else, almost turned mad by what he was witnessing.

Solomon leaned down and spoke directly into his ear. "Seer! It's Pawn! He's here!"

For a moment, the boy thought his companion might faint. He reached out and grabbed him. As Solomon looked back across the tent he could see the short showman with the big belly, standing beside Pawn, pointing at them, his face red with excitement. Somehow, the Seer, following Solomon's gaze, saw them too. He instantly picked up his big jar, took his friend's hand, and yanked him along their row of seats out into the aisle. They pounded down the steps toward the grounds. The stands were shaking with the stomping of feet and cheers of the crowd. When they hit dirt, Solomon looked up and across at the nasty showman and Pawn. Their enemies had more rows to negotiate, were higher up in the stands. They were shoving people and racing downward.

The Seer still held Solomon's hand. His was sweaty and gripped his taller companion's hard.

"Where are we going?" Solomon shouted. He couldn't imagine that they would just run for it. The other two would surely catch them here. He and the Seer had been lucky the first time. He doubted they could get away in Moffat's Grove Park — there'd likely be no lady excursionists, no perfectly placed policemen to help.

But the Seer didn't seem to be headed for the exit. He made for the performers' entrance. It was a smart move, because all eyes were on Cleopatra.

The two friends raced to the entrance and slipped past the show attendants who were meant to guard the area, as they, still mesmerized by the human cannonball despite having likely seen it hundreds of times, stared toward the other end of the tent. Once in the tunnel that led out from the performance area, Solomon and the Seer were quickly in a little village of trailers, unhitched from their horses, set up for their stay in Buffalo. None of the performers were there — all had gone into the tent to see Cleopatra's feat. The Seer chose the first trailer, in fact almost made a beeline for it, as if it were his intended destination all along. It was the shabbiest of them all. The Seer seized the handle on the door and turned it. It was open! They barged in.

The instant they closed the door, they could hear the sounds of the performers returning to their trailers, remarking on how well the cannon girl had done. Then, within seconds, they heard the short showman's voice too.

"Excuse me, madam," he gasped, obviously out of breath. "I am looking for two individuals who may be hiding out in your homes."

Frantically, Solomon and the Seer looked around inside the trailer. Where could they hide?

"There is no one here but our own esteemed performers," replied a snotty female voice, with a drawl almost as pronounced as her interrogator's.

"I must ask you to allow us to investigate," growled Pawn, his deep voice making Solomon jump.

There was a pause. He and the Seer stood stock still, as silent as possible, the boy terrified that they had made a big mistake. First of all, they should have kept running — they were now in an enclosed space with no way out. Secondly, they had chosen the wrong trailer. This one obviously belonged to someone at the lowest level of the company. Though it was neat and tidy, it barely had any furniture. They should have picked a trailer belonging to a star performer. There was nowhere to hide here — it was a cramped space with a crude straw bed with a single blanket and a small pillow, a little ice box on the floor, and some clothes, tattered ones at that, thrown over a small bench at the other end of the room. There was a stack of books in a corner.

Or had they chosen the wrong place? Though the Seer was obviously scared, his face twitching with excitement, he also seemed moored in this spot, his feet planted, as if it were important that they be in this particular trailer. It didn't make any sense.

"I must insist!" barked the showman.

"Make way!" cried another voice.

Solomon held his breath.

Suddenly, the door opened, and someone came quickly through it, almost as if thrown in. The figure had been wearing a sparkling cloak, but it was torn away from her as she was pushed inside.

Before them stood the incomparable Cleopatra dressed in her skimpy gold costume.

The first thing Solomon expected was a scream. But she looked at them with interest and brought her finger to her lips to indicate that she wanted them to be silent. A smile spread over the Seer's face.

"What about this trailer?" Solomon heard Pawn growl. He was standing right outside the door.

"I told you, sir, that you will not be entering our homes."

"And who is going to stop me?"

"We have gentlemen here who can deal with you," said the woman who didn't sound the least bit afraid. Solomon thought of the muscular men who had raised Cleopatra's net.

"Now, now," said the nasty little showman in a softer voice, "there is no need for an altercation of any sort. We are simply in possession of the knowledge that two business associates of ours, with whom we would like to confer, have entered your premises. Might we enquire if anyone has seen them?"

"If persons without credentials are within our prohibited area, we will attend to them and expedite their removal, thank you, sir."

There was another pause, then the little showman spoke again, his voice somehow even more syrupy.

"Might I introduce myself, my dear, charming lady? I am Aloysius H. Booth, and this is my assistant, Mr. Pawn. We are former members of the inner circle of one Leopold J. Coop."

The Seer uttered a little whimper and staggered. Cleopatra and Solomon both glared at him, and he gathered himself.

"Coop?" asked the woman. "You are acquainted with Coop? He owns a good portion of our enterprise here."

"His inner circle, I believe I mentioned. He owns a good portion of nearly every diversions enterprise, my dear. Control amusements and you control America. I believe that's his plan."

"When were you in his, as you say, inner circle?"

"As late as last year."

"And why aren't you with him now?"

There was a slight hesitation.

"We are pursuing our own business interests at this time."

"Interests?"

"We are setting up our own show … with the great Coop's blessing."

"How do I know you really knew Coop? Our Skeleton Man, Spratt, once met him. Mr. Spratt!"

"Yes, ma'am?" They heard a thin voice say as someone approached.

"These two say they were in Coop's inner circle — you were once allowed into his steam train carriage, were you not?"

"Yes, ma'am. It was extraordinary."

"It has pink curtains throughout," offered Booth.

"That's correct, ma'am."

"Anyone could —"

"His desk is made of mahogany with a gold encrusted telephone machine."

"Correct again."

"But once more, anyone —"

"His toilet has a gold seat, as well."

"I was never in his water closet, ma'am, wasn't allowed."

"Hmm."

"Might we simply make enquiries?"

There was another pause.

"If you do not cause a scene, and speak quietly and politely, you may ask those performers whom you encounter about the people you seek. You may knock on a few doors, as well."

"Might we look in the trailers?"

"Why would you need to do that? First, you said these individuals you seek were hiding out from you, and then you said they were business associates. Which is it?"

"I would say a little of both, madam. They are children on the run, possessed of talent but highly strung and unaware of their value upon a stage."

"Ah, children, why didn't you say so in the first place? You may do as you please."

Suddenly there was a loud knock on Cleopatra's door. All three inside froze.

"But not that one," remarked the lady.

"Why?"

"That's where the cannon girl lives. No white folks are allowed in there. She will be out in moments to wash dishes and then dig out the toilets before her bedtime. You may speak to her when she appears. It won't be long. We'll rouse her out if she isn't out soon."

"We don't need to talk to the Black one," remarked Booth derisively.

When Solomon turned to Cleopatra, he could see the shame in her face. Though North Britain too had once enslaved Black people, they had been free for nearly a century there. That wasn't the case in the American Empire. They had certain rights here now, but they still couldn't vote, and there were still a few remaining slaves, mostly old people in the southern part of the country. The Americans had almost had a civil war over the question of slavery several decades ago, but the presidential candidate who said he would do whatever it took to free them, even go to war, a tall Illinois lawyer named Abraham Lincoln, had been assassinated during a public debate with a man named Douglas as both vied for the Republican Party's presidential nomination. No leader had pursued the ideal of absolute freedom since, though President Douglas had made a compromise with the South during his second administration: He had gotten them to agree to stop the importation of slaves and the acquisition of new ones but had allowed the southern cotton plantation owners to keep the ones they had. So, slavery was slowly dying out, was almost dead, but the lives of most Black people were still desperate. There was a white world and a Black one in America. Cleopatra was from the South and the descendant of a slave. Solomon hated slavery. He didn't know why he had such an extreme view because many others, even in North Britain, looked down on folks from other races. The First Inhabitants, who had been the first to populate the land up there too, and had lived in large numbers in olden days, were few in number now and had suffered terribly because of the attitudes of many white North Britains throughout history, and even now. North Britains hadn't attacked the First Inhabitants like the Americans or virtually wiped them out — they had been more clever and subtle in their plans.

"Who are you two?" she whispered.

"This, Miss Cleopatra … this is a man named Seer. He can't speak or read … but he draws very well."

The Seer was nodding vigorously.

"Draws?"

"And I am Solomon Hunt from North Britain and seeking my fortune. I am trying to support my family, financially, in the meantime. I helped this little fellow escape from a sideshow in York."

She smiled, and when she did, it nearly melted Solomon. No one had ever made him feel the way Cleopatra already did. It was as if something changed inside him when he looked at her, like God was in him at that moment. Part of it was because she was, to him, a genuine star, but it was much more than that. She had dark eyes, beautiful brown skin, and lips painted with red gloss. She had seemed so small and fragile on the big extravaganza stage, but now he could see that she was just as tall as him, her arms and legs strong. He could see an inner strength in her expression too, an intelligence waiting to be put into action.

"If you helped him escape, then you are a good man."

She had called him a *man*. The Seer glowed up at him and took his hand. He frowned and shook it off.

"He seems to have some abilities," said Solomon.

"Abilities?"

"I don't know. I can't explain it. He's made us money and does it with ease."

"Money?"

The Seer smiled and pointed at the big jar.

"We'll explain later. Those two — Booth and Pawn, the ones asking questions out there, are the people who had him. They want him back. They *desperately* want him back. I don't why. But it seems like they'd do anything to retrieve him, like they believe he's special or something."

The Seer nodded sadly.

"I think they'd kill me to get at him."

Cleopatra sat down on her crude bed. She motioned at the Seer. "He's smart?"

"Very."

"Smart enough to get me out of here?" She sighed as if suggesting something impossible.

The Seer nodded vigorously. He dropped his jar, raced over to her, pulled out his pencil and paper, and began to draw. Very quickly, an image of the streets of New York City emerged, like those Solomon had seen in illustrated newspaper dailies, the twin State Buildings with their electric dollar signs and "Diversions!" billboards at the center of the sheet. It was the downtown area, known as Gotham Town. Then the Seer drew the three of them — himself, Solomon Hunt, and the great Cleopatra — holding hands, walking into the picture.

"New York?"

"You want us to go there?" Solomon asked his friend, his heartbeat increasing. *New York City!*

"That's where Coop is now, I hear," said Cleopatra. "The red pages say he's talking to people there about forming a new political party. What he wants to do scares me."

The Seer rose to his feet with a start. He quickly crossed out his picture. He thought for a moment and then began drawing a map of the western part of America. He made a dot for Buffalo, then Detroit City, then Chicago Town. At the latter, rapidly growing metropolis, he penciled in an exclamation mark. Then he drew the Mississippi River, several stops on it, including St. Louis, Memphis, and another big dot all the way down the river at New Orleans. Though he didn't know how to write the names of the cities, he knew where they all were — Solomon liked maps, loved to dream about traveling, and recognized the locations that all the dots indicated. As the little man drew, he made a thick line connecting each place. From Louisiana, the line moved west to the great Texas cities, then into outlaw country in the New Mexico Territory and then Colorado and the mining towns of Cripple Creek and Denver City, then Mormon Salt Lake City into Reno, Nevada (where he drew a cowboy), on to San Francisco (a dandy and a beautiful lady) and finally to small but growing Los Angeles in southern California, the warm, palm-treed retirement town for the wealthy, a distant-but-heavenly place. Solomon had read that the moving-picture industry was now working there in the winters, making American plays and stories look like sun-drenched dreams on film.

The Seer seemed to know all these cities. And along the thick line that wound its way through the Empire, he kept drawing the three of them: taking showboats down the Mississippi, riding horses in cowboy hats out west, and strolling down the boardwalks of San Francisco dressed to the nines. He drew Cleopatra performing her feat, he behind the cannon, lighting it, Solomon in the big jar, just his face glaring out at him. Behind them, he drew short, rotund Booth and huge, pumpkin-headed Pawn, and a man dressed as the Devil carrying a sign that read "SHOW OF SHOWS!" all in pursuit of the three allies. For his final touch, he drew Cleopatra, Solomon, and himself one last time, their heads floating in the ocean just beyond Los Angeles … smiling.

It actually made the three of them laugh, but it also stirred something deep within the North Britain boy. He felt a yearning. Oh, to be out there like that in America, heading west, seeking his fortune, with the famous Cleopatra and the Seer, performing, and maybe, just maybe, in his own way … being someone, admired in a way his father never could have imagined. It was a wonderful story … and he was ready to be a character in it.

"That's funny," said Cleopatra, "but ridiculous."

"Why?" Solomon asked, without thinking.

"I'll never get out of here, and even if I did, a Black girl and two white boys, or at least two who look like boys" — she glanced at the Seer again — "who look mostly white … we couldn't survive, even if we got away."

"Oh yes, we could," Solomon said. He wasn't sure why he said it, but as he did, he looked at the Seer, who was nodding vigorously. "The Seer … he gives us a chance."

The young artist leapt to his feet and took his comrade's hand, shaking it violently, and then gluing himself to him in a tight embrace. For a second, Solomon couldn't breathe. He pushed him away.

"You can't be serious, my friend," said Cleopatra. "What exactly is it that he does? How could he help us?"

"I can't explain, but you'll see. This might be one of the few chances you will ever have of getting out of here. If he can come up with an escape plan, will you give it a try?"

She paused for a moment, perhaps thinking of the consequences of getting caught.

"What do I have to lose?" she finally said, as if to herself. "I'll do it." She smiled and took their hands. The touch of her flesh, soft and warm, almost made Solomon's knees buckle.

"Good," he said, his voice breaking. She laughed and regarded him, but the Seer was instantly on his feet in front of them, pacing and thinking. Then, he snapped his fingers and began miming something. He dropped his head down toward a shoulder, held his hands together under it, and pretended to be sleeping.

"We should sleep?" asked Cleopatra.

The Seer shook his head and pointed outside the trailer toward the other extravaganza people, trying to form a word on his silent lips.

"When they are sleeping?" Solomon asked. "That's when we move? Tonight?"

The Seer nodded, and then mimed the three of them sneaking on tiptoes out the door.

"But we can't get beyond the trailer area," said Cleopatra. "There are always employees at all the exits and entrances."

The Seer shook his head.

"Yes, there are," she insisted.

"Wait a minute — I don't think he means that. Uh … we aren't going to go out an exit or an entrance … is that what you mean, Seer?"

The little man nodded.

"Then, how?"

He wouldn't say anything else. He was maddening in that way. It was as if he had a sense of drama about everything and when he had an exciting plan he wanted played out … he'd never give away the rest of the story.

Since the white show people wouldn't enter Cleopatra's trailer, the three friends didn't fear anyone finding them in there. She hung a cloth up from a string that went along the ceiling and changed out of her costume. Her dress was brown, old and plain, made, it seemed, out of sackcloth. But she had kept it clean and, of course, looked every bit the lady in it, even when she also wiped the paint from her face. She went out to do her dishes and clean the water closets and was back just before it grew dark. She brought her two new friends a little food, and they shared the chunk of bread and warm gruel she would have normally had to herself, adding the only item in her icebox ... a single, limp carrot. When someone yelled "lights out," she turned off her oil lamp and they huddled in the darkness. Despite the lamps being doused, the extravaganza people had gone outside and were drinking and talking. Soon, the noise increased. It sounded like some of the men were tickling the women, who laughed and sometimes shrieked with delight. People seemed to be chasing others around the lot. As this went on, Cleopatra packed all her clothes — just a brown bonnet, a change of underclothes, and her costume, and put them in a sack, along with a thick book from the tall stack in the corner. She found a pair of ratty old performer slippers and gave them to the shoeless Seer, who glowed back at her. A few hours later, the drinking and carousing stopped, and silence descended. They waited another hour and then sneaked out the door.

The Seer took the lead. Curiously, he headed back toward the performance area. They had to make their way around several showpeople who were snoring on the ground, a few men and women wrapped in each other's embraces. And finally, sitting there, right near the opening of the tunnel, was a heavily bearded woman with thick, hairy arms, fast asleep (or so it seemed), propped up on a broken-down chair. Though her eyes were moving frantically inside her lids, she didn't budge as they slipped past her and into the big top tent. Solomon's heart swelled when he looked up at the empty theater, its eight thousand seats yearning to be filled, the very air awaiting a show, remembering the spectacles that had been.

And there the cannon sat, at their end of the tent, right near the entrance to the tunnel, looking terrifying and warlike in the darkness. Solomon could see, when they reached it, that it wasn't a real cannon after all — it was much larger. The muzzle was tipped at a 45-degree angle.

The Seer motioned to it. It took the other two a few moments to realize what he wanted. He kept pointing up at the mouth.

He wanted them to get in.

CHAPTER TEN
THE POWER OF FLIGHT

He made Solomon get in first. Then Cleopatra slid down, holding her sack. She and the North Britain boy were face to face and pressed against each other — in fact, she was almost lying on top of him. At first, it was pitch dark, so though they could feel each other breathing, their chests slowly (not so slowly in Solomon's case) moving up and down, they couldn't actually see each other. It was a strange feeling, being that near someone, sensing them almost completely, but not being able to see them. Slowly, her eyes began to appear in front of his.

"This is a little close." She smiled. He just kind of nodded.

But they didn't have long alone together because very shortly they could hear the Seer grunting and groaning as he climbed up the cannon from the rear — he wasn't tall enough to jump and catch the mouth — and then his face appeared. In an instant, he was sliding down at them at full speed, clutching his jar. One foot landed on Solomon's head and the other on Cleopatra. They both cried out. Then they all started to laugh, so hard and for so long that the tears rolled down their cheeks and their ribs ached.

It was probably the first time in many years that any of them had laughed so fully. Finally, there was silence. No one said anything.

Solomon lay there in the dark cannon, pressed against Cleopatra, the Seer's foot on his head, wondering what in the world his accomplice was planning to do in the morning.

They were awoken by a sudden jerk. The cannon was moving. Up above, Solomon could feel the Seer shaking with excitement. He looked into Cleopatra's eyes, their noses almost touching.

"What's happening?" he whispered.

"Ah!" she said, nodding her head. "Now I know what the Seer is planning."

"You do?"

"Since we couldn't get out of the tent on our own … he's letting the people who wanted to keep us in … *take* us out."

"What?"

She grew quiet, not wanting the workers to hear them. Outside, men were huffing and puffing as they strained to move the cannon.

"It's heavier today, Jimmy."

"Yeah, sure, it grew overnight, you moron."

"I swear, it *is* heavier," said a third voice.

"Shut your cakehole and put yer back into her."

The valuable cannon had to be kept inside at night, but then moved out every morning so it could make glorious entrances into the tent for performances. The Seer had known this.

Solomon looked up and could see the roof of the tent moving. Then he saw a ceiling he didn't recognize … then the early morning sky. Not long after, there was silence.

"Uh!" grunted the Seer.

"We need to get out, now!" Cleopatra wasn't whispering anymore.

"But —"

In an instant, she had shoved the Seer up so hard that he reached the mouth of the cannon. Solomon saw his butt at the top and then saw it disappear into the sky.

"You go next, Miss Cleopatra. I'll push you up, then edge my own way out."

She giggled. "How manly, how gentlemanly of you, Master Hunt … but I think we should do it the other way around."

"We should?"

"Uh-huh."

He began to protest, but she put two fingers on his mouth. She was being polite, not wanting to explain out loud that she was likely stronger than him, certainly more skilled at demanding physical feats, and knew how to get in and out of this cannon better than anyone on earth. Solomon shut up and allowed her to grab him by the hips and shove him upward. She clutched his feet and pushed him out.

He had the presence of mind to get out of the cannon slowly. He gripped the edges with his hands and peeked out. They were outside the extravaganza tent; in fact, a good fifty yards away and far from the trailer village too. He could see the showhands who had pushed them out here returning to the big top tent, their backs to the cannon. Solomon looked down and saw the Seer, grunting and frantically motioning to him to get out.

Cleopatra was standing beside them in less than a minute. At first, the three of them ducked down behind their iron Trojan horse. Her face was tense but full of anticipation. "They won't have their backs to us for long. … Run!" she cried.

A temporary fence surrounded the entire grounds, keeping spectators away from not just the big top, but the back lot too. They made for it.

"HEY!" they heard someone yell. The three friends picked up their speed. None of them dared turn around. This was life and death. Cleopatra reached down to pick up the Seer, but he shook her off and kept to his own pins. She hadn't seen him run before. He moved, once again, at lightning speed. They hit the temporary fence at a sprint, scaled it, got over it quickly, landed on the park ground on the other side, and rolled away. Getting up and looking back, Solomon noticed that no one was following them. The yell they had heard must not have been directed their way.

"Calm," Solomon said. "Let's be calm, let's walk slowly, and just move toward the gate and out of the park without attracting suspicion. Let's pretend we are normal people."

They couldn't suppress their laughter, again.

"Where are we going?" asked Cleopatra.

"Chicago Town, I believe?"

The Seer nodded with a smile.

They were in downtown Buffalo a short while later and made for the steam train station on the run: Booth and Pawn had easily tracked them to this city and the extravaganza, so their enemies were capable of moving with haste. Then, Cleopatra, rushing along looking happy and scared, told them about a former policeman with flaming-red hair and a long needle nose who ran security at the show and had been instrumental in her "capture." He would be coming after her now. She feared what he might do to her if he caught her. The words "dead or alive," a phrase Solomon had read in western novels about cowboys and First Inhabitants, rang in his head. Getting away from all their pursuers would take every skill they possessed. At least they had each other.

But … they didn't have enough money to get to Chicago Town. Cleopatra had nothing.

Despite being the headliner, she wasn't paid a dime to work on *The Show of Shows.* Held like a prisoner, all she received was room and board. There was an unfair pecking order in the diversions industry and non-white performers were at the bottom.

They investigated the cost of three tickets to their destination. The Seer and Solomon then emptied their pockets … and found they were an American dollar short.

Though the boy groaned and threw up his hands, the little man didn't show any frustration. He sat down, the jar between his legs, and began tapping his forefinger on his chin again, deep in thought.

"Another jar act? I'll do it."

"I've been meaning to ask you about that. What's the big jar for?"

The Seer shook his head, looking over Solomon's shoulder into the crowd, appearing frightened by the very idea.

"Yes, you're right. That would draw too much attention."

The Seer nodded.

"Too much attention? What's the jar for, Solomon?"

"I get into it."

"Hmm. Flexible, are we?" She grinned. "Always helpful."

Suddenly, the Seer leapt to his feet. He dug into his pocket and pulled out some sheets of paper. Solomon was anticipating another drawing, but the little one didn't retrieve his pencil. Instead, he got down on his hands and knees and started folding the papers. One, two, three, four of them, he turned them into marvelously complicated shapes — a long tube and involved pieces that were attached to it.

Everything came to points at their ends. Once he'd made all the shapes, he connected them, and when he was done everything — in a matter of three or four minutes — he held a sort of thin airship in his hands ... one with wings. Then he started scurrying around the steam train station. Cleopatra and Solomon shrugged at each other and followed, moving quickly to keep up.

"Seer, what in the name of the monarch are you doing? We can't waste time like this. We have to go — maybe we should just travel to Detroit City for now? We can afford that."

But the little man turned around and shushed his friend with a harsh look, though as he finished, he glanced past him and his expression changed. A big grin grew across his lips. Then he started walking as fast as his legs could carry him.

The other two followed him until he came abreast of a wealthy white man in an expensive black suit and checked waistcoat with a monocle in his eye. He was marching across the station toward the First-Class carriages with a chubby little boy, also wearing an expensive suit with waistcoat and tie (though his outfit was orange). The man was veritably dragging the child.

"I shan't go, Father. There is nothing amusing for me at Grandmama's."

The Seer tapped the gentleman on the arm, rather hard.

The man stopped and indignantly looked around, at first seeing only the heads of other pedestrians in the station. Down below, the Seer tapped him again, this time on the hip, and the man looked toward the floor.

"Oh my God, it's a dwarf!" he cried. "And he touched me!"

Solomon frowned at the man. But the Seer simply held up his sleek airship with wings, as complex a paper model as one could wish to see.

"Daddykins! Look at that!" exclaimed the kid.

"Why … yes, yes, it is rather … do you like it, Laurence?"

"I want it … and I won't go to Grandmama's unless I can have it!"

The man hesitated. A smile began to slide across his lips. He arrested it.

"So you *will* go if you *can* have it?"

"Yes. That would be a deal."

"How much for your contraption, little man? … Speak up!"

The Seer extended his index finger.

"Cat's got your tongue, does it? Oh well, a dollar it is."

The man pulled on the chain at his waistcoat and released his wallet. A crisp dollar bill was retrieved.

"I will do it if it can fly," said the boy suddenly. "Only if it can fly."

"You little bas —"

But he didn't get his words out because the Seer stopped him by raising his arm straight up above his head and presenting four fingers to the gentleman's face.

"Four dollars?" asked the man, who apparently understood the language of money. He paused and thought for a moment. "Listen, if it can fly, and I mean *really* fly, I mean a good twenty feet or more, I will give you *five* dollars, dwarf, and you, young man," he added, turning to the boy, "will be visiting your grandmother not only this week but next week as well. On the other hand, if it cannot fly, this little man shall have his single dollar, and you shall be coming with me today anyway."

"Deal!" said the boy.

There was an expression on the Seer's face that told Solomon he had known all along how this conversation would go. He turned and faced the full length of the hall. His tongue darted out the side of his mouth. He looked across the station as if gauging distance and height; he licked a finger and held it upright to estimate wind velocity. Then he set himself comfortably on his legs, one in front of the other and wide, took the winged airship in one hand, drew back ... and released it at a calculated angle.

It flew. Goodness, did it fly.

The two-foot-long paper air machine left the Seer's hand and lifted into the train station sky as if God had sent the wind beneath its wings. It climbed at a steep angle until it was halfway to the beautiful, painted ceiling with its images of great white American warriors of the past, leveled off, and then sailed thirty feet above the heads of the crowd. It seemed like everyone stopped for a moment and watched. Across the great space it went — ten feet, twenty, thirty, fifty, one hundred, two hundred — all the way from one end of the gigantic station to the other, impossibly, magically ... flying. Solomon had read in the York news dailies about inventors in North Carolina, America, trying to create machines that could fly, fast and efficiently, faster than the passenger balloons. But so far, they had not succeeded. No one had. Nothing could really fly in the American Empire.

Until now.

The chubby boy ran after the flying model, screaming with delight, and the gentleman, his eyes wide with astonishment, pushed the five-dollar bill he had been fingering back into his wallet, took out a ten, and handed it to the Seer, his eyes still cast upward.

A short while later, the three adventurers were boarding a steam train for Chicago Town.

CHAPTER ELEVEN

IN SEARCH OF OTHER WORLDS

They took the cheaper fare, which meant their steam train would be following the long route to Chicago Town: through Cleveland first, then northwest to Detroit City, before veering slightly south again to their destination. This was perfect for them because their pursuers were not likely to take the longer way, and with waits in the big cities, the entire trip would stretch over the coming night, which meant they had a place to sleep. It gave Solomon time to talk with Cleopatra too and that suited him just fine. They ignored the looks of other passengers and their snarling comments about "that Black girl with those white boys," spoken so loudly that the whole train could hear. Not that the Seer's size or bronze complexion endeared him to others either, and nor did the trio's youth. The three friends found places in fifth class, far away from the others.

For the most part, the Seer occupied himself with drawing. Solomon noticed some of his pictures. There were a few of his two companions, lovingly done, and another of a sort of catapult.

It seemed a curious thing for him to draw.

"I don't know anything about North … North what?" asked Cleopatra.

"North Britain."

"What part of America is that in?"

"It's not. But it's the closest country to yours. The Empire pretty well surrounds it. You must have studied it in school."

"I don't have any formal education, Solomon. Though, to be honest, I don't think most Americans know anything about North Britain either, even white folks. I've never heard one person ever speak of it. We don't say much about places outside of the Empire in my country."

"You talk awfully well for not having any schooling."

"Thank you." She smiled. "My parents were readers, and they made sure I was too. I'm sorry I don't know about North Britain. It just wasn't in any books I read."

"You are forgiven. Are you really the granddaughter of African royalty?"

"Great-granddaughter. That's why I read. My great-grandfather was a slave but because of his heritage he was offered one privilege by his owner. So, he asked if they'd let him learn to read English. He was the only slave allowed. He made sure my grandparents learned too, and they passed it on to my mother and father, and that gift came to me."

"I love to read too," Solomon said. "It takes me away to other worlds. I've been missing it lately, too much going on, too many diversions." He slung his satchel down off his shoulder and pulled out his well-thumbed books — *Gulliver's Travels*, *Adventures of Huckleberry Finn*, *The Time Machine*, and *Anne of Green*

Gables, though he kind of hid the latter, worrying that it was sort of girlish. Then, he felt sheepish for thinking that way since he loved that book so much.

She smiled and picked up each novel, her eyes sparkling as she looked at them. "That's why I had those books in my trailer and why I took one with me when we left, an important one — the most important one." She tapped the bulge of the big book in her sack. "I used to get into trouble in the extravaganza for reading when I should be working."

He smiled back. "So did I. My father said I would never amount to anything. He said that a lot."

"We can share our books, Solomon, visit other worlds together, ones where we feel free."

He wanted to take her hand but didn't feel worthy of the great Cleopatra.

"So," he finally said, "how did you end up there, in that show?"

For a moment the boy thought she was going to cry. She took a deep breath and sighed.

"After many years, my parents were released by their owners. They had vowed not to have children and bring them into a world of enslavement. But when they were liberated and came north, they had me, even though Momma was almost fifty years old. We got by, my father working on the docks in Boston City, but it was hard work, just as demanding as in the cotton fields. At least, he was free. But it wore him out. He died when I was thirteen and Momma went within a year. I had nowhere to go, no profession. Moseley, the ex-policeman I told you about, he found me on my own in the City the month after my mother died. I was starving and ready to do almost anything. He said that I looked big and strong for a girl and that I had the appearance of an

African princess. I told him I was. I remember his eyes widened when I said that. He offered me a wage in the extravaganza … but, as you know, they haven't paid me anything since the first day I entered the big top — apparently Coop has separate non-white performers' contracts for his shows. I've wanted to run away many times, but they watched me carefully and told me I would die out on the streets alone anyway. They might be right. They gave me a few books — that's the only nice thing they did. Though I don't think any of them read. One of them told me it was too slow and boring, that books should be burned because they aren't needed."

"I hate them."

"I like Shakespeare," she said, pulling the big book out of her sack. It had the great writer's name on its spine. "It's hard reading at times, but it comforts me and it's beautiful, even when I don't understand it. I think his plays say that we all take on characters to give meaning to our lives — sometimes the roles we play are awfully sad, sometimes funny, and ridiculous — but underneath, we are all kind of equal … and everyone returns to dust in the end. I like that, even though it's sad."

She paused. "Books have been my only friends for a long time." Solomon could see tears welling in her eyes. But she was tough, show-business tough, as tough as a cowgirl on the frontier, and she stopped the tears in their tracks. "I think human beings like stories because we all want our lives to be stories … good ones. You have to stop me when I get rambling on like this."

"Miss Cleopatra, I would never —"

"Don't call me that."

"I'm sorry, I —"

"My parents called me Cleo … you can too."

"I … I'd be honored."

"Cleopatra just reminds me of bad things now … It's nice to have two good friends."

The Seer, who, unknown to them, had been listening carefully to their conversation, suddenly burst into tears. It took all the way past Cleveland to comfort him.

Nothing of any significance happened in Detroit City … until the steam train was pulling out. Solomon had stared up at the tall buildings on the way in — they were just as tall as the ones in Buffalo, though they were newer, and yet somehow, dirtier. Detroit was known as a place that made the most and the best of these newfangled motorized vehicles. Clouds of their exhaust hung in the air, and the city looked gray and brown and the station smelled. It was noisy too. Once the train came to a halt, there was a long wait. Black people were checking the steel wheels and hauling in coal and working on loading luggage on board — all the folks getting on were white. Solomon didn't want to watch. There seemed to be a lot wrong about America. He slouched down into his seat next to Cleo. They were both exhausted, no longer needing to be on the alert. They closed their eyes.

But the Seer was never at a loss for energy and always curious about everything. He pulled the window down and stood up, staring out into the station, like the meerkat he was. The steam train gave a little jolt and began to move.

Suddenly, Solomon heard someone shouting.

"HEY! Is that who I think it is? Right there! I can't believe it. I MAY HAVE JUST SEEN THE SEER!"

The fugitive's violet eyes bulged. He abruptly closed the window and sat down with a thump, his head out of view to anyone who might be trying to look into the train, his eyes cast to the floor.

Solomon got to his feet and peered out. He hadn't recognized the voice. It wasn't Pawn or Booth, and when he searched the people standing nearby and found the face that was shouting, now noiselessly because the window had been shut, it obviously wasn't Moseley, the needle-nosed, red-haired ex-policeman whom Cleo feared so much. It was a slick-looking man in wired spectacles, with a straw hat cocked at an angle, wearing a loud white suit with red pinstripes. He looked excited, like a fan. He was running along beside the steam train as it pulled away, yelling both at a nearby man who looked a lot like him and up in the direction of the three friends' window. Soon, he faded into the distance and the train steamed out of the station.

Solomon sat down.

"Seer?"

The little one looked up at his friend.

"Who was that?"

He shrugged his shoulders.

"Is there something you aren't telling me?"

He looked away.

"We can't be recognized everywhere we go," said Cleo. She looked frightened. "That man didn't seem like simply someone who had seen our friend do his geek show."

"Was he an extravaganza man?" Solomon asked the Seer.

"Looked like a talent scout to me," said Cleo.

"A talent scout?"

"Someone who finds acts and then works with diversions people and extravaganza owners to make them stars. He didn't seem like a small-time man either, and neither did the fellow who was with him. I'll bet they've worked with the big shows. Maybe even with Coop. I think they're insiders."

"Insiders?"

The Seer still wouldn't look at his companions.

"Will those men follow us? To Chicago Town?"

The fugitive shook his head, but Solomon wasn't convinced. Now he and his friends would be running from *five* people, a veritable gang on their trail.

"What do you think we should do, Solomon?"

The Seer leapt to his feet and looked at them, anxious.

"Maybe we shouldn't stop in Chicago Town?"

The Seer shook his head vigorously, putting his hands into his trousers and pulling out his share of their remaining money. He had equally divided what he had made among the three of them. He held his up in front of their faces.

"He's right, Cleo, we don't have enough money to go past Chicago *and* pay for a place to stay *and* feed ourselves. We have to *make* money there, not avoid the city. It's by far the biggest place on our route."

Now the Seer was nodding his head and smiling ear to ear. He reached over and made the two of them hold hands — which they were all happy to do — then he took both of their free hands in his, creating a little circle of friends. He glowed at them.

"He wants us to stick together."

"Do you think he can make us money in Chicago Town?"

"He did it before. And I have the feeling he has bigger plans now. Remember his map." The Seer had kept it with him. Solomon could see it bulging in a trouser pocket, the other pocket still full of blank sheets. He kept his pencil behind an ear.

Cleo pulled her hand away from the Seer's and patted him on the shoulder.

"I'll give him two days. Then, I'm sorry, but I'll have to make plans of my own. And if I see that red-haired devil, I'm heading for the hills … alone."

Solomon looked at the Seer. He sure hoped he had something up his sleeve. Not only was the boy desperate for Cleo to stay, but they were on their own and wanted, on the run … moving deep into the American Empire.

CHAPTER TWELVE

THEIR KIND OF TOWN

Chicago Town was incredible. It was big and loud and confident, and everything seemed new, like it was a gigantic child that had just learned to walk and yet somehow was instantly ready to run. This city had recently exploded in size.

Solomon gazed at it as they entered: such tall buildings, higher than the others in Buffalo and Detroit City. Dozens of huge passenger dirigibles, most as white as the clouds, hung in the sky, tethered to the roofs. The North Britain boy had read about the height of this city's structures in news dailies, but to see them was something else. "COOP INCORPORATED — Entertainment is Everything!" flashed a sign at the top of one of the tallest cloudscrapers. Many of the buildings were made of concrete, but there were some with panoramic windows wrapping around almost every floor, and others painted unusual colors. It was difficult not to stand and gawk upward. Solomon felt as though he were in a fantasy world, as if the buildings were made of mammoth marshmallows or towering candy sticks and sugar. This city was a symbol of the incredible growth of the Empire, its spread westward.

Chicago Town was also known for its sporting teams, kings of rounders and American rugby, and the Near-Death Bare-knuckle Fighting League, which performed in massive stadia in the outlying neighborhoods, its players celebrated like kings and truly important people in the red pages that dominated the city's many news dailies, some of which Solomon had found discarded on the train seats. Betting on the matches was a burgeoning industry too — there were even leagues of betting teams! And Coop seemed to be a big player in that world too. Amusements abounded in Chicago Town. If you wanted to make your mark, it was no longer enough to be celebrated in New York, Boston City, and Philadelphia. You had to come west to this big urban child on Lake Michigan too.

The Seer obviously knew this. He got off the steam train like a hunting dog. The other two had to step along to keep up with him and his head never turned once to the left or the right. He was on the scent of something.

Just as in Buffalo, he found it before he even left the steam train station. There, near the revolving glass-and-brass doors at an exit, on a billboard the size of an omnibus, next to another portrait of President Self and one of a rounders star, was an advertisement for "*THE BIGGEST SHOW ON EARTH!*" The Seer looked it up and down.

Solomon watched the excitement spreading across his face. *Why was he always drawn to the extravaganzas? What were the details, swimming in his brain, of the plan he had drawn up on his picture-map?*

"I thought he couldn't read," said Cleo, glancing around to make sure no one was observing them.

"He can't."

"So, what is he doing?"

"He seems to recognize show business posters. I'll bet he knows this show and has some idea about the acts in it. I think he knew all about you, even which trailer you occupied."

"He did?"

The Seer turned to her with a grin and nodded.

"But how?"

"That's what I'd like to know. If we knew that, maybe we'd know why those two goons are after him and why that other man was so excited to see him."

"There really is something about him, isn't there."

Solomon nodded. "There *really* is."

The Seer wasn't listening to them, or at least, he didn't seem to be. His gaze remained focused on the many sheets that made up the impressive poster. *THE WORLD'S MOST DANGEROUS ACTS!* read a headline smack-dab in the middle of the particular one in which he seemed to be most interested.

Solomon kept examining him, trying to figure out what he was seeing, where his attention was shifting. His eyes didn't linger long on that headline. They dropped down the page to the fine print at the bottom. *"Freaks!"* read a small word.

Immediately, the Seer was off.

The other two followed him. Gripping his big jar in both hands, the little man headed north along Michigan Avenue, a great wide street flowing with crowds of pedestrians, and past walls of department stores and other businesses. People were rushing as if their very lives depended on getting where they were going. The men wore colorful suits and straw hats and thrust out their chests, the ladies displayed themselves in tight dresses that jutted out at their behinds and revealed the lower parts of their legs above high-heeled boots. Amongst all of this, the poor, many of them Black or from the Realms of Asia or First Inhabitants, walked about, some even lying on the sidewalks, holding up their hands, some frighteningly emaciated, ignored by the busy pedestrians. There seemed to be so many more struggling people here than back in North Britain.

It took a while to get out of the business area, but eventually the buildings got smaller and soon the trio were in residential neighborhoods. The avenue they kept to was wide and filled with little stores, tanneries, blacksmith shops, and doctors' offices, Down the smaller streets past the stores, they could see endless queues of pleasant homes, all looking the same, set back on small lawns, newly planted trees lined up like soldiers by the sidewalks.

Every now and then they spotted a poster pasted to a building or tacked to a pole. Solomon had seen one that simply shouted "EXTRAVAGANZA!" as they left the business area, and there hadn't been any after that for a while, but now they increased in number. "*Right this way!*" read one. "*The biggest is up ahead*!" said another. "*Freaks, my friends!*" cried a third. And then, as they approached a rounders stadium three times the size of the one in York, a huge sign warned:

"BEWARE! Danger looms at GUM FIELD!"

Solomon knew about this stadium. He had read about it in the more slender red pages sections in the York news dailies. It was the home of the Chicago Bear Cubs, one of the most famous rounders teams in America. Gum Field was brand new. Even the home of the Gotham Yanks in the nation's biggest city couldn't match it. It was made of shining red brick — ivy was beginning to grow along the walls that surrounded its playing fields. Just this year, the first photo-picture ever reproduced in the *York Globe* had shown Alexander Spalding, a deep fielder and bowler with the Bear Cubs, about to touch the fourth post in Gum Field and score a key rounder in a match against the Cincinnati Red Legs. You couldn't see the crowd, but you knew that more than 30,000 people were cheering wildly.

Solomon could hear them now. He imagined that he was Spalding, the famous sportsman.

"UH!" exclaimed the Seer. His voice broke the boy out of his reverie.

He was pointing up at the red flags fluttering in the breeze high above the stands of Gum Field. They bore the name and colors of *The Biggest Show on Earth*. The Seer tossed Solomon his jar and started marching toward the huge front doors.

"Uh, Solomon," said Cleo, "it's the middle of the afternoon. The show won't start until five o'clock. They haven't even done the outside rope walk for the kid show. What are we doing here?"

The North Britain boy looked up and saw the high rope ascending from the ground outside Gum Field, running above the stands and into the stadium.

"Is that the one they use?"

"Yes. An aerialist, usually a woman without a lot of clothes on, walks it before the show begins. It's like a moving billboard. It draws people to the extravaganza."

She looked toward the sun. "But that's more than an hour from now."

The Seer was still striding away.

"Seer!" Solomon cried out. But he didn't look back. When he

got to the front gates, he veered past them and began walking under the awnings along the outside of the stadium.

"I can't go near this show," said Cleo. "Someone might recognize me!" She stepped back from her friend, looked behind her, then crossed the street and moved under a big oak tree into a shadow.

Solomon glanced toward the stadium. "Seer? Where are you going?" But he kept walking and as he rounded the curving exterior of Gum Field past the ticket booths, the boy noticed the same sort of gathering of trailers they'd visited at Moffat's Grove in Buffalo. *What was the Seer interested in? The so-called freaks? Performers? Or something even weirder?*

"We aren't going with you!" Solomon cried. The Seer kept walking. "We'll wait here!"

The North Britain boy wasn't really in a mood for waiting, though if he had to choose one companion to stay with for a while, it would be Cleo. He crossed the street, and they sat down in the shade under the oak tree, the big jar at their feet. They started talking. It was easy for them. It always would be. They could talk at the drop of a hat and never stop. He told her more about his life, the iron-fisted rule of his father, his dreams; she entertained him with stories of the great extravaganza. She talked about her book and her favorite plays in it — *As You Like It*, *Hamlet*, and *The Tempest*. She even quoted her favorite Shakespearean line: "All the world's a stage, and all the men and women merely players." She spoke too of her fear of Coop's new political party, the Fundamental American League, who wanted the Empire to stay the way it was, in fact, make businesses and the rich even richer, and what that would do to her and others like her. "He's said that Black people should never vote, and neither should First Inhabitants or immigrants." President Self was growing old, and Coop would be opposed by a new candidate who wanted to change America. "But Coop will make Americans fear that," insisted Cleo. "He is already saying that his opponent has *foreign* views. Coop's great business success makes him admired beyond everyone else in the Empire."

Solomon spoke more of the Seer's fear of the famous showman too, but said it seemed more personal. He tried to cheer up Cleo by talking about their adventure and of books again and they grew happier. Time flew past.

Suddenly, they heard a shout. It sounded like the Seer crying out. They looked across the street and saw him running toward them. There was a giant by his side who appeared to be about three times his height, sprinting too ... both pursued by ten showhands!

"UH!!" shouted the Seer.

Solomon leapt to his feet and was about to rush after them when Cleo pulled him down. "Don't run!" she said under her breath. "They don't know we're with the Seer."

The fugitive glanced at his two friends as he swept by, looking pained at first, but having the good sense not to give them away. He and the giant turned south and headed back down Michigan Avenue. But the others — big, powerful men with hairy forearms bulging below their rolled-up sleeves and shoulder muscles on display in sleeveless undershirts — were gaining on them. An escape had been perpetrated, and the showhands had been caught off guard, but now they were in full flight.

The giant, it seemed, was holding himself back. He was slightly ahead of the Seer and glancing around at him. The showhands kept gaining. Cleo and Solomon stood up and watched them from behind as they disappeared into the distance, silently cheering for their friend and his latest accomplice. But the others were getting closer. One began reaching out for the Seer. Then something remarkable happened. The giant leaned back, picked up the Seer by the scruff of his dirty white shirt, and lifted him into the air. Then he increased his speed dramatically. His stride lengthened and he immediately put distance between himself and his pursuers. The Seer's legs kicked violently in the air, and he swung his fists at the giant, but he couldn't reach him. In moments, the pair was out of sight. Seconds later, the extravaganza men came to a halt, leaning over, chests heaving, trying to catch their breaths.

As Cleo and Solomon walked down Michigan Avenue, Solomon carrying the jar, eyes to themselves, Cleo with her head down and neither saying a word, they passed the showhands walking back up the street, looking distraught.

"How'd that little devil get in?"

"Weren't the door locked?"

"He's got magical powers. I'm willin' to lay coins on it."

"Don't matter, magic or not, the boss is gonna lose his brains. They was groomin' the big one for somethin', somethin' important."

"He'll fire the lot of us, sure as shootin'."

About ten blocks down Michigan Avenue, a pair of enormous hands reached out from an alleyway and pulled both Cleo and Solomon out of sight. The boy was so shocked that he tossed the jar into the air.

The giant stood before them. He had instantly released Solomon and caught the jar, high in the air, with one hand. The boy gazed at him. On close inspection, he wasn't at all what he had appeared to be at first sight. He wasn't a fully grown giant. Oh, he was tall all right, incredibly tall, nearly eight feet high, with a head the same height as the distance from the tips of Solomon's fingers to his elbow, but he was still just a kid. It was amazing. Solomon guessed he was maybe fifteen years old. Like the Seer, despite his larger size, he was perfectly formed. He wore a cross on a chain around his neck.

"Uh Uh!!" said the Seer, and he stamped his foot and gestured toward the giant. If he'd been able to speak, he likely would have exclaimed "TA DA!!"

"Hello," said the giant in the strangest voice Solomon had ever heard — a kid's voice, but deep and resonant and gentle. "Why did he help me escape? I'm free, that's a marvel, for sure. I thank God for it. But ... what do you want with me?"

"I don't know," said Solomon.

"You don't know? How can that be?"

"You will have to ask the Seer."

"Is that his name? He can't speak, can he?"

"No, he can't."

"Then, how can we ask him anything?" As he glanced at Cleo, he did a double take. "Say" — he smiled — "aren't you Cleopatra, the human cannonball girl from *The Show of Shows*?"

"Yes, but my name is Cleo," she said, reaching out for his hand.

He set the jar down and took her hand into his, and it looked like it disappeared. "I'm Angus," replied the big boy with a smile.

"And I'm Solomon, and our friend here has some explaining to do."

The Seer was already down on his hands and knees and drawing. What he came up with was, of course, remarkable, and he did it in a flash. It depicted two scenes, one a flying trapeze performance and the other an acrobatic act. But they weren't just any two gymnastic turns — they were performed by a giant; and not just any giant — the gigantic child who towered over the other three in this very alleyway in Chicago Town.

"H-How does he know that?" said Angus in a quavering voice. "How does he know that?"

"What do you mean?"

"That's a secret … a *big* secret! I'm still in what they like to call 'the Freak Show,' but not for long. They are training me, forcing me, to be an acrobat. Word is orders came all the way down from the top. Someone up there found out I could do things no other giant has ever been able to do. Most people my size are awkward. And I'm still growing. Some people think I'll be over nine feet tall." He looked sad. "They're forcing me … they keep me locked up."

It wasn't that Solomon was hard-hearted, but he wasn't thinking about what this prisoner from *The Biggest Show on Earth* had gone through. He was considering something else. *What an extraordinary idea!* He couldn't even imagine what it would look like in person — a giant, this unbelievable boy from a strange dream, turning somersaults, flying through the air! Solomon didn't know a lot about extravaganzas, but he was willing to bet that nothing even remotely like this had *ever* been seen before … anywhere.

"How … how did this little one know?" exclaimed Angus again, taking a giant step back from the Seer, who grinned up at him with a devilish look.

But, once again, Solomon wasn't concerned about Angus's fears. Something had dawned on him. He suddenly realized, standing in that alleyway in Chicago, that he had become part of a mission, an adventure with a plan, one that he hadn't understood. But now he did, at least to some degree. *The Seer was putting together a show!* That's what the two of them had been doing since they'd come to America, since even before that: picking up unique and spectacular acts, all performed by kids. First, the world's only female human cannonball, and now its sole giant acrobat, to go along with Solomon Hunt's boy-in-a-jar display, everything staged by a mysterious and gifted young ringleader. Solomon turned to the Seer who looked back at him. That gleam was still in his eye, and it still appeared a little evil. What were they going to do next? How did the Seer know about these performers and how to spring them? Why did those other men want him SO badly? *Who, in this world, was he?*

CHAPTER THIRTEEN
A CLOSE CALL

This was how their act started in Chicago Town. Solomon was rolled out, inside the jar, into a square in the center of the city. The square was awfully busy, so no one noticed at first, just a few folks glanced at the head jammed inside the jar — chocolate brown hair smeared against the glass, blue eyes staring out. Then, a few ladies screamed. Within a minute, a huge crowd had formed around him, like a mob gathered at the site of a spectacular accident.

The Seer, somehow making himself look even tinier than he was and dressed in his Tarzan skin, emerged out of the crowd, approached the jar, and motioned toward it with flair. Slowly, ever so slowly, Solomon uncoiled himself from his impossibly small confines, exactly as he had been instructed to do. The applause was thunderous. It echoed off the big Chicago buildings.

Next up was Cleo. She came shooting into the air out of the midst of the crowd, somehow ejected upward by a magically powerful force. She turned four somersaults in the air before landing on the hard surface beside Solomon Hunt, bending her knees perfectly, taking the force of her descent with ease.

The Seer had vanished from their street stage, bowler hat in hand, catching the coins that were coming his way. As he did, up from the ground, from the very spot where Cleo had been fired into the air by his gigantic arms, rose a surreal boy … eight feet tall, his huge head high above everyone else. One could hear the whole audience gasp.

But that wasn't all.

Angus began to move, and as he moved the crowd parted to let him through. He jumped onto his hands, his big boots skyward. The crowd gasped again. Then he undertook ten somersaults on solid ground, springing through the air like a whirligig, covering half the square until he finished right between Solomon and Cleo. As he came to a stop, the Seer threw his bowler hat like a dart, and Angus put his arms in the air and caught it, then held it out at his waist.

As the crowd erupted into another enormous cheer, money came flying from every direction toward the big boy, who looked up to the sky in thanks.

That was it. That was their entire show at that time. They had rehearsed in the alleyway for half an hour, the Seer as director. It was designed to be dramatic, to have an impact, and most importantly, to get them onto the stage and off in a flash.

People were coming for them — there was no doubt about it: Pawn, Booth, the red-haired devil, maybe the talent scouts, and certainly all those showhands from *The Biggest Show on Earth*. Those last folks were probably beginning to scour the city now. All the young performers' pursuers intended to imprison every one of them … or maybe worse. Solomon wondered if he would soon be in some tawdry freak show … or dead. What would happen to his family then? In hours, maybe minutes, word would shoot up Michigan Avenue toward Gum Field that a female human cannonball, a contortionist, a little person, and (most importantly) a giant boy had brought down the house in a square in the center of the city.

So, the minute the quartet was done, bogged down a little now by coins, they were running away. They made for the steam train station. There was such a necessity for speed that they almost literally ate as they ran, stopping in a tiny place jammed between a big lending house and a betting business on Michigan Avenue, run by an Italian who made something he advertised as "Pizza Pie." It was cooked dough topped with tomato sauce and cheese, and shaped like a pie too. It was quite a concept. They bought it and four glasses of lemon drink and rushed back out into the streets.

But at the steam train station they encountered a problem. The next locomotive for St. Louis didn't leave for an hour. They sat on a wooden bench against a wall in a corner, consuming the last bits of their pie, and growing more and more frightened.

They couldn't help looking in the direction of the doors that opened onto the street.

They all imagined the showhands were streaming down Michigan Avenue toward them.

But the danger they soon saw didn't come from there, but from *inside* the station, from another steam train … arriving from Detroit City.

The Seer saw them first. Solomon felt a hand grip his arm, and fingers (and fingernails) sink into his flesh, and couldn't believe the strength that came from such a small frame. The Seer didn't say a word; he didn't even grunt. He didn't need to — Solomon turned his head from the outside doors and instantly saw what he was looking at.

Booth and Pawn were stepping down from the latest train from Detroit City and their eyes were scanning the crowd. Behind them, almost as if on cue, a red-haired man with a needle nose was exiting the very next car. Cleo, who had noticed when Solomon's head darted around, gasped and instinctively dropped to the floor. It was a simple but good plan, at least as a start. Solomon descended too and so did the Seer. Angus, who had been slouching on the bench to hide his size, quietly saying a prayer, his coat pulled up on his neck to disguise the enormity of his head, didn't notice what the others were seeing and wouldn't have been worried if he had — he didn't know about these pursuers. However, his companions' quick reactions, their palpable fear, scared him, and he instantly tried to drop down too.

But Solomon wouldn't let him … because an idea had immediately come rushing into his mind. He turned onto his back in a flash, planted his feet under the giant's enormous thighs, and shoved him upward.

"What are you doing?" cried the huge boy in what he thought was a whisper.

"Sssshhh! Stand up!"

"Stand up? Are you crazy?"

"Yes, but do it anyway. Stand up, way up!"

"But —"

"I know, everyone will notice you. You will draw a crowd. That's the idea. We have ten minutes until our steam train leaves — track five, remember. Start running toward it in nine."

The giant rose and Solomon motioned to the others in the direction of two nearby washing rooms, a Ladies' and a Gentlemen's, and they moved toward them, low to the ground. Cleo slipped into the first, the Seer and Solomon into the other.

A moment later, the North Britain boy crept out to the door and peeked into the hall. A big crowd had formed around the uncomfortable giant. As Solomon had suspected, Booth, Pawn, and Moseley were searching the train station, likely intent on examining every inch. But the commotion around the sky-high boy was too much for them to resist. They joined the crowd. The three men stood within a few feet of each other, Booth and Pawn not knowing Moseley, unaware of their similar missions. Solomon thought to himself that he had never seen three more repulsive people.

Behind the crowd, a ten-foot-tall clock loomed on the wall. Their train would leave in exactly seven minutes. The American Empire Steam Railroad was known for its punctuality.

Six minutes later, the trio emerged from the washing rooms and started to run. Ten seconds after that, the giant burst from the mob that still stared at him and broke into gigantic, loping strides.

Solomon, Cleo, and the Seer were closer to the track than Angus — they had a substantial head start.

The steam train whistle blew, and a porter shouted, "All aboard!"

Solomon turned his head and saw Angus coming toward them at incredible speed; behind him were all three of their hunters. They were pointing as they ran, their faces turning red, Booth and Pawn indicating the Seer and Solomon Hunt, Moseley focused on his Cleopatra.

The steam train started to move, but the porter spotted the late arrivals rushing for his car. He held his door open. All four raced toward it. Solomon glanced at Cleo and nodded. She seized one of the Seer's arms and the boy grabbed the other. They lifted him into the air, his legs kicking in resistance, and threw him through the opening and onto the train. Remembering the human cannonball's ability, Solomon went next. He was inside in a flash. He imagined Cleo's face behind him, the last of the three of them to get onto the train, but as calm and calculating as she had been during her act. She raced along, and once Solomon was safely on board, leapt on herself. They all turned, on their knees, and looked back out the door. Angus was coming, moving as fast as the chugging train. He leapt, one big foot aiming for the opening … and landed inside. "Thank God," he said quietly. Their pursuers were left in the steam train's dust.

But the young quartet saw the three of them cursing and shaking their fists. Only the Seer responded. He pushed his head out the window, taking the blast of air, sticking out his tongue, placing his thumbs in his ears and wiggling his fingers at them. The sounds he made seemed like curses.

As the three men faded into the distance, the four friends saw them stop gesturing at the steam train. Booth and Pawn had noticed what Moseley was doing … and he them.

Not long after, Solomon, the Seer, Cleo, and the giant curled down onto their wooden benches in fifth class, still breathing hard, hearts still pounding. They were heading south now. This train would stop twice in the state of Illinois, briefly in Peoria and Springfield, before it moved on to St. Louis in Missouri. The Seer's map noted that last city as a stop on their travels; so, that's where they were heading. They didn't know what awaited there, but they could tell by the grin on the Seer's face — made a touch anxious by the fact that his pursuers had come so close to him and had seen where the train was going — that he knew exactly why the four of them needed to get there. He wasn't sharing it. They would get off in St. Louis and nowhere else. They could only hope that the men who were hunting them would search Peoria and Springfield first. They could only hope.

CHAPTER FOURTEEN

WHO THEY MET IN ST. LOUIS

They moved through miles and miles of farmland and past country villages carved out of the wilderness, taken from the First Inhabitants who used to live here less than a century ago, and stopped briefly in Springfield. Solomon wished they could visit this town, the home of Mr. Lincoln, the man who, it seemed to him, could have been a great force in American history, who would have tried to free the slaves long ago, had he not been killed on the steps of the capitol building in this very town. But they were quickly moving south again.

Angus told them more about himself. He'd been raised in Baltimore, Maryland near the eastern seaboard, in a poor family who, despite their son's remarkable ability in school athletics, had grown ashamed of him and frightened by his size and sold him to a traveling showman. That man, after presenting him for a year in a tiny tent in which his head nearly went through the ceiling, had, in turn, auctioned him to *The Biggest Show on Earth*. They, with their unparalleled gifts for entertainment and advice from Coop's people who had invested in their company and watched the boy rehearse from high up in the stands, quickly understood that he could be so much more than a sideshow giant. He, like Cleo, had often tried to escape, but his ability and size made him so valuable to the extravaganza that its owners made sure he was watched twenty-four hours a day. He was a religious boy, a Christian, and his trust in his God was remarkable for someone who had been through so much.

"I don't try very hard when they train me. They don't know half the things I can do."

The Seer grinned.

It grew dark. Solomon sat there feeling guilty, but not about their adventures. He was thinking about home. He had gotten so caught up in the things he was doing with the Seer, with the danger, the excitement, the entertainments, the thrill of meeting Cleo … that he had momentarily forgotten about his family. He made a vow to find a way to send them money as soon as he could. It wouldn't be long before they would be destitute.

The Seer sat near him, looking at his map in the dark and drawing. He continued to work on that strange picture of the catapult. It was coming along.

Solomon intended to ask him about it but drifted off to sleep.

It was about midnight when they reached St. Louis. They came in from the east side of the Mississippi River and the city was almost all on the western shore. It wasn't as huge as Chicago Town (which was the third largest metropolis in the Empire, behind New York and Mexico City), but it was more than twice the size of York, and larger than Montreal, the other urban center in North Britain. Solomon had read that St. Louis had a bit of a southern feel to it. In fact, he'd heard that there were still slaves in the city. That was difficult to even imagine.

They were just downriver from the land of Mark Twain and his Tom Sawyer, Huck, and Jim, an author and characters Solomon loved.

Being here seemed as impossible as actually stepping into the *Adventures of Huckleberry Finn*. America had always been like some sort of fantastic hologram in the North Britain boy's imagination, now it was right here in front of him, wonderful, and terrible too ... and he was walking about in it.

You could almost sense the East and North fading behind, and stretched out ahead was not just the South, but the West too, the Wild West. In the quiet station in the midnight hour, a man walked past them in a cowboy hat with a dirty kerchief around his neck, no guns on, but dusty and mean looking, as if he'd come from somewhere where saloon brawls and showdowns were common.

The Seer seemed to know where he was going here too. This time, he didn't pause at any of the billboards and posters (plastered on the walls so many places in this great country, where money and sensation ruled). The bronze-faced little man marched right out of the station this time, with Solomon, Cleo, and the young giant in tow. They were quite a sight.

A young woman, well attired in a long, tight dress and matching blue bonnet with frills, obviously catching a very late train with her soldier-husband, quickly clung to him when she saw the strange young quartet and had to put her hand over her mouth to keep from crying out.

When the four of them reached the nearly deserted street that fronted the station, big buildings rose up in grids before them, all dark at this hour with just a few of those new electric lights on. It looked like a city abandoned after a battle, though they saw a few tough-looking people, who seemed to have emerged at night out of the underground of St. Louis.

The Seer didn't even look at them and neither did he glance at the few horses and carriages that rattled past, the odd sputtering motorized vehicle, and the silent passenger balloons docked high above the buildings. He kept marching, this time not into the center of the city and along a main street, but to his left down a smaller artery and then on and on, walking for what seemed like an hour, first under gas lamps and then into almost complete darkness in the suburbs, his route lit only by the odd light in the houses. Eventually, it began to feel like the four companions were completely out of the city, but then a constellation of dimmed lanterns appeared up ahead, slightly lighting the darkness in a field.

After a few strides in pitch dark, Solomon almost ran into a fence. Somehow, the Seer had walked right through it! Then the boy realized that his friend had actually gone between the posts of a wide gate while he had collided with one of them, a very tall one. When Solomon looked up, he saw "*ST. LOUIS FAIRGROUNDS*" written in ornate letters on a big golden arch. He caught up to their guide.

"Fairgrounds, Seer? What are we doing? I don't see an extravaganza. Wouldn't it be lit up like a Christmas tree? Even at this hour?"

But, of course, the Seer said nothing. Solomon could see his eyes now, focusing on what was out in front of him.

In moments they were in strange surroundings indeed. It was like being inside an elongated horseshoe, with what appeared to be low buildings forming walls on three sides. But as things became clearer, illuminated by a lantern here and there, Solomon could see that the buildings were actually wagons and tents with great painted canvases and small, fold-out stages. They all faced inward toward what, during the days and evenings, would be captive audiences.

The four of them were standing in the middle of a carnival.

While Solomon stared, Cleo and Angus nodded their heads in recognition, and the Seer looked to be figuring something, his tongue slipping out of his mouth, his eyes moving back and forth, observing the canvases and tents as if searching for something.

The artwork was remarkable — blue, red, gold, green, and purple and every lurid shade of color known to man or the devil. And what they depicted was even more devilish. "*The Living Dead*," "*The Lincoln Assassination*," "*The Wild Man of the Borneo*," "*The Elephant Skin Man*," and all sorts of other attractions loomed over the four of them in frightening hues. The presidential candidate's head was exploding as a bullet entered it; his corpse lay in a coffin as visitors were depicted examining it; the Wild Man glared out at them; the creature with the Elephant Skin looked like he was half pachyderm. The North Britain boy's eyes actually bulged.

But the Seer was all business. He had spun around examining the show tents and found the one that he wanted. "*The World of Edgar Allan Poe!*" read blood-red writing across the top of it and below were slightly smaller exclamations:

"*Experience the Horror!*" "*Discover the Macabre!*" The paintings exhibited a huge razor-sharp pendulum swinging toward a torture victim tied to a board, an orangutan murdering two women, a masked figure in a crimson cloak with the words "*Red Death*" written across its blotchy forehead, and a pale woman rising from a coffin. Solomon loved the frightening tales of

American writer Edgar Allan Poe — they were inventive and scared the liver out of him ... so he couldn't resist them. But this was indeed a strange way of presenting them. During the afternoons and evenings, Poe's dark tales were alive inside this tent!

The Seer walked past the little stage that sat up high in front of it.

"That's the bally," whispered Cleo to Solomon. "There's always a talker there, dressed up real fine, who draws the audience into the tent with his talk, tries to make the show so enticing that they can't resist. The idea is to keep all the acts hidden inside, make them seem irresistible, get the audiences to pay, and then bring them in. Get the money first, that's always the plan. It's an American ethic."

Solomon doubted that he would have needed any enticing.

They clambered up the stairs to the door of the big Poe tent in the dim glow from the lanterns, as silently as they could, barely able to see the steps. But then the Seer stopped in his tracks. Solomon could see why. A guard, a very large man, as fat as an enormous rubber ball, his face as round as the moon and featuring three chins, lay fast asleep in a gigantic chair at the entrance. Solomon had never seen such an obese man. They carefully stepped by him and entered the exhibition tent.

Curiously, the door was unlocked. That seemed unusual. In fact, it worried them. The Seer motioned for Angus (who would barely fit inside anyway) to stay outside near the guard and wait for them. The door clicked shut behind them.

It was dark and spooky. They could hear the tick-tock of the razor-sharp pendulum moving back and forth, and as they edged along in the big tent through Poe's horror stories, unable to see things until they were almost a foot in front of their faces, barely avoiding falling into a pit, seeing the living female corpse, Lincoln's dead body, and the masked figure of Red Death in the crimson robe, they all tried to not cry out. It was difficult. Some of the characters popped up at them as they walked about, their movement apparently tripped by the three intruders' footfalls on the floor nearby. When an orangutan, *a real one*, suddenly reached out in the darkness for Solomon's neck, Cleo had to seize her friend and pull him back and put her hand over his mouth. Curiously, the big monkey didn't make a sound. It was obvious that during the days it screamed at the suckers who came in here, but now, looking sleepy, it just seemed curious, unable to muster a cry and seemingly uninterested in making an effort to terrorize someone when it wasn't getting paid. It grinned at Solomon Hunt.

Then they heard someone speak.

"Intruders," said a hideous voice. "You are all about to die."

The blood ran cold in Solomon's veins.

But the Seer didn't hesitate. He walked toward the source. Solomon gripped Cleo and pulled her back, but then they heard a different voice, a much nicer one: that of a young girl.

"Hello?" she said sleepily. There was the sound of a match being struck and then a small lantern appeared, floating in the darkness in the girl's hands, her face ghoulish above it.

Solomon and Cleo moved toward the Seer, who was looking at the girl and holding his finger to his lips in an effort to have her talk quietly.

"Who are you?" she asked, a slight foreign accent now evident, looking a little afraid, though not as frightened as one might have thought a teenage girl would be when confronted by silhouetted strangers in her bedroom in the middle of the night. But then again, they were all in an Edgar Allan Poe story.

An enormous raven sat in the shadows in a fake window above her head. There was a chair and a writing desk with a quill and ink bottle nearby. The girl had been curled up on a chest, under a single, thin blanket, in this re-creation of a dreary little room. She was dressed in a man's black suit with black southern string tie, a fake black moustache above her upper lip, matching her medium length black hair, parted severely in the middle like a man's. The whole scene was creepy.

"Intruders," repeated the raven. "You are all about to die." Then it examined the visitors. "Nevermore," it said, almost apologetically, without the energy it obviously usually employed, as if simply remembering its line.

The girl turned to it. "Ssshh, Edgar."

"Nevermore," it whispered.

"Nevermore, nevermore, nevermore ..." said a chorus of other voices in response, some echoing others, all speaking softly.

The three friends looked questioningly at the girl. She stepped to the side, switched on the electric stage lights that lit her set, and suddenly that end of the room was filled with a blazing bright light. The girl's skin looked shockingly pale now, almost the alabaster of a statue, and behind her a whole unkindness of ravens was suddenly visible, jammed into a cage meant for a quarter of their number.

There must have been more than half a dozen.

"Uh," said the Seer quietly, pointing at the girl, then at them, then toward the way he and his companions had entered.

"Doesn't he speak?" she asked.

"My name is Solomon Hunt, this is Cleo the human cannonball, and we have a giant named Angus waiting outdoors. May I introduce the Seer … I think he wants you to come with us. We are seeking our fortune and our freedom. We won't hurt you. In fact, we want to help you. Does that make any sense to you?"

Tears formed in her eyes.

"Yes," she said, "yes, it does. I've often dreamed of something like this."

"I'm not surprised," said Solomon, glancing at their leader.

"But it's impossible. This might as well be a dream." Her accent, though slight, was unusual, unlike any the North Britain boy had ever heard.

"What do you mean?" asked Cleo.

"There's a guard outside and —"

"Asleep."

"That doesn't matter … unless your friend is holding the door open from the outside."

Solomon remembered the click of the door as it closed behind them.

"He isn't," said Cleo.

"A magician rigged that door so that intruders can easily open it and come inside, but once it is opened, it locks tightly both ways. You … you are trapped in here with me."

Solomon's heart began to race. The canvas walls of the tent were as thick as brick — you couldn't knock them down or even slice through them. The door was sealed into it with heavy brass hinges.

The Seer took the girl by the hand and raised her to her feet.

"He will find a way out," said Cleo, looking unsure.

"But it's impossible."

"That usually doesn't concern him," said Solomon. He and Cleo glanced at each other, worried.

"I'm Marilyn," said the girl, "or at least, that's what they call me here." She seemed awfully shy for a showgirl. And as she rose to her feet, Solomon could see that she wasn't very tall, petite next to Cleo. He could also tell that her skin wasn't as white as the bright light had made it appear and that she had bits of white powder on her face, as if she hadn't been able to fully wipe it off after her performances of the day before.

The Seer reached out and ripped the mustache from her lip.

"Ouch!" she cried but then smiled. "I've wanted to do that for a long time!"

"You said they call you Marilyn," said Cleo. "What's your real name?"

"I am really Ayesha." It sounded wonderful when she said it.

"Uh!" remarked the Seer, stamping his foot and pointing at her.

"I think he wants us to call you that."

The Seer held out his arm and the huge raven fluttered onto it. It was as black as the night, its head nearly a third the size of the little man's.

"Oh my goodness!" cried Ayesha. "How did he do that? Edgar never goes to anyone other than me."

But the Seer wasn't offering explanations. He motioned to Cleo and Solomon to take up the cage with the tightly imprisoned ravens and bring it with them.

"Oh, no," said the girl, "you don't need to do that." She reached up and opened the little door. "Allan," she said clearly, "you lead the way, then Lenore, then Eulalie. Ulalume, Berenice, Eleonora, and Morella are next, and the rest of you just keep up."

The biggest raven hopped out, followed by the others.

"We won't be flying for now," added Ayesha. "I expect you all to do your best to resist that. Allan and Lenore, you are to keep the others in line."

As the whole troupe made their way back across the tent, the birds followed, hopping behind the human beings, not one of them making an attempt to fly.

Solomon pinched himself on the arm, good and hard, but he seemed to be wide awake. He looked at Cleo, but she wasn't looking back. She didn't appear to care about how remarkable this scene was — her face was grim. And she was right. It didn't matter how amazing the birds were, or this girl, or even the Seer. Not one of them, or anyone, could save the four friends from their predicament. *They were locked in.* Their ringleader had finally made a mistake. A big one. They had imprisoned themselves for the carnival people to find in the morning — and Solomon had heard that carnies were the meanest and toughest of showpeople.

But the Seer didn't seem to care. He led the way, focused on getting back to the entrance without incident, looking optimistic. Could he have actually anticipated the rigged door? Obviously, he had a plan. It turned out to be simple.

When they reached the entrance, he mimed that he was very tall and that he was grabbing the door and ripping it back with great savagery. *Ah, yes*, Solomon thought.

"Angus," he called out, as quietly as possible.

"Yes," said his deep voice on the other side, too loud.

"Don't say anything else," Solomon replied quickly in much softer tones. "When we opened the door, it locked on both sides. So, just do what I say ... Rip it from its hinges."

There was a long pause.

"What?" he finally said, too loud again.

"Keep quiet ... then rip the door out."

"But —"

"Uh!" barked the Seer as loudly as he dared.

There was another long pause. Then the door trembled, then the whole tent seemed to shake, and seconds later they could see Angus, from the belly button down, standing before them, the entire entrance in his long fingers. The magician who had rigged these locks hadn't counted on the abnormal strength of an eight-foot giant.

The fat-man guard awoke at the sound of the door being torn from its hinges, took one look at Angus and the man beside him who looked about a quarter his height ... and fainted back into his chair.

Ayesha stepped outside. She gasped and then put her hand over her mouth.

"Fly," she whispered, a tear rolling down her cheek. The ravens lifted into the dark sky. Only big Edgar stayed with her. Now, in the moonlight, Solomon could see that her skin was actually even darker than he had thought as she self-consciously wiped more of the wisps of white stage makeup from her face. She looked like women he had seen in photo-pictures in books about the Levant and the Kingdom of Syria and the girls in the story about Aladdin and his magic lamp. Cleo took her by the hand and ushered her down the stairs. Though the lanterns offered only dim lights in the night, the petite girl actually held her hand up to shelter her eyes.

Angus stood in front of them, still holding the door in his massive mitts, his mouth gaping.

"Close your mouth ... and the door," Solomon said. "Let's get out of here."

But the giant remained there, gazing at what he had done. "Uh," said the Seer and reached up and patted him on the thigh.

"I think he is saying that you don't know your own strength," Solomon remarked.

In minutes, the five of them were gone from the fairgrounds and walking back toward downtown St. Louis, the ravens unseen, flying high above them. But before they got far, the Seer turned their path toward the Mississippi River. Solomon thought of his map. The city of Memphis, deeper into the great South down the magnificent waterway, was next.

The North Britain boy came to a halt.

"Seer," he said, "I have something to do first."

His friend didn't even look around. He simply motioned to Solomon to keep following.

"I said … I have something to do first."

The Seer stopped and looked back, those violet eyes suddenly piercing, and shook his head.

"I have to send money to my mother. I should have done it long ago. That's the whole purpose of my having left home. I need to find a posting office."

The Seer shook his head again.

"I'm not coming with you until I do."

The Seer jumped up and down and his face began turning red. He looked like he was about to fly into a tantrum.

"Fine, then, this is the end of the line for me," Solomon said.

"Uh!" screamed his friend and turned and started walking toward the river again. The giant followed him and so did Ayesha and her ravens, though she looked back beseechingly. Cleo stood between them, not sure what to do.

Solomon moved toward St. Louis. And within moments … they were all with him, the Seer pounding his feet into the ground as if he wanted each step to explode the earth beneath. His face was almost purple now and he kept holding up one finger as if to say he was giving Solomon Hunt one minute, a curious deadline since it would take at least twenty to get back to the business area of St. Louis, and several hours before any office opened.

"Are you sure this is wise?" asked Cleo by Solomon's side. "They were right on our trail in Chicago. They must have known we were coming to St. Louis. They could check our train's destination, couldn't they?" She looked toward the city. "They'll be there."

The boy kept walking.

"Solomon, I'm scared."

But there was no point to anything he was doing unless he got to a posting office, no matter how dangerous it was to retrace their steps. He had to do this.

CHAPTER FIFTEEN
CAUGHT

On their way to the carnival, they had passed a suburban house with two fine fruit trees — apple and pear — in its front yard. As they neared it on their way back, Angus reached over its white picket fence and way up and plucked a few giant handfuls of samples from each. He handed them out. It had been a while since they ate the pizza pie, and it felt good to put something into their stomachs.

But none of them were thinking happy thoughts, even as the fruit went down their throats. They eyed the dim space in front and behind them while they walked, looked down streets and alleyways, and even toward rooftops. Slowly, their surroundings became a little brighter, the buildings taller, but in some ways their worries increased. Others could see them more easily now … and there were more of them.

In the American Empire, posting offices were marked by large pictures of a horse with a rider in the saddle, toting sacks and letters, waving them high in the air. This was in tribute to the Pony Express, a service that used to move mail and other things across the Empire on horseback, gaining fame in the recent Wild

West days. Some places, it still existed. Americans loved to think of themselves as having a romantic history. Solomon thought he'd seen one of those pictures on a big building on the way in. Sure enough, it wasn't long before they found it. But it was still the early hours of the morning, so just as Solomon had figured, they had to wait. That wasn't entirely a bad thing — they needed to sleep.

They all curled up on the stone steps of the Posting Office, a motley crew leaning against each other, Cleo with her head on Solomon's shoulder, which he certainly didn't mind, but the Seer, unfortunately, with his cranium on the other. And so, they drifted off to sleep.

"Intruders!" came Edgar's alarm just as the sun began to rise.

They all awoke with a start to see a thin man with a starched collar, little hair, and rimless spectacles staring at them. He was standing back a distance, almost in the street, as if trying to decide if he should be calling a sheriff. A few carriages were rumbling past behind him, almost running him down.

Solomon leapt to his feet.

"I … I would like to avail myself of your service."

"You would?" The man gasped as Angus stood up to his full height.

"Nevermore," said the raven.

"Ignore him, sir."

"I shall try." His voice was shaky. "Do you … do you have money?"

"Oh, yes."

"How much?" He looked sceptical.

The Seer had remained meticulous about sharing everything they made equally, bills as well as cash. Now, each one of them pulled out a big handful and displayed what they had, the coins glittering in the rising sun. This was the way to do things in America.

The man's face brightened. He pulled a key from his pocket. "Yes, well, let me just open up and we will help you with that service you spoke of."

The five friends gathered behind him, all of them anxious to get out of sight. The ravens settled on the building across the street, although Edgar came in with them. There was a high ceiling in the office, made of white plaster with a fancy design and centered by a chandelier. The floors were plank and creaked when you walked them. The front quarter of the room was a waiting area with wooden chairs and the back three quarters office space, separated from the front by a wooden half-wall decorated with carved figures of horses. It rose only to about chest height and then continued upward as thick iron bars for another five feet and in the middle of it was an open counter about two feet by two, where customers spoke to the clerks. The posting office man found another key and pushed a door in the wall, walked in, locked it behind him, and approached the open counter from the inside.

Leaning against it, Solomon glanced around at the inner area. There were desks piled with letters and parcels and all sorts of objects meant to be shipped somewhere across the great Empire. A gun rack, filled with rifles, loomed on the wall in there, to his right. At the back of the room, he could see a cage of carrier pigeons and through a back door that now opened, he saw a cowboy step inside, a real cowboy with cowboy pants and a cowboy hat. There was a gun belt slung across his waist, weighed down by two six-shooters. Outside, several horses were tethered to a post. The Pony Express wasn't entirely dead.

Solomon nearly emptied his pockets of bills and coins, leaving one note behind. He had confidence now that the Seer could get them more. The posting office man's beady eyes examined the boy through his spectacles. "That's a heap lot of coinage for a man of your vintage," he said. He seemed a lot braver now that he was locked behind the barred counter. "Young folks shouldn't be out and about on their own." Behind him, the cowboy stopped as he noticed Solomon on the other side of the bars.

The boy told the clerk where he wanted the money sent.

"North Britain? What part of America is that?"

Solomon explained.

"Another country, huh? Well," he chuckled, "I sure hope it gets there."

The cowboy grinned too. But his grin didn't last long. He started looking at Solomon like he recognized him, then turned and walked out the back door. As he disappeared, the boy saw his hand move to his gun belt.

Solomon didn't know it then, but the Seer had been darting around the room behind him, making each of his party give him a couple of coins. As the boy was filling out a form, the Seer dumped them on the counter in front of him, the money rolling about on the wooden surface before settling. His eyes peered up at his friend with warm affection. Normally, Solomon would have shoved him away, but this was very kind. He patted his friend on the shoulder.

"Thank you."

"Uh," said the Seer, and pulled on Solomon's sleeve, trying to tug him away from the counter.

"I have to fill this out first."

The Seer went up on his tiptoes and looked into the office, as if searching for someone. The cowboy was gone.

There were three forms to complete. Solomon started into the first one, finished it, and then turned to the second. A big clock ticked loudly above them. The Seer kept pulling on his sleeve. When that didn't work, he started to pace, grunting to himself.

"Solomon," said Cleo anxiously, "The little man is awfully worried. I don't blame him. We need to go."

The giant opened the outside door, bent over, and looked up and down the street.

"Just a moment," said Solomon, "I'll just be another moment or two."

The instant Angus closed the door, it slammed open again, almost knocking him to the floor. There stood the cowboy, thrusting money into his pocket. He stepped aside and revealed three figures behind him — a needle-nosed man with red hair, a little showman with a big stomach, and a tall man with a head the size of a pumpkin, all of them out of breath.

"You do indeed know everything that goes on in town, Mr. Mix," exclaimed Booth with a smile.

The Seer cried out. It was the sound of a baby or a small animal about to be attacked by a predator. In an instant, Pawn, vicious and skilled in street fighting and therefore aware of whom his most dangerous enemy was, had Angus by the throat and backed up against a wall with a long, thick arm. The giant was extraordinarily strong and yet no match for Pawn. Neither could Angus match him in attitude. Solomon noticed, for the first time, that Moseley, the needle-nosed man, carried a cane. From it, he now unsheathed a sword and held it out toward Cleo in a menacing manner. This meant that the villains had their two most dangerous foes at bay. Tears began to roll down the Seer's face. He quivered where he stood. “Intruders,” shrieked Edgar. “Bad men! Bad men!”

“A ridiculous assessment,” said Booth. “We have merely come for our property, Mr. Coop’s little treasure, now ours.”

The Seer’s eyes grew large with fear.

“Is that who that is?” asked Moseley, his jaw dropping. “You didn’t say anything about that. Is he really the Seer?”

“Never you mind who he is,” growled Pawn, driving his hand harder against Angus’s throat, holding him so tightly against the wall that the big face was turning blue. “You get yours and we get ours. That was the deal. That’s the end of our partnership.”

Moseley looked unsure. “Is that *really* him?” he repeated.

“Sir,” said Solomon, turning to the cowboy, his voice quavering, “how much did these gentlemen pay you?”

The Seer gave a little shriek and smacked himself in the head, his expression suddenly looking happier. Booth had been trying to corner him in the room, but the fugitive now temporarily eluded him, rushed over to Solomon, and pushed him toward the cowboy.

“None of your business, lad,” said Booth. “We are deciding what to do with you. Silence will help your cause. Shut your mouth or face the consequences. You have occasioned us a heap load of trouble.”

“How much?” Solomon repeated, looking straight at the cowboy.

“Umm,” he replied, looking at Booth, then back at the boy, “I reckon it was a goodly amount.”

“How much!” Solomon demanded again.

“I reckon … ten Douglas dollars.”

"We can offer you twenty, right now!"

The Seer jumped up and down with joy, seemingly as excited about how the tables had been turned as he was about the drama of it all.

Solomon turned and scooped up his coins from the counter, holding them in a basket that he formed with his shirt, and motioned to the others. They dug into their pockets. Solomon dropped the coins on the floor in front of the cowboy and the others tossed theirs toward him too. They would only have a few dollars left, but it was time for a desperate measure.

The cowboy paused. He looked at the glittering cash, then at Booth and Pawn, then back down at the money. In an instant, quick as a man in a showdown, his right hand darted to his gun belt and one of his six-shooters was ready for action.

He pointed it at Pawn's wide head.

"Step away from the big lad!" he barked.

The posting office clerk ducked down below the counter and let out a whimper.

"You are not serious, boy!" shouted Booth.

The cowboy snatched up his other six-shooter and pointed it directly at Booth's heart. "As serious as any American making a good old American decision."

"All right … now just relax yourself, sir!" the short showman sang.

Pawn released Angus, smacking him hard against the wall and growling at him.

The five runaways took no time at all to leave the building. And when they got to the street, they began to run, back the way they had come, out of the city and down toward the Mississippi River.

Solomon was the last one out of the posting office, and as he'd exited, he'd heard Booth say in a sickly sweet voice, "Surely now, Mr. Mix, we can work something out."

The showman was about to make the cowboy even richer. Money more than spoke in the American Empire. It shouted. It veritably swore. They'd be on the young peoples' heels in moments.

And so, the friends ran.

After five or ten minutes of running and fast walking, the neighborhoods became poorer and the buildings more sparse — Solomon could see the wide, muddy Mississippi River between the structures to their left. Up ahead, in the water, he spotted a riverboat heading south. The Seer, in the lead of course, seemed to be on a direct line toward it, as if it were their destination — this, despite the fact that it was a good two hundred feet out in the water.

Solomon stayed to the rear with Ayesha, who was having a hard time keeping up. She was breathing heavily, terrified, Edgar bobbing about on her shoulder, yelling "RUN!" and the other ravens up above were all cawing at them too, doubling back every now and then, as if scouting for the pursuers. Solomon kept glancing behind. As the Seer finally led them directly toward the water, between two ramshackle houses with crowds of poor people standing on what passed for front lawns, the boy glanced back again.

His heart froze. There they were, coming around a corner: Pawn out in front, gaining on them, followed by Moseley, and little Booth far behind, huffing and puffing, his face red and looking like it might explode.

"Seer!" Solomon cried. "THEY'RE COMING!!"

The Seer stuck out his chest, pumped his arms, and really began to sprint. There was such fear in his attitude that Solomon truly believed he didn't care one ounce for any of others at that moment. He simply wanted to get away. He feared Booth and Pawn the way a convicted murderer feared a hangman.

The land went from lush green grass to dirt and then to mud as it began to descend in banks to the edge of the river.

Solomon glanced back again. Their pursuers were rapidly closing in!

There was the riverboat, coming almost even with them now. The boy could make out its two prominent black smokestacks, its two fenced floors of verandas, and its big paddlewheel at the back churning up the brown water. The Seer didn't hesitate when he reached the edge of the Mississippi. He jumped in, fully clothed. The giant followed suit and so did Cleo in her boots and dress. Solomon took Ayesha's hand and pulled her with him. She stumbled and fell into the mud!

"I'll have you!" cried Pawn, no more than a dozen steps away. *What was to be done now,* thought Solomon. He couldn't leave Ayesha behind; Pawn would brutalize her right in front of them to make them give up the Seer. In the water, the little man cried out.

But they had to get away. Solomon let go of Ayesha's hand for an instant, unsure. Pawn reached his big claws for her. Edgar swooped. He darted at the pumpkin head and scratched his face. The big man cried out and swatted at the enormous raven. One of his fists caught it and it gave a shriek and fell to the ground. In that instant, Solomon reached back, grabbed Ayesha, and rushed her to the river. In fact, he pushed her in. He immediately followed and in seconds they were in deep water. Ayesha turned in the river and looked back toward her beloved pet, weeping. But then, almost as if in response, Edgar began to rise, flapping on the ground and then into the air, and heading toward her. In moments, he was perched, dry as a desert, on his mistress's head.

That gave the five friends little relief though. Unfortunately, the bird hadn't caught Pawn's eyes. The big man was rising now too, wiping blood from his cheek, hatred in his expression. Moseley neared him. They rushed toward the water.

Out in front of him, Solomon heard a curious noise. The Seer had begun to laugh. It was a strange sound, like someone gargling at a high pitch. Solomon yelled at him, "What are you doing? They will be on us in seconds!" But as the boy glanced at his friend, he could see him pointing toward their pursuers, his face resplendently happy, that weird laugh still in his throat. He knew something about Pawn and Booth, something that wasn't good for them at this moment, and he had just discovered that the needle-nosed man was afflicted with the same problem.

"You can't swim either!" cried Booth, glaring and shaking a fist at his new partner, who had pulled up like a frightened mare at the edge of the Mississippi. "Pawn hates water ... he absolutely hates it! The sissy!" The short showman wasn't mentioning, of course, his own childlike fear of the depths. He turned toward his prey out on the water and glowered.

The Seer didn't stop laughing all the way to the riverboat.

CHAPTER SIXTEEN

MEMPHIS MUSIC TO THEIR EARS

Never was a group of young people as fortunate as they were that day. The riverboat was nearly empty … except for two boys — one Black and the other white, a veritable Huck Finn and his good friend, Jim, no more than sixteen years old but on the job, taking the boat south past Memphis to New Orleans for its owner for a few coins. Jefferson, the white one, even jumped into the river and helped the five young friends, or at least the two females (though Cleo needed the least aid of any of them). He did yeoman work getting them all on board, weighed down as they were and struggling in their soaking clothes. Jackson kept his hand on the wheel up above.

"My, my, you surely is a sight for sore eyes," said Jefferson, staring at them once they were all lying on the deck, panting and gasping for breath. "Clumb up here, set down, and let's have a stare at y'all. What is you, a freak show of some sort? Tarnation, I never thought in all my life I could even dream up a group as wonderful as y'all. And who is those folks on the shore shouting this here way? Runnin' from them, is you? Well, now, nothing we like more than a good race, don't we, Jackson?" He turned to his partner.

"Y'all know we do, 'specially when the folks that is doing the runnin' is grownups and the folks that is being chased is the young 'uns!"

"Recalls our boyhood days, don't it, Jackson?"

"Does too, Jefferson. When we used to steal a thing or two."

"But we is respectable now, ain't we?"

"Yes, we is, respectable as all get out. We in bidness together. Whatever you needs done, we do it."

And that was the way it went, all the way down the Mississippi to Memphis and beyond. Rarely had Solomon met two people who could talk more than Jefferson and Jackson, and most of it nonsense. They were like characters in a play with far too much dialogue.

But the five companions didn't mind. The other two were friendly and helpful, and shared their food — their collard greens, chitlins, and fried chicken — provided for them, it seemed, by wealthy owners who trusted them to move their boat at a very reasonable rate.

"We likes the company!" cried Jackson.

Eventually, the little troupe fell asleep, despite it being midmorning. They hadn't slept much all night. The hot Missouri and Kentucky sun dried their clothes as they lay there, sailing south. But Ayesha was too excited, and couldn't drift off, so Solomon stayed awake with her, unable to settle himself, deeply upset by his failure to get money to his family, waiting to talk with her until after she got on her knees and looked to the east in the boat, praying to Allah, just as she had done the night before outside the posting office. When she was done, she turned to Solomon and, with Jefferson and Jackson's constant chatter in the background, and the green shoreline of the Mississippi passing by, she told the North Britain boy about herself. He sat there transfixed by her tale. She had indeed been born in the Kingdom of Syria, but her parents were killed in the never-ending wars there and she fled the Levant, a mere child, a stowaway on a boat across the ocean to the American Empire for a new life. There, staggering homeless and starving into the countryside near the city where the ship had docked, she was picked up by a band of Romani people and adopted by a caring man and woman. She began traveling the roads of America with her new family, given the care of their seven ravens, with whom she developed a magical friendship. When their wagonload of family and friends were arrested as vagrants and thieves in Vancouver, New Columbia, on the west coast of the Empire two years ago, the local government tried to place the children in homes in the city. Ayesha ran away, only to discover that her Romani parents had been released and expelled from the area. She began traveling on her own, seeking word of them, knowing little about making a living and not good at begging. Sitting alone one day after prayers in a park in Oregon State, her ravens displayed behind her in a tree like an art exhibit, a carnival owner heard her speaking with them in full sentences. Within an hour, she was being fed and given a new change of clothes; but ever since that day, ever since he enticed her, she was never allowed to leave the carnival company. They called her Marilyn, shone that bright light on her white powdered face during performances, and always kept her and her ravens locked indoors.

"They thought that only Edgar spoke more than a word or two, but my birds can do so much more than they know. Word is Coop has been trying to buy us."

On the deck, the Seer, whom Solomon had thought was asleep, grinned.

In four or five hours, the great state of Tennessee appeared to their left, Arkansas to the right. The poverty they could see from the river was alarming. But on the rises in the distance, they also spotted huge mansions. Solomon wondered if some of them were former plantations, where wealthy owners had kept their many slaves.

Cleo and Solomon grew even closer on this boat ride. They spent more time talking and reading aloud to each other from her Shakespeare plays. She teased him about his chocolate-brown hair and red freckles and bright-blue eyes, which she thought was a funny combination. They started laughing more together, and she took to calling him "Solo." He liked that.

But the heat became almost unbearable. The sweat poured down the northern boy's face without his even moving a muscle. In fact, for the most part, it kept him very still. It was a relief when the sun began to lower in the sky. As it did, the hosts told their guests that Memphis was approaching and they would have to stop for a while, check in at the local docks, and confirm by carrier pigeon that they were on schedule.

It was a much smaller city than even York. In fact, it seemed to Solomon that he could see most of it from the boat, its lights beginning to come on in the dusk. The five of them were happy to stay on board, not wanting to chance meeting their hunters. In fact, they had a perfect view of the brick railroad station and its comings and goings from their dock, its sign peeking up above the two- and three-story buildings near the water, as high as the tallest structures in town, which appeared to be the churches.

Here they saw cotton being loaded on to other riverboats in huge bales, the workers bringing it to the docks by horse and wagon, few of them with more than rags for clothes.

The five unusual friends peered over the edge of the railing on the upper deck of the riverboat, looking out across Memphis, scanning the road leading to the dock for any sight of their pursuers, praying that Jackson and Jefferson would come back soon. The Seer nervously worked away on a drawing — that catapult picture again. It was beginning to look like a medieval weapon of war.

It didn't take their new friends more than a couple of hours to return and shortly after that, just past suppertime, they cast off and the riverboat began drifting south toward the great Mississippi delta and the magical city of New Orleans.

But before they did … they took on a new passenger.

"This boy done play this Spanish guitar like a magic man!" exclaimed Jefferson as he introduced them to the young fellow he and Jackson had picked up on a Memphis street named Beale, where they had slipped in to buy some provisions.

"And he sing like the devil hisself."

"He needs a ride, and it is our pleasure to accommodate him."

Maybe sixteen years old, he was a captivating young man. Cleo and Ayesha couldn't help but stare at him, for despite his ragged clothing, he was as handsome as an Arabian prince in a storybook, with a light-brown complexion. It was even more difficult to not *both* watch *and* listen to him when he began to play. To say that Solomon had never heard the like of the sounds he produced would be an understatement.

Most music that Solomon knew was slow, melodic, and conservative. It was meant to soothe its listeners or lightly entertain them. Much of it was church hymns. Outside the worship halls, musicians played fiddles, pianos, or brass instruments. The snotty folks listened to hard-to-understand operas or solo singers performing highfalutin songs. Everything Solomon had ever heard had a beat that was slower than the human heart. That was what music was to him … until he heard Robert Elvis McTell.

It was like the boy attacked his guitar when he played it, like three men were playing, like God, or the Devil, had given him strange powers. His guitar throbbed with a frantic beat, and over that he played intricate melodies, loud and strong and filled with emotion. When he sang in his high-pitched, sometimes moaning, sometimes thrilling voice, it made Solomon sad like he'd never felt before, or excited in a way that almost alarmed him.

Even more amazing was the fact that Robert Elvis McTell couldn't see the guitar he played — he was as blind as a mole. His head rocked back and forth as he performed, his sightless eyes rolled up in his head, his whole body entranced by his songs, seized by some power that made him play the way he did.

The Seer was fascinated.

Solomon was also intrigued by Robert's stories about being the son of a Black slave and a rich white woman and being thrown out of his plantation for it, his existence denied by everyone he had known, both Black and white, left to walk the streets of the South, gifted with an ability to play his instrument from the moment he found it, dusty and unused, as if left there by some supernatural element, at the crossroads of two railroad lines between Tupelo and Greenwood, Mississippi, where he was born. People would throw him coins when they heard him sing in the towns, but others hated him for it, especially rich white folks who said that when he played and sang, it corrupted their hearts and the hearts of their young people, got them worked up, too excited, and unnaturally aroused. But the Seer didn't seem to care about his life story. All he wanted Robert to do was sing and play.

And when he did, the little man would pace, as if he were calculating something.

He would bob his head to the pounding beat, thinking.

Whenever the Seer settled, he'd pull out his map. Solomon could see his eyes following the route down the Mississippi and through the Wild West to Los Angeles and to their three smiling faces, drawn so lifelike, severed from their bodies and floating in the Pacific Ocean.

And so they drifted south from Memphis into the tropical brown and green of the Delta at the center of the American Empire, sleeping in the muggy air on the deck at night, listening to Robert Elvis McTell moan and shout, to his guitar throb, the beat much faster than their hearts, heading by Arkansas, then Vicksburg, Mississippi, where Cleo stared out at a group of Black men chained to each other in a prison gang and wept, and past the docks at Natchez and Baton Rouge in Louisiana, and then … toward the one and only New Orleans, the city at the mouth of the great river.

CHAPTER SEVENTEEN

THE BIRD BOY OF NEW ORLEANS

New Orleans was a mixture, with people and music and cultures and colors as blended together as the jambalaya stews the citizens ate. New Orleans was English and French and Spanish; it was brass bands and accordions and banjos and guitars; it was bland old-fashioned food and spicy meals that nearly lifted the roof off your skull. Solomon loved it and couldn't help thinking that it was what all of the American Empire should have been like.

They came in during the early morning, but it felt like midday heat. It wasn't so much the sun but the thick humidity, so dense it seemed like warm water was hanging in the air. Their clothing stuck to them. Just south of the city was the Gulf of Mexico and beyond it, the equator, like some sort of danger nearby.

They said goodbye to Jefferson and Jackson at the docks, and the other six entered the city like actors walking onto the stage of New Orleans, which, everywhere they went, seemed to be in the midst of a party. The Seer had given Robert Elvis a coin and convinced him to come with them — he seemed to have plans for him. While Angus, Ayesha, Cleo, and especially Solomon gawked like children at what they saw, the Seer seemed completely unimpressed. Once again, he was searching for something or someone. This time, he didn't take his little troupe to the outskirts of the city. Carrying the big jar, he led them right into the core, directly to the French Quarter, the most colorful and dangerous part of town.

Here, Solomon saw couples glued to each other in ways you would never see in the North. Men and women, and sometimes women and women, and men and men, kissed openly; they danced to music played by bands in the cafes, and held and caressed one another as they swayed to the beat. Solomon was afraid to look at Cleo as they walked along those avenues. Robert Elvis couldn't get enough of it, his body veritably vibrating to the beat of the city.

But again, the Seer paid no attention. He took his gang down a main street, swung into a smaller one, and then walked up to a wooden entrance in an alleyway.

He thumped on it.

The door opened a crack.

"Yes?" It sounded like a boy.

"Uh!" said the Seer.

"There are no squatters here. We don't need for anything either. Thank you for your interest."

The door closed.

The Seer pounded again.

This time the door opened slightly wider. Solomon could see an eye looking out and likely all it could see was him.

"Who are you?"

"Solomon Hunt."

"Don't know you. What do you want?"

"I don't know."

"You don't know?" The door opened a little wider. When it did, Solomon could see that their prospective host was indeed a boy, about his age. He was barefoot and his dirty trousers were held up by suspenders hanging over a red-checked shirt, though he had tied a rough bowtie around the collar. His reddish-black hair looked like it hadn't been washed for a year and stood up in in high coils on his head as if in alarm. But he wore a pair of spectacles.

"Well, well, who do we have here?" he asked, smiling at the strange group.

The Seer pushed the door open wide and strode in. The other five followed. The room was almost bare except for a wooden table filled with test tubes and flasks and books. Something was boiling and an awful smell, like rotten eggs, filled the space. Another boy, looking afraid, sat on a chair at the far end of the little room saying nothing. The Seer nodded to him, but he looked down.

"What is the meaning of this intrusion!" exclaimed the first boy, shocked that all six of them had traipsed right in.

"We don't know," said Cleo.

"Say, aren't you —"

"Yes, I am, but it's him you'll want to talk to." She pointed at the Seer.

"Him?"

"I think he's come here to see you."

"Me? Why on earth would he want to see me?"

The Seer set down the jar, looked straight at the boy, and began to flap his arms like wings.

The boy turned pale. "Is he with Coop?"

Needless to say, the boy's question nearly floored Solomon.

The Seer was violently shaking his head. Then he crawled up onto the table and leapt off, flapping his arms again. The boy in the corner looked alarmed.

"He knows!" cried the young host, his eyes growing even wider now under that high reddish-black hair, then darting back at his friend.

"Knows what?" Solomon asked.

"*How* does he know?"

"I'm afraid he doesn't speak. Whatever you think he knows, you will have to tell us."

"Doesn't speak? Who is he?"

"We have no idea," added Cleo, "but he's called the Seer."

"The Seer? Why do I know that name?" The boy looked to his friend again, who shrugged his shoulders, silent as ever.

"He's actually afraid of Coop, that much we *can* tell you," added Solomon.

"That makes two of us."

"Well, why are *you* afraid of him? Let's start with that."

"I'm not sure I should be saying anything to you. I've worked very hard for many years to keep my secret. But I will tell you this, since you've come, you say, to meet me. My name is Napoleon LaJoy, and I am an inventor. … I shall assume that does not ring any bells and you have mistaken me for someone else. Good day."

That explained the mini science lab on the table.

"It's nice to meet you, Napoleon," said Cleo, ignoring his obvious intention to see them out. She shook his hand. "But what does this all have to do with the Great Coop?"

The New Orleans boy paused. He looked at them, the fear in his face not abating, aware that he was outnumbered. "Nobody knows my secret except for Coop, his people, and me." He glanced at the Seer in wonder. "Or at least, that's what I used to think."

"Secret?"

The Seer tore a page out of one of the books on the table, quickly creased and folded it, and then fired it across the room. It flew just as wonderfully as the flying machine he had made in Buffalo.

"He's doing it again!" exclaimed Napoleon. "How … how does he know that!"

"He knows lots of things," said Angus, who was bending over so his head wouldn't hit the ceiling.

"What … what do you want?" asked Napoleon, backing away.

"It is my experience," Solomon said, "that the Seer wants only good things for the people he recruits." The fugitive smiled at that and tried to take Napoleon by the hand. The young stranger shoved him away.

"Recruits? What do you mean by that?"

"I think he wants you to come with us. You must have some special talent."

The Seer nodded his head vigorously.

"You don't look like you are doing very well here," Solomon added.

Napoleon sighed, turned, sat down next to his silent friend, and took his hand. The fact that these visitors hadn't harmed them yet seemed to be calming both of them a little. "My inventions don't always work. Or at least, I can't convince others to buy them. Maybe the color of my skin doesn't help." He looked up at these six strangers who seemed so genuinely interested in him, all about his age, and his face began to relax more, as if he were beginning to believe that they were indeed there to befriend him. "My parents had high hopes for me at first, a diamond in the rough, a poor Black boy who could figure, imagine, and extrapolate better than any boy his age. But they sent me away when I wouldn't stay at my studies. I didn't have time for all that schooling nonsense. It was holding me down."

"Why was Coop after you?" Solomon asked, trying to cut to the chase.

"Because … because there is one thing I invented that really works. It has the potential to change life itself. Coop found out about it. I don't know how, but his people came here. They treated us like dogs." He glanced back at his young partner.

"His people?" asked Cleo.

"A little showman with a southern accent and a tall one with a huge head."

Every one of them nearly fell over.

"But …" Ayesha said, "that's those men, Booth and Pawn."

"How … how do you know their names?" Napoleon got to his feet. "We barely escaped them."

"They are chasing us too."

The boy's face relaxed again. "They *are*?"

"They want him," said Cleo, pointing at the Seer.

"And it isn't just because they want to use him in their awful show," said Solomon. "It seems like he's much more to them than that … like he's some sort of savior or something."

"I never showed them my invention," said the boy. "I never explained it, even when they beat me."

His partner nodded his head gravely.

"Explained what? Napoleon, what did they want from you?" Solomon asked.

"That may be why the Seer brought us here. What is it that you do?"

Their little leader flapped his arms again.

"I ..." said the boy, "I've learned how to fly."

After they told Napoleon that Booth and Pawn, along with an ex-policeman from *The Show of Shows*, had been right on their trail in St. Louis and knew that they were heading south on the Mississippi from there, he didn't take long to throw his lot in with them. In fact, he didn't even bother to gather up his test tubes and hoses. He simply put on his boots and retrieved a big brown sack, like Solomon had seen workers stuffing cotton into, and went immediately out the door with them.

Or almost immediately. Before that, Napoleon took his friend in his arms and kissed him tenderly on the lips, lingering there. It was remarkable. Then the boy inventor pressed his head to his partner's head and mumbled something about being sorry to leave him behind, but that he had to go with these people, that his friend needed to return home and somehow make amends with his family. The boy nodded sadly. Then the Seer crossed the floor, got up on the chair, and kissed the boy on the lips too, a tear in his eye.

Out on the streets, when they showed Napoleon (still wiping his own eyes) that they had some money left, he took them to a dingy little restaurant on Bourbon Street where they were fed a stew with more spice in it than Solomon imagined there was in all of North Britain. It made him sweat and his nose run. He had to eat several bowls of rice and drink a vat of water to cool himself off. That made Cleo laugh, which was good to see.

As they walked down Canal Street a few minutes later, the

Seer kept pointing to the west, so they turned that way. After a while, as he continued to point in that direction, it became evident that he wasn't just leading his companions to a western part of the city but wanted to go much farther … way west … continue toward Texas and California.

Solomon remembered the route on the Seer's map and the storybook places he had noted in the Wild West. When his friend first drew them, it didn't truly sink into the boy's mind that they might really be going all the way there. Now it did. And it amazed him.

"He wants us to go to Houston," he told Napoleon.

"Houston, Texas?"

"The very one."

"But why?"

"I'm not sure. Maybe it's the best way to flee, maybe it's something else. So far, he's kept us alive and fed, and mostly in the dark."

"I'm for Houston," said Cleo, smiling at Solomon.

"We're all strangers in New Orleans, except you, Napoleon," said Solomon. "What's the best way to get there from here? We are almost completely out of money." (That fact was scaring Solomon more and more, not just because it imperiled the seven of them, but because he still hadn't sent a single coin back home. He wasn't sure how long his family would last on what his father had left behind.)

"Let me think," said Napoleon, scratching his chin as they walked.

"We don't even have enough for a steam train," said Cleo, "and we were lucky to get onto that boat. We could try to board another one in the Gulf, but the only way to do it is to stow away. I don't want to risk that."

"We could put on another show," said the giant.

The Seer shook his head.

"A show?" asked Napoleon.

"That's how we make money," said Solomon. "I'll explain later, and you'll see soon anyway, I hope. But the Seer doesn't seem to want that now. And when I think of it, I understand. Those goons are likely coming down the Mississippi right behind us, so we shouldn't draw attention to ourselves. If we can get out of here immediately, they will have to find our trail before they can trace us. As far as they know, we could be headed east. Houston — that should be our next show. It has to be."

The Seer nodded and reached up and patted Solomon on the shoulder, like a big brother might.

"I have an idea," said Napoleon.

He took them north out of the city to a junkyard. There they bought a used motorized vehicle's steam engine and carriage, along with an old wagon meant to haul cattle, for their last three Douglas dollars.

"It won't be fast, " said Napoleon, "but I think it can pull us and this wagon at least some of the way to Houston. All I need is water to boil in the engine. We can keep to the old Lake Charles Road down near the Gulf, which should take us straight west. "

They hooked up the wagon, poured water into the engine, lit one of the matches Napoleon produced from his pocket, saw the machinery and its pulleys and belts sputter into action, then got into the wagon and moved out, not much faster than they could have run. Until they left the more populated areas, they were a bit of a spectacle, which worried Solomon.

But at least the little troupe was moving. And they kept moving, along a dirt road, then nearer the water, its deep blue surface stretching as far as the eye could see. They struggled past swampy bayous, the road patched in places with logs laid right on its surface, filling their tank with salt water from time to time, everything around them lush green, avoiding lurking alligators in the swamps, moving on through Louisiana in the night, and toward the Texas border, palm trees above them, some of their number sleeping, others taking turns steering or just staring at the starlit sky.

It took them a whole day to get to Texas, and two to reach Houston. They found farms and orchards where they stole enough food to survive. Their vehicle gave out before they reached their destination, but it had gotten them most of the way. They were near a town called Beaumont and only had to walk the last fifty miles.

They avoided towns and villages on purpose. And the few people they did see barely glanced their way. The heat seemed to make these poor folks tired and uninterested in everything, even in their unusual group.

But the six of them knew that mixed races knowingly traveling together, with seven ravens flying above them, stuck out like an unwanted extravaganza.

So, they veered a little south as they neared Beaumont. They'd been hearing talk of oil from the locals ever since they entered Texas, but it had increased lately. "Black gold" some of them called it. People were saying that it would soon be found here in millions of gallons, and when that happened Texas would change forever; it would explode, the towns would grow into cities and the little cities into booming metropolises, and the rich would get even richer. America would become even greater. Diversions and entertainment would spring up everywhere.

Straight south of Beaumont on a hill, they saw a huge wooden cone or at least the skeleton of one, stretching up into the Texas sky.

"Oil derrick," said Napoleon.

Solomon stood and stared at it. They all did. It looked like a primitive church steeple in the devilish Texas heat. As the boy gazed up, he imagined black oil soon gushing out of the top of that derrick like a geyser of gold. "Spindletop Oil" read a sign at the top of the giant cone.

"Solo," said Cleo sharply, sounding concerned. When Solomon looked at her, she was nodding at two figures coming down the hill toward them with a dog by their side — a big, nearly hairless white animal with a black circle around one eye. As they neared, Solomon could see that both men wore sweat-stained cowboy hats and had holsters with six-shooters, bullets strapped to their trousers, and rifles in hand. One was over six feet tall, the other barely five. Their faces were tanned and dirty and appeared as if they'd been shaved with dull knives, their mustaches cascading from their lips and down their chins in strips like drips of crude oil. The dog was growling.

"We should move."

But the men quickly stepped into the road in front of them.

"Whoa!" cried one of them.

"What have we got here?" said the other.

"Nothing," said Cleo and tried to walk by them.

"Now, now, dark little filly, not so fast," said the smaller one, seizing her by the arm. "You is surely a pretty piece of nothing."

Solomon stepped toward him.

"Don't be a hero, young feller," said the other, drawing a gun from his holster.

"Besides, we just want to ask you a few questions," drawled the short man. Solomon didn't like the way the cowboy was gripping his friend. He held her tightly by the upper arm and had pulled her close. "You got some dark ones with you, boys and girls. And little black ones in the Texas sky too." He leveled his rifle at the ravens, who began to fly off.

"No!" screamed Ayesha.

"Just target practice, ma'am," said the short one, who started to squeeze the trigger. Angus, who had knelt for a rest as they looked at the derrick, somewhat disguising his size, suddenly rose to his feet and caught the rifle's barrel in a huge mitt, ripping it from the cowboy, whose eyes grew to the size of goose eggs. The gunshot echoed in the hot day. The taller cowboy raised his pistol and aimed it up at the giant's head. The dog snarled and began to bark, showing its teeth as it moved toward Angus.

"Enough!" called a voice from up on the hill. A man was standing there in a bowler hat and, unbelievably, a shirt and necktie. "Let them pass. Get up here! Come on, Bull's Eye!" The dog turned and ran toward the derrick.

"It's Mr. Bush," said the shorter man, grabbing his rifle out of Angus's hands.

"We'd best get back."

The other one turned to the seven friends, spat thick brown liquid on the ground, and snarled. "Y'all don't be stopping on the Texas roads and staring at others' business or it may not go as well for you next time. We are the law for the Spindletop oil field, and we don't appreciate folks, especially Black ones" — he glared at Cleo and Napoleon — "and those who choose to associate with them" — he stared at Solomon — "nosing about."

"We were just moving through," said Solomon.

"Good," the man replied. He spat again and the two of them began to walk up the hill toward the derrick. Then he turned back to the troupe for an instant. "Where you heading?" he barked.

"Houston," said the giant.

"After this here place in Beaumont gushes black gold, and it will soon, Houston will become the biggest city in the American Empire, mark my words. And me and Will here, we will be rich as them pro rugby players. We'll set up in Houston and have us a harem each … of all colors!" He gave Cleo an ugly look. "When you get to Houston, y'all will feel it. Oil is coming and the big times is coming too. It's already commenced."

He walked away, but his smaller partner stopped again.

"You go to Houston," he called back, "but walk on through. The oil ain't for you. It's our place. It's a Texas place. God's country … And you best move in appropriate colors when you get there too!"

The friends took his advice. Most certainly not because they agreed with him, but because they valued their lives. Though Houston was nowhere near the size of New Orleans, it was easy to see on approaching that it would be even larger one day. The seven of them walked on a road along the brown Buffalo Bayou River into town, Cleo keeping behind with Napoleon, as if in another group, guiding Robert Elvis McTell by the hand. Even a distance from the city, there was a veritable flow of people moving with them and many steamboats on the bayou coming up from the ports on the Gulf. The residential neighborhoods turned to business areas, the buildings grew taller, and everywhere they could hear the sounds of hammers and saws and new places rising. They even saw an enormous stadium going up for the new American Rugby League team that would soon play here. One building had a makeshift sign on its growing skeleton reading: "COOP INCORPORATED — Entertainment is Everything!" Just seeing the all-powerful showman's name on the empty structure, his brand spreading west, frightened the troupe. They walked by quickly.

"The rich folks building all these entertainment places and stadiums know what they're doing," Solomon heard Napoleon say behind him. "I've heard it said that Americans spend more than half their incomes on diversions these days."

The troupe needed the essentials of life to survive — just a little money and proper food — but the Seer wasn't letting on how he planned to get either. He didn't seem to be headed for a train station or looking for posters or a field where an extravaganza might be. Did many even come out to Houston yet? (They would soon, no doubt.) In fact, he looked tired and uninspired.

Here Solomon was, thousands of miles from home in an exotic but dangerous place, on foot and with little to live on, still pursued by evil men, and depending on this young genius who seemed to have lost some of his will. They were melting in the heat.

But circumstances were about to intervene. Up ahead, near the corner of Main and Congress Streets, near the County Court House in the market square, an enormous crowd had gathered. They sounded bloodthirsty.

CHAPTER EIGHTEEN
LICKIN' ANY MAN ALIVE

Someone was fighting in the market square in Houston and the police or the sheriff and his deputies or whoever was responsible for keeping the peace didn't seem to care. (In fact, they were part of the audience.) It may have had something to do with the combatants.

Three men were fighting a woman.

And the woman was winning.

Solomon shoved into the crowd, the Seer pushing through legs next to him, clutching his jar, his face lit up with excitement. Any time there was a large gathering of people, especially people looking at something, he was enthralled. Cleo, Robert Elvis, Ayesha, Napoleon, and the giant all kept close now, since no one cared to look at them: everyone's interest was elsewhere. Men and even women and children were shouting, cheering on the fighters … or at least, one of them.

In the middle of the circle formed by the spectators, a young woman, or girl (it was difficult to tell her age; she appeared to be not much older than Solomon and about his size, and wearing a dirty dress that showed her hairy calves above her manly boots) was surrounded by three large men, all taking swings at her, all missing by wide margins. And it wasn't that they were clumsy or unskilled at pugilism. She was just incredibly elusive. Her face was in front of them but when they swung … it wasn't. She seemed to be trying to get them to stop, just avoiding their blows, but every now and then she'd reply by staggering them with sharp cracks to their heads with the edge of her hands, or thundering kicks to their legs, delivered with sudden pivots that marshaled her lower-body power. Each time, the men would fall back, sometimes they even dropped, but on every occasion, they came at her again. All three were hulking fellows.

"What is happening?" Solomon asked a man with a different complexion than his by his side. At first, the man seemed surprised that this boy would speak to him but then responded.

"That powerful gal is kicking those brutes' hides all around the Houston market square, that's what's happening."

The mob roared with delight as each male blow missed and each female one found a bruising mark.

"Why?"

"The four of them tried to rob someone and that gal stepped in."

"Four of them?"

He pointed to another man, lying face down on the pavement, out cold.

The Seer was jumping up and down.

"Seer, I'm surprised at you!" said Cleo. But he was riveted on the violence. The only time he looked away was to gaze at the big crowd in wonder, searching individual faces it seemed, as if intrigued by their intrigue, and counting their numbers.

"You give me no option!" cried the young combatant, suddenly rushing at one of the men, seizing his shoulders, and delivering a knee into his midsection. The man folded up like a concertina and dropped to the ground, heaving, little air left in his lungs. The crowd roared.

The young woman turned to the other two.

"Now, leave this be."

The men hesitated and then advanced on her again.

"I will have to finish this," she warned them.

Solomon felt the Seer tugging on his sleeve. Down below, he was setting the jar on the ground. He looked up at Solomon and pointed into it.

"You want me to get in? Now?"

The North Britain boy's first inclination was to tell him he was loony, but his stomach was rumbling, so he obeyed. No one noticed at first, so fixated was everyone on the brawl. The Seer turned to the rest of his crew, pointed down at Solomon Hunt, and then motioned for them to disperse. They all knew what to do — everyone except Napoleon, who looked at his companions with a puzzled expression. The Seer picked up the jar and began carrying it and its contents out into the fighters' circle, bringing Robert Elvis McTell along by shouldering him in the lower back, letting him know that he was to come with him.

The little person with his big jar and his musician appeared just as the young fighting girl dispatched her last two opponents, knocking them down with sharp hand-edge blows to their respective necks, apologizing to them as they fell. The policemen advanced at the same time, obviously intent on arresting all five combatants … *after* they'd had a good view of the contest. But they were stopped in their tracks, as was the entire crowd.

Before them appeared a miniature man bearing a human being in a jar, a blind mixed-race boy with a guitar walking beside them. It was a sight none of them could even imagine. Everyone — police, mob, and fighting girl — went silent.

The Seer set the jar down in the center of the square and everyone looked at the face, pressed against the glass, peering out — wide blue eyes, smeared chocolate-brown hair. Then Robert Elvis McTell sat down next to the jar, nudged there by their leader. And immediately the young artist began to play and sing. It was mesmerizing. His fingers flew across the frets, and the sound of three guitars came from his, the beat pulsating, faster than the human heart, his voice soaring above it as if amplified by magic, sounding in parts sad, pained, and aroused. And as he sang, the human being began to climb out of the jar, directed by the little person.

The policemen stood stock still, their mouths open.

And when the being in the jar rose before them, about five and a half feet tall, a nearly fully grown boy, everyone still looked on in wonder. But then, in the sky, an unkindness of ravens appeared out of nowhere and began calling to the audience.

"Look here! Look this way! Spectacle! Spectacle!" they cried. And directly below them, out of the midst of the mob, came a sort of rocket woman — a Black girl as beautiful as a princess — supernaturally ejected into the air, turning somersaults seven feet high and landing gently next to the jar. "Look back! Look back!" screamed the ravens. And everyone looked to the spot she had come from. There, a giant rose from the crowd, drawing oohs and ahs before he performed his amazing somersaults on solid ground, whirling like a gigantic top until he landed in the center of the ring.

The troupe had reenacted their Chicago bit with a few brilliant Seer-directed twists. The applause filled the square, even the policemen clapped. And in amongst everyone, the Seer was running about, holding out his hat, as it was laden down with coins.

But the magic didn't last. Suddenly, it was as if someone flicked a switch, or clicked their heels, and the fantasy world of the performance vanished.

One of the policemen shook his head and shouted. "You!" He was pointing at Solomon Hunt. "Y'all can't bung up our square like this. This is a civilized place. And you is all below age. Y'all is under arrest by a law of the glorious state of Texas … whatever that law may be! And you five …" He turned his gaze to the fighters — the adults were groggily getting to their feet — "You are under arrest for public brawling, by a law of the glorious state of Texas … whatever that law may be." He turned to the mob. "Disperse!"

And so they did, in all directions.

That was a godsend to the seven friends.

Solomon picked up the jar and began to run. Angus lifted Robert Elvis into his arms and took off too. Cleo, Ayesha, and Napoleon were instantly on their heels. In seconds, the Seer had raced across the square, darting through the dispersing mob toward his companions. But as he approached, he did something surprising — he seized the fighting girl by the hand and pulled her along with him. About to be arrested, she didn't hesitate to move.

Half an hour later, they gathered in a field of orange trees and watermelon plants west of Houston, huffing and puffing, and out of sight. They hadn't stopped running since the moment they began. Every one of them slumped to the ground.

"That was quite a show," grinned Napoleon. "Can I join?"

The Seer, who had begun to count the bills and coins from his hat, stopped for a moment, smiled, and nodded vigorously.

"Who ..." began the fighting girl, "... who are you people?" She had a somewhat manly voice, or at least a tomboy's.

"Solomon's Stupendous Traveling Spectacle of Life!" said Cleo with a smile and out of breath. "No adults allowed!"

Solomon *really* felt like someone now. "Who are *you*?" he asked their new acquaintance.

"I'm John Sullivan Chan," she responded quickly and proudly.

There was silence as they all looked closer at her.

"Or Joan ... sometimes I use Joan."

They could see now that their acquaintance not only had Asian features but despite her long hair, boy's features too, a little bit of fuzzy hair on her cheek, a pronounced though powdered nose, and an Adam's apple moving in her throat when she swallowed. But she didn't seem confused about anything and certainly wasn't lacking for confidence.

"Well, it's nice to meet you, John," Solomon said. "Or Joan ..." He paused, then pointed at their fearless little leader. "He has plans for you."

"He what?"

"Where did you learn to fight like that?" asked Ayesha shyly.

"I am trained in a mixture of pugilism and martial arts."

"Martial arts? What's that?"

"Something that's unknown in America, though I'm guessing lots of people will know it someday. My father was an acrobat from the Realms of Asia. He was taught martial arts fighting as a child. Then he came to America in a troupe and stayed on to make up his own show. He was a theatrical genius."

It was as if she were giving a speech on a stage. She crossed her thick young arms over her chest and dug in her feet, shoulders width apart. The Seer got up, glowing at J.S. Chan.

"He married an Irish American showgirl in San Francisco, " she continued. "Her father was a pugilist prizefighter who taught her how to use her fists. They taught me what they both knew, to defend myself in this world. No one can match it."

"Wow," said Solomon.

"My parents were killed a few years ago, when the stagecoach we were on in Arizona was robbed … so I'm on my own."

"I'm sorry," said Cleo.

But J.S. didn't seem to be looking for sympathy. She somehow stood even more bolt upright. "I guess I was born to be the equal of any man."

The Seer dropped his coins and jumped up and down, ecstatic.

"What's wrong with him?"

"I think he sees something in you that we could use," said Solomon.

"Use? I'm my own woman."

No one said anything.

"Well, I've always felt like I was a woman, from the time I was little. My parents were okay with me being different." He looked at them defiantly.

"We're all different," said Napoleon. There was an instant murmur of agreement.

"But anyway, you aren't more than seventeen or eighteen, by my reckon," said Cleo finally, "and you don't exactly look like you have much more than the clothes on your back. You'd do well to come with us. We share everything we make."

"I do just fine. I get odd jobs everywhere I go. I survive. I just change my clothes for some of the work I take."

"Bet they call you names, no matter what you are wearing," said Robert Elvis. "The American Empire is the land of opportunity, the greatest country in the world ... if you have the right complexion, and other stuff."

"Or unless you're on a stage," said the giant. "That's the great equalizer."

J.S. Chan didn't reply. The Seer stepped forward and patted her on the arm. "Come with us!" cried Edgar on Ayesha's shoulder. That broke the tension, and they all laughed.

"Come where?" their new friend asked.

Solomon looked at the Seer. "Ever been to the New Mexico Territory and the Wild West?"

The Seer gave his friend a nod and a wide smile.

CHAPTER NINETEEN
OUTLAW COUNTRY

As always, the only way for the Seer was west, so they headed that direction from Houston, but at first that didn't seem like a good idea because even though they now had all sorts of money, there was basically nowhere to spend it nor anywhere for Solomon to arrange to have some sent home. The minute they'd made more in Houston, he'd wanted to find a posting office. But they had to keep moving and now their surroundings were awfully desolate. The land was getting less green and rising. They passed a single village, north of the dirt road they followed, but were reluctant to enter it with their mixed company. After that, they saw a few houses here and there, and way off the road, big ranches with mansions rising in the distance. When they finally stopped for their second night to lie down under the stars, they were all exhausted and hungry and the last sign they'd seen, wooden and dusty, said it was still forty miles to Austin, the state capital.

They rose early the next day to get a good start and could feel Austin nearing in about five hours. By that time the sun was high and hot in the big blue Texas sky. About ten miles from the city they came upon a building covered with crude signs advertising hot meals and another indicating "No Black Folk Allowed." They left Cleo, Napoleon, and Robert Elvis outside in the shade with the tethered horses around the back and ate the beef and rice they ordered as quickly as they could. It was delicious, cooked on a big grill and seasoned with spicy sauces, washed down with a cold strawberry drink. But thinking of their hungry friends, they didn't linger. The owner and his helpers, all big men with big bellies and greasy hands and forearms they wiped on the kerchiefs around their hairy necks, watched them in silence as they ate, not sure, it seemed, if they should be allowing a giant, a little person, and a rather manly young woman in their establishment and equally as undecided about so many kids with money to spare. For a while, Solomon was worried their brutish hosts might rob them. Every time the men looked away, each of the friends cut off portions of meat and scooped rice into their pockets to secret out the door to their three friends, and Solomon drank just half of his fruit drink and somehow took it with him, still in the glass. They didn't mosey along when they left — and their hungry companions ate as they walked.

Though Austin was the capital and had a palace-like State Building of pink granite with a huge cupola and arched entrance that towered over the town, it seemed about half the size of Houston, and certainly didn't have the boomtown feel of that city. The Seer wasn't interested in staying here or in putting on a show. Their pockets were still full of bills and coins.

But he did seem to be looking for something. The eight others walked the streets behind him, Solomon's attention focused on spotting a posting office, Cleo, Napoleon, and Robert Elvis McTell keeping a distance away, and the giant trying to be as inconspicuous as possible (which didn't work and never would throughout their journey).

The northern boy found what he was searching for before their leader encountered his. In minutes, with the Seer impatiently pacing outside while the others took time to rest, Solomon had sent some American Douglas dollar bills off to North Britain. He feared sending too many, in case they were lost or stolen. And the group couldn't spare much either. But, at least, he had done something.

Back out on the street, the Seer immediately marched them away and they walked for another long stretch. Finally, he stopped and grinned. What he was looking at was a corral on the hilly land on the northwestern outskirts of the town … full of horses.

Solomon had ridden horses before, but his father had only owned Clydesdales, working animals with big backs and legs, usually harnessed to plows, with slow, lumbering gaits. The horses their leader was eyeing in this Austin corral looked more like the ones the California Kid or Buffalo Bill rode in western novels. There were chestnuts, palominos, and dapple grays. They all looked like they could gallop like the wind through a western landscape. Solomon's heart started to pound. "Rides to Colorado" read one sign with an accompanying price. The little troupe had enough money to rent some of these animals. Colorado was to the north, but more importantly, it was west and on the route the Seer had laid out back in Buffalo.

It turned out that they couldn't move very fast with their horses. Cleo, of course, was fine on hers, John or Joan was as smooth as an outlaw, and Napoleon and Solomon, while not as good, were at least able to stay aboard. But Ayesha was frightened by the animals and had to take turns riding with others, as did

Robert Elvis McTell; and Angus had his own horse but exhausted it after just a few miles. He had to walk it for long stretches and seemed to feel sorry for it; there were moments when Solomon thought he might actually pick up the horse and carry it!

The Seer had his own horse too, and despite the fact that his feet didn't reach the stirrups, had magical control over his steed.

So, off they went into western Texas toward the New Mexico Territory, the ravens flying above them. Soon, the land became more like what the North Britain boy imagined the terrain to be in all those cowboy novels. Texas Rangers passed them in a troop at a crossroads, sporting ten-gallon hats and badges, and they spotted a battalion of Buffalo Soldiers in the distance later on. Solomon watched all these folk heroes move past in awe. But other than them, they didn't see many people, just the odd tumbleweed town. They were heading upwards: up to the Rio Grande and beyond … into outlaw country.

It seemed to take them forever to get to the border. The land continued to rise and then became a huge plateau of desolate plains and then rose again. A couple of days passed, sleeping under the stars, getting by on the food shared with them by the few folks they met, including First Inhabitants who were particularly kind. They saw a few more towns, each looking like a Wild West place, with ranches in the surrounding areas. But they didn't want to linger, afraid of the reaction their presence might bring. So, they stayed away, just sending a couple of their troupe into the settlements to buy flasks of water.

Finally, they got to the New Mexico Territory and headed into land that seemed to change every few hours, desert-like at times with picturesque mesas in the distance, then almost mountainous, and sometimes relieved by green valleys. It grew punishingly hot, though it was now September. All of them began to grumble, a few even said nasty things about the Seer, who didn't seem to hear and certainly didn't respond, as he rode up ahead, his nose pointed west, seemingly never tired, leading them, they worried, to their deaths. *What was his plan? What was he after?* On their third day from Texas they came to a sign, wooden and battered and driven into the ground by the side of the dusty road.

"Lincoln County" it read.

They were all as hungry as wolves and parched that day. They'd used up their food supplies, their water was gone. From a rise, they could see a town in a valley.

This time, they weren't going to avoid it. They were all going in, no matter the reception.

It was another Wild West town — a couple of saloons, sheriff's office, and a blacksmith's shop at the center of a cluster of about fifty or so houses — but even from a distance they could see that something was going on in the main road.

As they rode closer, Solomon realized that they were about to witness a "showdown."

He didn't even think they really existed. He thought they were just bits of drama written into western novels to get readers excited. But here before him, in the business area of Lincoln, New Mexico Territory, were two men facing each other about forty paces apart, obviously intent upon doing each other terrible harm. A score was about to be settled. A crowd had gathered on the plank boardwalks, keeping their distance, but not moving. Faces looked out of windows and others stared down from balconies in the town's two wooden hotels. The Seer dug his boots into his horse's sides and raced down the hill and into town. The others followed at a slower pace. As they entered from the east, they could see the two contestants more clearly. One was definitely a gunslinger, and his very presence struck fear into Solomon's heart. He was dressed in dark clothes and a cowboy hat, with a black leather vest and chaps, and spurs on his boots, and a big, black handlebar mustache drooped over his mouth. His gun belt was slung low on his waist and his left hand was twitching near the handle of his six-shooter as he eyed his opponent with a greedy grin. His enemy looked frightened — a thin man wearing a saloonkeeper's apron, a gun in his hand but held low, as if someone had set it there and he was reluctant to use it. In fact, he didn't look like he knew how to employ it at all. But he glared back at his opponent, trying to surmount his fear. Not far from him a woman in a billowing dress and bonnet wept, holding two small children by the hands.

Solomon couldn't believe how thrilled the Seer was — it was disgusting. The young fugitive moved quickly to a spot near the sheriff's office, directly between the two gunfighters; he had a perfect view. The sheriff himself stood there, arms folded across his chest, two deputies by his side, all with starred badges on their chests, doing nothing. They looked like they were trying to hide their fear. They were going to let this happen. Solomon wished to God that he could do something about the murder they were about to witness.

The two men on the street were just staring at each other.

"You make your move, partner," growled the gunslinger.

"Don't do it, Hank!" shouted someone, then shut his mouth.

The friends got down from their horses, tied them to posts near a water trough at one of the hotels and climbed up onto the wooden sidewalk. No one even glanced their way. A boy stood next to Solomon, slightly behind him, in the shadows. He was dressed in strange clothes, halfway between a First Inhabitant's and a cowboy's, with a loose blouse under a vest, baggy trousers, and a colorful cloth belt around his waist. He wore a white hat with a wide brim, which offset his almost copper complexion and long black hair. He turned for an instant as Solomon neared him and the North Britain boy glimpsed two Colt revolvers with gleaming nickel finish and ivory grips facing out, hidden under his vest.

"He's got to do it!" shouted the gunslinger. "He insulted my reputation. You don't asks John W. Hardman to leave an establishment."

"I would do it again! We don't want your type around here," said the saloonkeeper in a shaky voice. "It ain't safe with you here!"

"Keep quiet, Hank!" cried another voice in the crowd.

"Don't matter no more. I's going to shoot you here in cold blood in front of your wife and kin and all your friends. No one badmouths Dead-Eye Hardman. Now, you draw, mister. I'll give you first move."

There was silence.

"May God bless my wife and children; may God take me to heaven for doing the right thing," said the saloonkeeper. Then he put both hands on his gun and began to raise it toward Hardman. His eyes were closed.

Angus held his hands together in prayer and Ayesha looked to the east. Solomon brought his own hands up to his face but peeked through the fingers. The Seer stared wide-eyed in fascination.

A shot rang out, the saloonkeeper fired … and John W. Hardman fell to his knees. A bullet had passed through his left hand and his gun had fallen from it. And as he raised his right hand to grasp his mangled left, another shot rang out and both his hands were bloodied. Solomon could actually see the big hole rip through his flesh. Hardman shrieked and held his wounded hands up to his face. The saloonkeeper's wife ran to her husband and the family held each other in the dusty main road.

Some looked at the victor in awe. He had done it! He had defeated Dead-Eye Hardman. But others, more savvy, looked around. They knew the saloonkeeper's bullet had missed by the width of a barn door. Someone else, someone in the crowd, had shot the famous outlaw, not in the heart or in the face, but in *both* hands! The gunslinger's career was over.

Others searched the roofs of the buildings. But Solomon knew where to look: right behind him in the shadows. The revolver-toting boy's eyes met his.

"An interesting posse you are moving about with, my brother," said the dark-haired kid. "I would lay a bet that you aren't too kindly taken to in these parts."

"Y-yes," Solomon stammered.

"You are in possession of information about me, I believe, about what just transpired here on the streets."

"I … I won't tell," Solomon whispered.

"Don't matter. I can look after myself. I was about to move on, anyway. Are you folks hungry? You look it."

"Yes," said Cleo, who had been listening to the conversation. "And we were about to move on ourselves."

He smiled at her and tipped his hat. "Well, you must have something to eat first. Will you be my guests in the saloonkeeper's establishment? I am guessing the charges will be reasonable this afternoon."

Minutes later they were gathered around the biggest table in the saloon, listening to the piano player play up a happy storm, treated to apple drinks and beans and potatoes by the relieved saloonkeeper. He didn't seem to bat an eye at the giant or Cleo or Napoleon or Robert Elvis McTell. They were all welcome.

Other customers didn't appear to feel the same way, but their young host sat at the head of their table with his vest pulled back, so those gun grips were visible and projected an air that told others he was willing to use them and knew how. So, everyone kept their distance. All except the sheriff, that is.

Just after the nine of them had settled in to eat, he appeared with his deputies inside the swinging outside doors and called out to the revolver-toting kid.

The piano player stopped performing.

"Boy! I know it was you who shot Hardman. And I'm a taking you in."

"No, you aren't, white leader. You just sidle on back to your office with those two sidekicks of yours, who did nothing when that depraved desperado was about to murder a good citizen, and tend to your proper duties. I am about to leave town anyhow."

"Boy, you are going to turn in your —"

Suddenly, their young host rose to his feet, reached his hands across his chest and down to his holsters, and snapped out both Colts. He trained the barrels on the sheriff in a split second, one hand crossed over the other. It took no more than the blink of an eye. The sheriff hadn't even moved.

"Yes … well …" said the lawman, "as long as you is leaving."

"I is, and thank you for the hospitality."

Geronimo Jones turned out to be not much older than Solomon too, the son of a First Inhabitant woman (or Mescalero Apache, as he pointed out) and a white lawman. His father had been gunned down by an outlaw two years ago. The boy, who had been taught how to shoot from childhood, perfecting a unique crosshanded style, had taken to the road after that, leaving his mother with her few remaining people in southern New Mexico Territory near the border of the large but very poor American state of Mexico. His parents' marriage had been looked down upon by whites and, to a degree, had led to his father's death — the dastardly man who killed him had bragged about bagging "that First-Inhabitant-loving lawman." Geronimo had vowed to live a lawful existence but to seek out and destroy evil wherever he found it, especially hunting the man who had killed his father.

"But I feel I want to change my life now," he told his young guests. "They say, in these parts, that anyone who kills another with firearms, for good reasons or bad, will die by the gun too. It is said that The Deacon himself, Jim 'Killer' Miller, is looking for me. Even Billy the Kid died young."

At that, the Seer leapt onto the table and danced down it toward Geronimo. His eyes were on fire. He grunted at him and began motioning with his hands, as if beckoning him to join him.

"What does he mean by that?"

"I think," Solomon said, "he wants you to come with us."

By noon the next day, they were far from Lincoln County, heading northwest, almost at the Rio Grande river, turning toward mountainous, gold-mining Colorado, keeping to the route the

Seer had laid out on his map. When they had risen that morning, he had taken them out into the country and led them in a rehearsal of a new show, one that incorporated all of them, including Napoleon, J.S. Chan, and Geronimo Jones. It was strange to be doing such a thing in the desert-like surroundings of the New Mexico Territory, their only audience the sky, the snakes, and the roadrunners.

Exactly what the Seer was seeking still wasn't clear. Solomon knew he was obsessed with taking them west, but didn't know what compelled him there; the boy knew too that the last stop on his map was Los Angeles but was puzzled by his depiction of their smiling faces floating there in the ocean. And he still didn't know why dangerous people were pursuing his friend. Booth and Pawn and the needle-nosed man could very well be near them here in the wilderness, on horseback, ready to kill all of them to retrieve their little prize.

But Solomon knew something else too ... he felt like *someone* when he traveled with the Seer and Cleo and the others, and when he heard that life-giving applause that greeted him as they performed. They were an amazing collection of young artists who could put on a show that would startle any audience and bring Solomon and the rest of them the money and freedom they all needed. This life was thrilling, and dangerous, and at any moment could come to a violent end.

Every night before he went to sleep, the same thoughts ran through his head, whether he was floating down the Mississippi or listening to the wild coyote call in the New Mexico desert.

"Who is this little man? Why do our pursuers so desperately want him? And what is his plan?"

CHAPTER TWENTY
COLORADO, BY AIR

Geronimo knew this territory well and had excellent vision — in fact, it seemed he could sense others at a distance, so he spotted it first. It was kind of like seeing a motorized vehicle in the streets of ancient Rome, appearing as a dot in the sky at first, coming up the deep canyon of the Rio Grande from the south. But it grew larger as it groaned along in the air toward the little troupe below.

An enormous passenger balloon!

And even more incredible than its appearance in this unpopulated and romantic land was the fact that when it neared, floating no more than one hundred feet above the ground so its inhabitants could see down into the canyon … it stopped. It was like a barn moving through the air, casting a long shadow over the nine friends. It descended slightly so it was only thirty feet above. Ayesha's ravens flew to it. Up there at the railing that surrounded the observation deck was a man in a smart blue uniform, his face mustachioed, looking down at them.

"Hello!" he shouted. He had a slight German accent.

"Good day!" Solomon cried back.

"What an interesting collection of humanity here in the Wild West! Where are you going?"

"Colorado."

"Well, so are we. Pikes Peak, Colorado Springs, and Denver City, a little touristing, you know."

"Uh!" shouted the Seer and motioned to the giant, who had been walking beside his horse, leading it. The little man threw his hands toward him in a theatrical gesture like a performer who had just finished a turn and was asking for the audience's appreciation. Angus understood, let go of the reins, and did a handstand. The passengers' applause immediately sounded above.

The Seer slid from his mount and set the big jar in the sand and motioned to Solomon, who got down and took off his boots and shirt and trousers and squeezed himself into it. The applause was even louder.

"Say," called out the Captain, "would you all like a ride? Consent to be our entertainment and it is free!"

It took about half an hour to get all of them up the ladder and into the huge dirigible — landing the giant was especially tricky. The branded horses had made this trek to Denver City in Colorado many times, so Solomon, Cleo, and some of the others slapped them on their behinds and off they galloped northward, happy to be on their way on their familiar route without loads on their backs.

Just a month ago, it had been amazing to the North Britain boy to simply see a passenger balloon. Now, he was actually inside one. The interior was remarkable. It was obvious that the hundred or so people on board, many decked out in suits and long dresses in the middle of the hot day, were wealthy, and their surroundings reflected what they demanded on a luxury cruise.

The planked deck upon which the little troupe first landed was cluttered with beautifully carved wooden deck chairs and everything was surrounded by a polished gold railing. Inside the glass doors was a stateroom with a gleaming wood floor and laid out with white-clothed tables for dining — the aroma of a lovely meal still lingered. A chandelier hung from the ceiling. The bedrooms were downstairs in a private area and (though the nine of them were never allowed near them) they could imagine how regal they must have been.

The Seer and friends were the entertainment for the next few days, all the way to Colorado. They slept on blanketed settees in the stateroom at night. During the days, they did their act, though the space was too confined for the entire show. But their well-heeled audience seemed to be enchanted. And so was the troupe, not by the passengers, but by the whole experience of floating high above stunning scenery. They looked down upon the Rio Grande, then spotted the towns of Albuquerque and Santa Fe, appearing like oases in a desert. Solomon imagined what was going on down there in those outlaw towns with their armed marshals, saloon showgirls, and hard-drinking cowboys. On one hand, he wanted to be there, but on the other, he and his companions were best up here, above the fray.

The Seer rarely did any sightseeing. When he wasn't helping with the acts, he liked to look at his map and draw. Solomon had thought the catapult picture was nearly done, but the little man kept working on it, making it more and more complex. When Solomon asked about it, he didn't respond.

Not long into the cruise, they began to see the magnificent Rocky Mountains to the west and soon those breathtaking elevations were all around them as the airship sailed into Colorado.

It took their breath away, almost literally, since it was harder to breathe at this altitude.

They passed over the mining towns of Cripple Creek, Pikes Peak, and Colorado Springs. This young state was still in the grip of its second great gold rush. Every adventurer in the world seemed to be coming here and excitement and danger came with them. Solomon had heard that the great scientist Nikola Tesla had an experimental station here too, where he created electricity, great lightning storms of it, in a madman's retreat. Napoleon, standing next to Cleo and Solomon at the railing, told them he had once sought out Tesla during a lecture tour in New Orleans and had learned about the applications of this new energy. He was particularly interested in how one might amplify music and the human voice. The three of them looked toward earth, imagining the thunderbolts the great man was summoning down there.

In another day, they were above Denver City. This was where they were to leave their horses and the most northerly spot on the Seer's mapped journey to the west. They descended. Solomon wasn't sure what the Seer wanted to do here in this isolated place and how they could get from Denver to California over the mountains. But he knew something was up.

A big crowd gathered below as they moored in a field on the outskirts of the city. It seemed that few passenger balloons came this way, so this was an occasion. The little troupe's unusual appearance didn't draw too much attention — either they were used to strange folks in the middle of the wild frontier, or the nine friends were simply entertainers to them, and they expected such people to be different from everyone else.

Denver was a beautiful spot because it sat next to the mountains, but in other ways it wasn't so pleasing. Due to the gold rushes and all the opportunity here, it had drawn more than its fair share of opportunists and con men and women. The community was full of them, and not just in the saloons and gambling halls and bordellos, but in the offices of the politicians too. In fact, it wasn't always easy to tell the difference between the con men and the lawmen; they split the power between them.

But Solomon didn't know all that about this outlaw society until later. As they disembarked from the dirigible that day, he doubted that Cleo or Napoleon or any of the others did either … except maybe the Seer. They began walking from the field, heading toward the surprisingly substantial skyline of Denver City, followed by a few folks who now gawked at Angus and the ravens and the rest of the motley young troupe. The birds occasionally cried out "Hello!" Solomon was guessing that he and his friends would soon put on some sort of show here. It seemed a likely place, since there was unquestionably money about.

The Seer was the only one who wasn't looking toward town. He walked with his arms crossed, deep in thought. It never seemed enough for him to *just* put on a show — it had to be a great show under riveting circumstances. *What was he considering now?*

In minutes, they were passing houses and businesses and then strolling along a gravel street that was widening. The buildings grew in height too. All sorts of folks passed by, from dirty miners to tanned-faced women in trousers, to fancy-dressed ladies and sly-looking dandies who looked like swindlers.

Many of the buildings, even the offices and stores, appeared like saloons and entertainment halls that had been stretched upwards. The city was bigger than Solomon expected, with a frontier bustle to it.

The little crowd that followed them increased as they neared the center of Denver. Solomon didn't like that. He looked at the billboards to try to get a sense of what made this town tick. But the big signs, though a little cruder than back in the center of the Empire, and specific to Colorado, had similar messages: *"America is the Land of Dreams but Denver Makes Them Golden"* and *"You are No One Until You Come to Colorado! Land for Sale!"* and ... *"The Tivoli Saloon, Where You See Stars!"*

That last message struck a tiny chord in Solomon's memory. He had just picked up a copy of the *Denver Pioneer Post* off the wide-plank sidewalk and had begun looking at a remarkable story on the front page, complete with a photo-picture of a gorilla, of all things. "SUDSY WANTS GORRILLA FOUND," it cried, followed by a sub-headline, "Fun from the Tivoli Saloon."

He began to read out loud, knowing the Seer would be intrigued.

"Sudsy Randolph says —"

"Uh!" exclaimed the Seer and stopped.

Solomon looked at him. He had cocked his head as if he recognized something and then motioned for his friend to continue. They all halted and Solomon read on.

> Sudsy Randolph says he wants his gorilla back. Citizens who haunt the noisy and glitzy interior of the Tivoli Club at 17th and Market — and that is most of Denver at some point, though many of you wouldn't care to admit it — will recall the marvelous ape that has, shall we say "graced" the Tivoli Stage of late, appearing right after the New York Dancing Dolls and George Beedle of British impersonating and vocalizing fame. Said ominous and muscular forebear of ours has gone missing. Sudsy "procured" him, shall

we say, in a little game of chance he "played" with Beans Beauregard of the Traveling Beauregards last month, then put him on stage to do his remarkable escape-artist routine where he was tightly handcuffed, hand and foot. by a local marshal before extricating himself in front of amazed onlookers to the tune of *I Am a Man After All and A Mighty One Too*, played on the Tivoli's ivories by the inimitable Reggie "Downbeat" Right.

And, of course, at the end of things, the gorilla turned to the audience and said, "thank you" or something much like that. But his act is no longer and Sudsy isn't pleased. The ape, perhaps unhappy with his pay, walked out on the Tivoli impresario sometime in the early hours of Monday morning and hasn't been seen in town for three days. Word is he is hiding in the mines, since he was observed strolling out in the countryside in that direction by young local lads not long after he was reported missing. There was no time for him to engage in conversation with the boys, since they hightailed it away at top speed. Sudsy says he will give anyone with information about the "Simian Houdini" a few coins (bite those hard before accepting) and anyone capturing him a cool $100 Douglas bill. (Good luck collecting!)

By the time the last word was out of Solomon's mouth, the Seer had snatched the paper from his hand and was racing ahead, looking at the street names carved into or painted onto the corners of the buildings. It was evident that they were on Market Street and that the next cross street was 9th Avenue, followed by 10th, and the Seer was recognizing numbers. Soon, he was sprinting. They all tried to keep up and once or twice a few of them were almost struck by carriages and buggies and a motorized vehicle or two (though there weren't many in this city). He stopped when he got to 17th. There was the Tivoli Club, a two-and-a-half-story building on the southeast corner of the wide gravel streets, with a wraparound veranda out front and big windows that went almost the full height of the ground floor. "TIVOLI" read a big sign in red on the roof. "Headquarters for Gentlemen, First-Class Goods and First-Class Attention. Diversions Daily. Open Day & Night, Wines, Liquors and Cigars."

Out from the swinging doors of the entrance came none other than Sudsy Randolph himself, his heeled, spurred boots smacking on the wooden veranda, his tall, lean frame dressed in a black suit with waistcoat and gold watch chain, bearded, long-haired, and sporting a cowboy hat tipped back on his head. A crocodile-skin gun belt with full holsters was slung low under his belly. When he stepped out the door, everyone within sight of him paused for a moment before walking on. This was obviously a man of influence in Denver City.

He took one look at the nine companions and their problems were over … sort of.

The Seer ran up to him and Sudsy instantly stuck out his hand in greeting. "Well, well, little man what do we have here?" He took his hand back from the Seer's, wiping it as he placed it into a waistcoat pocket, and glowed at the bizarre collection of youngsters.

"Uh!"

"I see, not a loquacious sort, are we?"

"My name is Solomon Hunt," said the North Britain boy, puffing a bit as he stepped up on to the veranda. Sudsy took his hand too, and shook it as he displayed his teeth, some glittering with gold.

"My guess is that you gentlemen and ladies" — he doffed his hat in Cleo and Ayesha's direction, and then luridly toward J.S. Chan — "are in the entertainment and diversion industry." His hair was greasy underneath. "I know you, don't I?" he said to Cleo.

"Human cannonball," she said, looking suspicious.

"Ah yes! The one and only Cleopatra! Now," — he ran his eyes over the rest of the troupe again — "I don't know that I am acquainted with you other folks, but I am guessing you all have, shall we say, particular talents? I must confess to not having seen the likes of your combination in all my born days. You are quite a sight! Welcome to the Tivoli Club. We offer libations, games of cards and chance, the charms of the fairer sex … and startling entertainment. Can you startle me? If so, you will undoubtedly startle the populace of Denver City."

"Uh!" shouted the Seer.

"What … what does that mean?"

"It means yes," said Cleo.

"You, my daring, dark-skinned, delectable miss, might be willing to spend some time with me, would you think?"

"I am not yet seventeen years old, sir."

"And?"

"We will perform for you," said Solomon quickly.

"Yes, well, come in." He kept his eyes on Cleo, though at times they lingered on J.S. Chan too.

Though all the gambling rooms and other chambers both upstairs and down were in full swing, the Tivoli's saloon and entertainment hall was still an hour from opening. On its little stage that afternoon, in front of empty tables and chairs and a few of the host's men and painted saloon girls, Ayesha made her ravens talk, Angus turned some acrobatics, Solomon did his jar act, Geronimo took out his ivory-grip Colt six-shooters and shattered a shot glass off a frightened employee's head, and J.S. Chan defeated one of Randolph's toughest thugs without ever throwing a punch. Sudsy insisted that "Miss Cleopatra" do nothing, except sit next to him while he watched. The Seer directed and when they were done, Randolph stood up and applauded. "Hired! One week at five dollars per performer … depending on liquor receipts, of course."

That didn't seem like much money and Solomon didn't trust this obviously infamous con artist, but the Seer leapt to his feet and shook hands. It didn't make sense. Solomon wondered if he had something else up his sleeve. If he did, it had better be well concealed, because in Sudsy Randolph the Seer was meeting his match.

The con man was sly all right. He treated the weird little troupe of youngsters like royalty. He had all their clothing washed and even provided them with new trousers and dresses made to fit. He was someone to watch carefully.

A curious incident occurred early that evening. Sudsy was feeding them, and the Seer was still leafing through the newspaper. Solomon wondered what an illiterate could get out of the *Pioneer Post* and assumed his little friend was looking at the pictures. But then the Seer stopped at a particular article and stared at it for a long time, his mouth wide open. Looking upset, he proceeded to rip the sheet out and walked over to Sudsy, who was standing by the bar. The Seer motioned at what he held in his hand and pestered Randolph about it, his face red. The first few things the con man responded didn't seem to satisfy the Seer, but eventually he appeared to tell him what he wanted to know, because the inquisitor stopped asking questions, balled the page up in his little fist, and stuck it into his pocket. He sat back down again, stroking his chin, thinking, looking frightened.

Solomon never once saw their leader smile again, all the way to Los Angeles.

They performed the show that night and it was said to be one of the greatest Denver City had ever seen. But not due to what they actually did. Their act, though interesting enough because of their unique performers, was really rather tame compared to what they had done in other places and what Solomon knew they were being prepared to do in the future. The Seer seemed to want it that way. Usually, he pushed them to do new and sensational things but had kept his directing to a minimum during the rehearsal and wasn't even in the saloon when the show began that night.

But he appeared before it was over, just as it ended, in fact. And that was what made their performance so great, made it one of the best in Denver's history.

You see, when the Seer appeared, the audience gasped. They had good reason.

He had Sudsy Randolph's gorilla by the hand.

CHAPTER TWENTY-ONE
OVER THE MOUNTAINS

It was like one of those dramatic moments from a cowboy novel where the whole saloon is full of noise and people are drinking and the saloon girls are kicking their bare legs high (or in this case, Angus is in the midst of a handstand) and men are shouting, and someone enters through the outside swinging doors, usually a bad guy dressed in black with guns drawn … and the whole place goes quiet.

When the Seer came in with "the Simian Houdini," silence suddenly reigned.

He strode up to Sudsy, who was sitting at a table near the front, Cleo installed beside him. Randolph's mouth was wide open. Then he drew his gun on the gorilla.

"Ain't you the clever one," he said to the Seer in a low voice, looking into the troupe leader's eyes with an expression Solomon hadn't seen on him before, as if he were searching for something.

The Seer held out his right hand, palm up. He wanted the one-hundred-dollar Douglas bill.

"Give it to him, Sudsy!" yelled someone. Randolph found the voice and offered its owner a black look. Silence resumed.

"Of course … I shall," he began. "A deal is a deal, after all. Let it not be said that Sudsy Randolph goes back on his word. In fact, I will do this gentleman one better," he announced to the crowd, which was a big one that night, jammed into the saloon and even sitting on the bar. "I will hand him a five-dollar Douglas bill BEFORE I give him the one hundred and I will ALSO give him a chance to make even more than the generous century note. That is just the sort of operator I am!"

He snapped his fingers and a shady-looking associate with dark eyes that shifted about under a black hat and who wouldn't even look at his boss, stepped forward and pulled a roll of money from his pocket and handed it to Sudsy. An empty table was set in front of him. The con artist selected four bills from the roll and gave it back.

The first was a five, which he gave to the Seer, who quickly pocketed it.

Randolph then turned to the audience.

"I hold in my hand TWO genuine one-hundred-dollar bills."

The audience gasped. He held them up to the light, turning them so everyone could see the portrait of former President Douglas on one side and American war heroes on the other.

"And one … not so genuine." He turned the third bill around so everyone could see that one side was blank.

"Many of you are aware of how I first made my name in these parts, as a soap salesman, but not of an ordinary sort. I sold, and still sell, soap that will cure your ills, whether they are balding of the head hair, women's complaints, or premature aging. Your skin, though beaten by the Colorado sun, will be as soft as a baby's bottom after using it. Why, simply look at my own youthful visage, my luxurious head of hair … and I have never received a complaint from a woman!"

He glanced at Cleo, who looked away, then extended his gleam to a few showgirls at the bar who smiled back at him and giggled.

"I am going to do the following for you, my little gentleman."

"No," Solomon said to himself.

"I am going to wrap these three bills around three bars of my extraordinary soap. You, sir, can then choose which TWO have the genuine one-hundred-dollar bills. You shall walk away with either one hundred dollars or … TWO hundred dollars. You cannot lose … unless, of course, catastrophe happens. This is, after all, a game of chance, and one must take one's chances. A bill or two may slip away somehow. But I shall promise you this, on my mother's grave … two of them are at this very moment real one-hundred-dollar bills and I will wrap this soap in front of your very eyes. Do you want to play? Do you agree to take all and expressed chances, scant as they are? You are certainly assured of gaining my bars of soap! Of THAT you can be certain!"

The Seer nodded his head.

"No," Solomon said to himself again.

Sudsy rolled up his sleeves to prove that there would be no evident shenanigans. He held the bills up for all to see, even let the Seer examine them, and then carefully wrapped each bar in front of the little man and the audience and set them down on the table. The pianist played as he worked.

"Now, sir … find your two one-hundred-dollar Douglas bills! *Bonne chance!*"

The piano man played furiously, and the Seer eyed the three bars of soap, then almost instantly nodded his head to indicate he had made his choices. The music stopped.

But the Seer didn't choose a bar of soap. Instead, he reached over the table and slipped his hand inside Randolph's suitcoat, locating an inner pocket in a flash.

From it, he extricated both one-hundred-dollar bills.

In the silence that ensued, Solomon Hunt heard the infamous Sudsy Randolph, never bested in this remarkable game of chance, say under his breath while glaring at the Seer ... "Who are you?!"

Solomon and his friends slept in an upstairs room of the Tivoli Club that night.

Or at least, his friends slept, and the boy tried to. For a long while, he couldn't close his eyes, believing that at any minute Randolph or some of his henchmen would murder them in their beds. And if not them, then Booth or Pawn would. The troupe was all in one room, lying on crude mattresses, Angus snoring like, well, a giant.

Finally, Solomon fell asleep. But he had only drifted off for moments when he felt a pair of hands on him, seizing him roughly by the arm. His eyes snapped open, and he likely would have screamed had the Seer not put his palm over his friend's mouth. He motioned for Solomon to get up. In the dimness, the boy could see that several of their party were already on their feet and the others were being quietly awakened.

There was no time to ask what was going on, nor was it wise to break the silence.

The Seer led them out the door and then down a little wooden staircase at the back of the building. Solomon assumed that they were going to get out of there as fast as they could. He was wrong.

Their leader left the others outside in the cool Colorado night and took Solomon down a flight of damp basement stairs. He pried a key from his pocket and opened the door at the bottom. They stepped inside. The boy could hear something breathing, something large, and then he heard the creaking sound of a cage opening. They turned and walked back up the stairs. When they emerged into the moonlight, Solomon could see that the Seer had the Simian Houdini by the hand, again.

"Thank you," the beast said clearly.

The North Britain boy didn't ask the Seer how he came to have the keys to that basement door and the cage inside, but it wasn't hard to figure out. The gorilla obviously didn't like Sudsy Randolph or any of his men but was as docile as a kitten around the Seer. They had likely asked the young genius to help them take the gorilla to his cage and the Seer had agreed, knowing that he could palm both keys up his sleeve when the job was done.

And so, the little troupe had their tenth performer.

Solomon thought of the next location the Seer had marked on his map: Salt Lake City, on the other side of the Rocky Mountains, the enclave of the strange and sometimes frightening Mormon nation. The boy had read many stories about them.

But how in the world were the ten of them to get there?

The Seer had a plan, of course. And, in many ways, it was awfully conventional. A railroad had just been built from northern Colorado west through the mountain passes at extraordinary expense. In fact, when they arrived at the Denver Steam

Railroad Station the billboards were full of praise for the "*American Ingenuity!*" that had built it. "*America, The Greatest Nation on Earth, Once Again Proves Its Greatness! Take the High-Wire Ride Through the Rockies!*" There were paintings of bridges and tunnels built into awe-inspiring mountain scenery. "*The Highest Steam Railroad in the World!*" exclaimed another sign. There were also images of First Inhabitants (Geronimo explained they were from the Ute nation) and of buffalo, though they had seen few of either and would hardly see any more. The people had been decimated and shuffled off to little reservations, and the buffalo killed in the hundreds of thousands.

It seemed to Solomon that this trip was going to be a high-wire ride indeed, but not just over the mountains ... simply getting their group onto the steam train would be plenty precarious.

The big clock on the wall was at five o'clock when they arrived in the empty terminus. It was still dark outside. There was an early train at seven a.m. Solomon strolled up to the ticket booth with the Seer, making sure their giant, their folks of color, their ravens, and of course, their gorilla, were tucked away out of sight. But when Solomon ordered the ten tickets, the man behind the bars asked to see their group so he could examine exactly who would be boarding his company's trains. Before they could stop him, he came out from his office, holding the tickets close to his chest, and looked across the marble floor at their bizarre companions. He gaped at them, but when he had taken them all in, he smiled.

"I am spotting a critter to which I am presently taking a shine, especially given that you are absconding with it from Denver City. Is that Sudsy Randolph's gorilla?"

"Yes, sir, it is," said Solomon.

"Well, here," he said and handed him all the tickets. "Get yourself onto the fifth-class car right away before respectable folks arrive and slouch down out of sight and stay that way for the whole trip; try to keep the gorilla and your ones who might draw unwanted attention hidden. I'll give you a blanket. You can throw it over the animal if you need to."

"Yes, sir," said Solomon.

"Sudsy Randolph took me for a load of dough," continued the man. "I shall personally tell him that you left here heading east … toward New York City! That wild-goose chase should cost him a pocketful!"

They did as he said and by seven o'clock, they were going north to Boulder and then straight west deep into the heavenly Rocky Mountains. Solomon counted thirty-three tunnels before they reached the Continental Divide that marks the spot where all the rivers and lakes run west instead of east. They went along mind-boggling switchbacks and over bridges that seemed to hang in the sky. They saw mountain goats and elk, and bald eagles among the few wispy clouds. Even the gorilla wanted to look out. The American Empire couldn't put billboards on these mountains or fence in this scenery for amusement parks or sell the wildlife, though Solomon was guessing they would have, if it had been possible.

The trip was more than five hundred miles and took them until suppertime that evening. They made just a few quick stops during the first half up to the border, one at a mountain restaurant and station, and then only a few more in Utah. Though it was just past mid-September now, they passed through a couple of snowstorms. Near the border, the land flattened out, but they were still at high elevation; they followed lower valleys the rest of the way. They saw six buffalo together once, looking lost, and a group of a dozen Ute people, with rifles and bareback horses, appearing equally forlorn.

As they traveled, the Seer spent a great deal of time looking at his map. He seemed awfully serious and even a little scared. Solomon noticed that his hand shook. Something had changed for him back in Denver. And a few hours into the train ride, he drew something new on the map, the first change he had made on it since he created it in Buffalo. First, he crossed out their three smiling faces floating in the Pacific Ocean near Los Angeles. Then he drew what looked like a pirate's chest overflowing with gold coins … a treasure.

The last hour or so of the trip was through a particularly steep valley. As the train emerged out of it, Solomon could see Salt Lake City in the distance.

About fifty years ago, the Mormons had come in wagonloads to this high, flat stretch of land to escape religious persecution and set up their own society here on the far side of the continent.

About half the size of Denver, this city looked like one tenth of the fun. Though Solomon was sure there were saloons and dance halls somewhere, he and his companions didn't see any. What they did observe was an orderly place with clean streets and horse-and-buggy traffic, moving slowly and considerately. Men dressed in old-fashioned black clothes and women in long plain dresses and monochrome bonnets. The troupe also saw the domed Mormon Tabernacle and a huge, white, Gothic cathedral.

They looked like something from outer space or from an Arthurian legend — impressive but a little frightening. It felt like the Wizard of Oz lived in there.

The Mormons appeared in many books and were usually the bad guys: dour men with long beards who hated fun, enslaved their many wives, and were violent with enemies. They were even the bad guys in one Sherlock Holmes book Solomon had read! But they didn't seem so bad up close.

But what was the little troupe going to do here? Hardly anyone stared at them ... the way they should have. Instead, folks turned away and simply ignored them.

That wasn't good for showpeople. They likely couldn't draw a crowd in Salt Lake City and their "sinful" show would be a bust.

Then it occurred to Solomon that this may have been precisely why the Seer had brought them here. Did taking a route through this distant city allow them to be inconspicuous? Booth and Pawn wouldn't suspect that they would come this way and Coop wouldn't either. And this unusual route would be the toughest to track. Out there trying to sniff the young troupe's trail, those evil men likely were depending on hearing about their spectacular presence up ahead, drawing crowds and making money.

Still, the group remained very much on the move. They had to continue west from here to keep to the directions on the Seer's map. He wanted to get to Los Angeles ... and that treasure. And so did Solomon — Southern California had intrigued him from the start, but now, with those gold coins on his mind, it was doubly enticing. The Seer's route went from here through Nevada to San Francisco, then south along the Pacific Ocean. So, why hadn't they simply gotten on another steam train at the terminus and headed that way? Or were there any trains from here to the coast?

They kept walking. The Seer was marching them right through Salt Lake City toward the west. Were they going to *walk* to San Francisco?

But before long they saw what he was after … *stagecoaches!*

Solomon couldn't believe it. He didn't know that they even still existed. But up ahead, he spotted a fenced-off depot filled with them, sitting at the end of the last wide dirt road they walked in Salt Lake City. The sun was setting now, so they would have to sleep outside nearby and catch a coach west in the morning. The man in charge of the depot, who looked decidedly un-Mormon with his clean-shaven face, fancy coat, and money-grubbing attitude, wasn't thrilled by their appearance. He tried to look away and not even serve them, but the Seer, an expert in what people want, especially in America, took out some of the change from their train fares and dropped it on the man's counter. Then, he dramatically set their remaining one-hundred-dollar bill beside it. In seconds, the group had ten tickets.

Their leader was obviously still worried about being followed, despite not having seen Booth or Pawn for so long. He was figuring that no one, not even their expert trackers, would imagine that they'd take a stagecoach from Salt Lake City to California. It certainly had never occurred to Solomon Hunt.

They walked out into the wilderness, a good half mile from the depot and far from any habitation (though they could see single lights far in the distance, likely from Mormon ranches) and went to sleep.

But they didn't doze for long. They were awakened by gunfire. It was coming from somewhere in the direction of those distant ranches. It grew louder. It was coming their way! They rose and kept low. Soon they could tell what was happening: About half a dozen men on horseback, a couple with lanterns and others with rifles, were chasing a single person who was on foot.

"Can you see her, Joshua?!" cried one. "We cannot let her get away!"

"I am sorry! I will leave!" shouted their terrified prey, a young woman, probably not much older than Solomon.

"Your fate is cast; your sin has been committed. God will take you where you should go with the aid of the bullets from our guns!"

"I was just 'aving fun with 'im. *He* said *'e'd* run off with *me*!"

"You don't arouse a Mormon boy's heart and body, you infidel! It is a serious matter! No one leaves the clan and anyone who entices our young men deserves death!"

More shots rang out and then there was silence.

"Is she hit?"

They heard the horses bridled and the men jump down from their steeds.

"There she is!"

For a moment there was no talking.

"Why, she seems dead! She isn't breathing. Her heart is still!"

Cleo gripped Solomon's arm.

"Jacob, we weren't to actually shoot her! That isn't right."

"No one hit her, Isaiah. There's no blood on her, no bullets in her. She must have died of fright, likely something wrong with her pumping organ. We should return home and leave her carcass here. She was just a drifter, a foreign floozy using her dark beauty. No one will trace her; no one will have any reason to suspect us.

Why, we live miles away. The birds will finish her. God makes his decisions. He judges Jezebels and tempting Eves."

The little troupe waited for several minutes after the sound of the horse hooves had thudded into the distance. Then they rose and sought the body. Solomon found it, a young woman indeed. She felt cold. The North Britain boy pressed his hand to her throat and then Cleo put a palm on her chest: the young woman's heart was definitely still. Ayesha sobbed and Solomon didn't feel much better. They all knew they had to leave this poor woman here to be picked apart by the vultures, likely far from her loved ones.

They got to their feet and began to walk away.

"Who are you lot?" said a voice on the ground behind them.

The dead woman had spoken.

CHAPTER TWENTY-TWO
THE DEATH GIRL

Zara Patel Chaplin had been dead a moment ago. There was no doubt about it. Now she was as alive as the rest of them, standing before the young party, regaling them in her working-class English accent inflected with a strong Indian lilt. But perhaps the most shocking thing about all of this was that her reappearance from the heaven or hell she had just visited didn't strike her as anything remarkable.

The Seer was staring at her, fascinated.

"Oh, listen 'ere, mates," said Zara as she got to her feet, and they gathered around her in the moonlight. "I've done that many a time — not the enticing-a-boy thing, which I'll 'ave you know I did not do — was 'im who was so interested — but the coming-back-to-life thing."

Her face and clothing were becoming more evident in the dark. A girl about eighteen with the night-black hair and eyes of someone from the Colony of India, wearing an undone, form-fitting dress with a spectacular peacock pattern that showed her bare ankles and oversized black boots. She sported a bowler hat, a little small for her head, an open and tattered suit jacket, and carried a bamboo cane. She was a sight to see in Salt Lake City. And a talker too.

"I learned that death-turn from a yogi back in India when I was a child, before the family moved to East London. 'e could stop 'is 'eart for five minutes at a time, 'e could. Mine 'as it at about two minutes, currently. I uses it to end me act."

"Your act?"

"Yes, me act. I comes to America because it is the land of opportunity, you know, the land of diversions. Entertainment is everything here. It is the place to become someone. My troupe played the 'alls in the big cities out east last month and then I comes west because I 'ears that Los Angeles will be the place to be soon — inventors is making moving pictures there now in the winters, and soon, amusement folks say, they will make them by the carriage full and all of the Empire will pay to see 'em."

Most of them laughed at that, but the Seer looked serious.

"I aim to be part of it all," added Zara Patel Chaplin. "Life is a show, I say, and why not be at the top of it?"

She started dusting herself off and doing up her dress and suit coat.

"But I gots meself into a fix out 'ere in this tame place. I was standing on the street corner doing me miming and some card tricks and intending to fetch coins out of people's ears to buys me a ticket on the stagecoach to experience the ride out west and, wouldn't you know it, even though I could get a few blokes to stop and 'ear me out, not one of 'em gave me more than a few pennies. They just like to stare at me, men does. That 'appens often. I use it when I can. Made a couple of pennies, and that's it. But this one boy, out on 'is own, kept *really* staring and emptied what 'e had in 'is pockets for me. Well, we got to talkin' and then he takes me out behind the cathedral where I lets 'im kiss me. Why not? You only live once and 'e was tolerably 'andsome, quite shapely beneath his clothes. Then, he tells me I can come out to 'is ranch and sleep in 'is barn the night, so long as I keeps out of sight. I could tell that 'e liked the kissin'. I can kiss with the best of 'em, you know. I could tell too that that was why 'e wanted me to come with 'im. I wasn't worried, I know a thing'r two about defending meself, believe me. Well, 'e couldn't get enough of it and came out to the barn with a lantern to see me at night. There I was, partly in me skivvies and partly dressed, and him a kissin' me when 'is father appeared, 'aving followed unbeknownst to 'im ... and you saw what 'appened after that."

"They are awful people," said Robert Elvis McTell.

"Well, no sir, I don't think they is, really. At least, not much worse than most of the rest of us. If I saw a stranger come from overseas and without 'er dress entirely on sneaking around me barn and a kissing me young son with relish, like I was, then I might ponder shootin' 'er too ... maybe."

Zara Patel Chaplin was a decidedly forgiving and open-minded young woman.

"And those men," she continued, "were firing over me 'ead, on purpose. They weren't so evil, not entirely. That's been me sense of them since I been 'ere. It's people that don't know 'em who is demonizing 'em in books, folks who want to put themselves up a little higher than them. For the most part, I figure that people is the same wherever you go, want the same things. We all just want to be respected, be recognized as individuals, and be worth something. These people who named themselves Mormons are making a mighty effort, taking on the role of God's chosen folk

— that's who they is telling themselves they is — and for the most part, they ain't doing any worse than the rest of us."

"Uh!" cried the Seer, who was glowing at Zara.

"Who is that little man?"

"He's our leader," said Cleo.

The next day the group had an eleventh performer with them as the stagecoaches pulled out from Salt Lake City heading west toward Nevada and California. "Stagecoaches," plural, because the eleven companions took up two of them.

It had been cold overnight and was still a little cool when they started off.

They traveled through the Great Salt Lake Desert, an ancient lake bottom made of white sand and salt and almost nothing else. It looked like an enormous, pale pancake. It wasn't until they reached Nevada that things began to change. It took them a few days to lumber through the area, the big steel and wooden wheels moving at a pioneer pace. It was like being back in time half a century. They kept to the valleys and rarely saw any trees until they were almost all the way to the western end of the state, just sparse desert grasses and cacti. They saw the odd jackrabbit, coyotes, and a few mountain lions in the distance.

What kept the little troupe intrigued was the thought of California, not so far up ahead now, the land of paradise, the bright lights of San Francisco, the palm trees and Pacific Ocean ... and whatever that treasure was waiting for them in Los Angeles. The Seer spent his time looking out the window, not even grunting, almost always facing ahead, westward. When he would glance elsewhere it was to look down at his drawings to make adjustments to his ever-evolving catapult, now appearing more ominous with each stroke. Solomon often watched him, fascinated. During one stretch, the Seer stared south into the desert and drew what looked like a plan for a new city in the Nevada wasteland, a unique place featuring only entertainments and diversions. But he kept returning to the catapult.

Solomon imagined that Booth and Pawn were long gone, off their scent and no longer dangerous ... but he imagined wrong.

CHAPTER TWENTY-THREE
TRACKED DOWN

On the third day, with the sun high above them in a deep blue sky, they passed through a surprisingly green valley and stopped at the little village of Loveland. They were told there that they would reach Reno by nightfall. Reno was the last stop in Nevada, right at the California border. It was also the final destination for their stagecoaches. The troupe was looking forward to it. Not only would they finally get out of these bouncing, banging little desert cabs, but Reno was also a much bigger place than any they had seen since Salt Lake City, a real town with about five thousand residents and a few comforts. Solomon was hoping for a hotel where they could get up some hot water for a bath.

Silver had been discovered in the Reno area about three or four decades earlier and a boom had gone through it for many miles around, an absolute bonanza, creating not just Reno, but the nearby state capital of Carson City.

No one in Reno noticed that they were a mix of races and sizes, or even that one of them was a gorilla, as they traveled along the dirt streets, sitting safe inside their stagecoaches behind small open windows. And though they received some strange looks once they disembarked at the yard on the southern outskirts, they had paid good money for the trip, so they weren't treated badly, just ignored. They wrapped their gorilla in their blanket so his face was barely visible — he looked like a large, ugly woman.

They gathered around in a circle to chat. As Solomon looked at them — their little leader holding the Simian Houdini by the hand, the ravens clustered on Ayesha's shoulders, Angus towering above everyone, Geronimo with his long, jet-black hair and his six-shooter butts jutting out from his shirt — it truly hit the North Britain boy what an absolutely bizarre group they were and the spectacular, unprecedented show they could now present. Something else occurred to Solomon Hunt, something that was obvious but that he hadn't really thought much about — they were all just kids.

"How much money do we have?" he asked everyone.

During the stagecoach ride, they had divided up their funds again, always their policy. They emptied their pockets and counted. There was silence for a moment.

"That will get us a nice hotel with quite a bit left over," said J.S. Chan.

"Enough for a train to San Francisco for all of us?" Cleo asked.

"Uh!" exclaimed the Seer, nodding his head.

"Just enough, I imagine," added Zara.

"Uh," said the Seer again, this time not as enthusiastically.

"And we'll need food for a day or two as well," said Napoleon, "so, we'll be pretty well empty by the time we get to Frisco."

"Uh," nodded the Seer one last time.

Solomon didn't say what he wanted to say — that he needed

to take a portion of what they had and send it home. But there obviously wasn't enough to spare. He had to trust that California would bring them much more — a gold mine, a treasure, financial salvation for his family. He was counting on it.

"What will we do then?" Solomon asked the Seer.

Their leader pointed at the jar.

The Cartwright Hotel in downtown Reno was classy for these parts, so much so that they all knew the instant they saw it that it wouldn't accept Cleo or Napoleon or Robert, maybe not Geronimo or Zara Patel Chaplin, and certainly not the Simian Houdini. But they were adamant they weren't going to leave anyone out this time. So, they came up with a ruse. The first thing they did was find a back entrance. Then Solomon and Ayesha (keeping out of the light) and J.S. Chan (with his/her hair tied back, men's clothes on, and earrings out), booked a room each on the ground floor. Next, they sneaked Angus in the back door and stationed him at the interior entrance, the one that led into the lobby and through which guests entered. He held it tightly shut while the rest of the group quickly came in through the back door and into their rooms — girls in one (including Joan Chan, of course), boys and gorilla in the other two. The ravens found a tree outside and were told, in no uncertain terms, to stay there.

But the birds didn't have to wait long. All eleven performers were up early in the morning and out the back entrance on their way to the Reno steam train station where they booked eleven tickets for San Francisco. They were allowed on board because they (again) arrived early, once more added a bribe to their payment (and bought the Simian Houdini a ticket to boot), and kept away from the other passengers. They purchased a little food for the trip and settled in.

When the steam train pulled out, Solomon was excited. And he was equally thrilled as they passed the beautiful Lake Tahoe area and then headed on through the stunning Sierra Nevada mountain range. But it wasn't until they were down out of the mountains, past the high lands and into the valleys and verdant lands of central California and on toward the gorgeous capital of Sacramento that he became almost beside himself with anticipation. The North Britain boy was right smack dab in the middle of California! He was thousands of miles from home after having crossed the great Empire. He couldn't believe it. The promised land of America! He knew that something awaited them here, if not in the legendary city of San Francisco, the Golden Gate of the West, then in Los Angeles where the Seer seemed to be promising them so much. It felt like they were in the greatest rounders game of all time, running around the third post and heading for home.

But then the steam train pulled out of Sacramento.

Napoleon was standing talking to Solomon, Cleo, and the Seer. The others were stashed in seats across from them: Angus slouched down, the Simian Houdini hidden under his blanket. Every now and then they spotted the ravens in the sky, flying along beside them — the birds would get behind, but caught up each time the train stopped. Cleo and Solomon were seated next to the window where he'd been staring out during their half hour wait, a book out, not saying a word, feeling happy and occasionally smiling at her. She smiled back. There was no other place in the world he'd rather be. Napoleon was nattering away at the Seer, talking about his flying invention and how he thought he was almost ready to make his dangerous leap into the sky. The Seer was the only one of their party who didn't look pleased. He was barely listening to Napoleon. Instead, he was working on his main drawing again, of that dangerous-looking catapult contraption, today adding a startling touch — a sort of cockpit into which a human being could fit. He had focused on this drawing once they entered California, and it was now full of details and appeared to be almost finished.

Solomon's gaze had been cast across the great crowds in the station, people-watching, and thinking about human beings and how everyone dresses to impress others and has their own style, however plain or ornate. It was all part of human desire. Some even had a style that said "don't look at me," but even that was a statement. He looked down at his own ragged outfit. He needed to buy new clothing. Was he "someone" yet or the useless human being his father had told him he was? He still hadn't really done anything for his family. He looked over the crowd to a big clock and a huge timetable on a stone wall to see the many scheduled steam trains to San Francisco, which was less than two hours away.

Above the faces in the mob, he saw a huge head … *the size of a pumpkin!*

Napoleon noticed too and suddenly stopped talking.

There was Pawn in the crowd in the Sacramento Steam Railroad Station! Booth was right beside him! And next to them was

Moseley, bearing his cane! They were shoving their way past others, heading toward the train that carried the eleven friends.

The Seer noticed his two companions' sudden silence. He stood up and surveyed the crowd through the window, spotted the pumpkin head in an instant, and let out a cry.

But the steam train chugged into motion.

Pawn, who had been scanning the car windows as he and Booth moved rudely toward the track, noticed the Seer behind the glass, peering out. He pointed a long finger at him and let out a growl.

They ran at the train, but it kept accelerating. In a minute, the little troupe was gone, and their pursuers were standing in the station watching them get away, just like in Chicago Town a few weeks ago. But Solomon didn't feel any relief this time. He remembered what he had seen on that train schedule. There were a number of locomotives to San Francisco that day. The next one left in a few hours.

CHAPTER TWENTY-FOUR
GOLDEN CITY

The two boys told the others what they had seen. Then they all sank into silence.

Napoleon and Cleo looked terrified, and Solomon imagined he did too. John and Joan S. Chan were balling up their fists as they sat there, looking calm on the surface, and Geronimo Jones kept his hands close to his gun grips. The Seer's reaction was different from everybody else's. He was pacing up and down the aisle, deep in thought. Then he sat for a while and then paced again.

Solomon kept thinking back to the sight of those three men glaring at them as their steam train pulled out, but it wasn't just them in the image in his mind. As the villains stood at the edge of the track watching, he'd noticed several other men — one, two, three, or more — emerge one after the other, each behind the other and well apart, way down the station next to the track. Were they all pursuing them too?

How had Booth and Pawn gotten so close? Had they followed the little troupe's unlikely route by passenger balloon and stage-coach? It didn't seem likely. Somehow, they had simply figured their prey were going to San Francisco, where fortunes could be made. They had likely taken the quickest way here — west along the Sunset Route of the Southern Pacific Steam Railroad from New Orleans to Houston, and straight through Arizona to California.

Solomon couldn't help feeling desperate. Cleo wouldn't look at him. She took his hand and stared at the floor. Their pursuers would be instantly after them. The Seer was set on getting to Los Angeles, but they didn't have enough money to travel that far now — they had to disembark in Frisco, at least for a while, to gain the cash they needed. They were boxed in. Could they reach their final destination before Booth and Pawn? What, in God's name, was this treasure ... and could it save them?

They sat stone silent for a long while. When they finally started to talk it was in quiet tones. They weren't going to think clearly in San Francisco if they remained so nervous, so to change the mood a little, Solomon tried to tease the Seer. He pretended he was going to stuff him into the jar. His friend's reaction was stunning. He fought the boy off like a wildcat, kicking and screaming, violently thrashing out at him and the jar. His eyes bulged with fear. When Solomon stopped, the Seer tried to attack him. The others pulled him off. Angus had stood up during the commotion, shielding the scuffle from the rest of the car. No one seemed to notice. The Seer sat alone again for a while after that, his face beet red.

Half an hour later he came over and settled beside Solomon and patted him on the leg, but didn't utter a sound. They were still seated that way when a man walked down the aisle toward their seats, slowed to look at them, and then passed by. A few minutes later he returned.

"Do you mind my asking if you folks are in the entertainment business? Diversions?" he asked. His voice was friendly and musical, and his face was shaped like a pie with a smile in it. His wire-rimmed glasses were circular too and his white mustache curved around his mouth. He doffed his straw hat and bowed politely to Cleo, Zara, and Ayesha, then touched it briefly, a little unsure, as he glanced toward J.S. Chan.

"Yes, we are," Solomon said. They weren't used to strangers speaking to them on trains.

"May I sit?"

Solomon moved over.

"My name is Cecil Griffith. I have just given up the trade myself and brought my little lady to the west coast to enjoy the fruits of our labors. It is a fine industry, isn't it?"

Solomon thought of who was pursuing them and didn't answer.

"Oh, I know there are some bad apples — it's tempting when there is so much money involved and reputation — but there is nothing finer than making folks laugh and entertaining them, giving them a little thrill. I am as proud as punch of what I did for a living. I ran five extravaganzas throughout my life and never had a complaint from a customer or an employee."

The Seer smiled weakly at him, the first sign of even the slightest bit of joy out of their leader since Denver City.

Solomon believed their new acquaintance. He seemed like a genuine sort.

"Sometimes, it is the biggest names who give our profession the lowest reputation. Take Coop, for example." The Seer turned his face to the window.

"He isn't said to be the most pleasant man in the Empire, cruel to his employees. I had a few peripheral dealings with him and that was enough for me. Unfortunately, he is a very powerful man, and some folks admire him just because of that."

"We have heard bad things about him too," said Cleo.

"The human cannonball!" replied Griffith suddenly as he looked directly at her. "I knew I knew you! It is a pleasure to meet you, madam!"

"It is just as well that Coop doesn't travel in the parts we're headed to, southward from here," said Solomon. "He is pretty stiff competition for the rest of us and likely cutthroat too."

"Well, usually he doesn't frequent south of here, yes, that is true."

"Usually?"

"It's the strangest thing. I read in the red paper sections just today that he is coming this way right now."

Solomon sat upright. "This way?" Curiously, the Seer didn't seem shocked. All he did was slouch lower in his seat.

"Well, not right here, but close. Word is he is coming to Los Angeles, should be there in three or four days. That far into the southern section of the state!"

"Los Angeles!" Solomon looked at the Seer, but he was slouching even lower, pulling his hat over his eyes and the jar up in front of his face.

"I agree, that is a bit of a shock," continued the friendly showman. "I could understand if he went to Frisco. You could play a week there. In fact, he did that twice before. But why Los Angeles? It's big enough now for some pretty impressive shows, but it is still marginal for him … though it *is* growing mighty fast, they say … and the moving-picture business does work there in the winters. In fact, they are likely arriving about now. That is a coming industry, you know."

"So I hear," said Solomon, his mind fixed on what the man had said about Coop.

"They say the great man cut his eastern tour short and headed this direction just a week or so ago and is coming the quick way through the Arizona desert. Curious."

Solomon couldn't help himself. He turned to his little companion. "Do you know about this, Seer?" But his friend looked away.

"Seer?" asked Griffith. "Is that what he's called? That rings some sort of a bell for some reason."

"I'm sorry about my little friend not being overly social," said Solomon. "He hasn't been feeling the best lately."

"Say what you will about Coop, he has always had a knack, a sort of sixth sense, you know, for what works in this business. He has always had the best ideas. Or at least he used to. The new show hasn't gotten very good reviews. Is the great Coop losing his touch? Maybe he's just getting old? People say he has been acting strange of late. That run for the presidency of his won't go well if his shows are declining in popularity. Lord help us if he gets elected. We worship at the altar of money enough as it is. Look out for each other, share, that's what we should be about."

The friendly showman stood up. He handed out old business cards as souvenirs to each of the members of the troupe (or at least to all but the Seer, who turned away, and the Simian Houdini, whom the showman recognized under the blanket but didn't bother — in fact, he put his finger to his lips in conspiracy with the young people) and bid them farewell and happy trails and "straw houses" and returned up the car to his seat.

"Seer!" Solomon barked, as soon as the man had gone.

But his friend still wouldn't look at him.

"Did you know that Coop was coming to Los Angeles?"

"Uh."

Solomon couldn't tell if that was a yes or no. Then something occurred to him.

He had been wondering about the Seer's mood change after Denver and recalled now that it had begun right after he looked at a copy of the *Denver Pioneer Post* back in Sudsy Randolph's Tivoli Club. He had torn out a red page and pocketed it. Solomon looked over now and saw the bulge still there in his trousers. He seized him, and despite a mighty struggle on his friend's part, pulled out the crumpled ball of paper and looked at it.

A huge drawing of Coop graced an advertisement. He was decked out in his trademark cowboy hat encrusted with diamonds, his buckskin coat, and his long white hair. "THREE DAY'S ENGAGEMENT IN LOS ANGELES, CALIFORNIA!" it read. "SEE THE GREAT COOP AND HIS GREATEST SHOW EVER, FOR THE FIRST TIME IN LOS ANGELES!"

The Seer couldn't read. But Solomon remembered him getting information out of Sudsy as he showed him this page in the paper.

"You've known since Denver City, haven't you?"

The Seer said nothing.

"I thought you were trying to avoid him! You're afraid of him, aren't you? I thought you were worried that he'd do something to you. What does he want with you? Does he know you?"

The Seer still wouldn't say anything. Cleo took his hand.

"Why didn't we turn around back in Colorado?" asked Solomon.

No response.

"Are we still going to Los Angeles?" Cleo asked softly.

The Seer looked at her and nodded. He seemed very sad.

"You have to go there, don't you, no matter what?" said Solomon.

His friend nodded again.

"For that treasure you drew?"

He nodded.

"What is it? Tell me. Draw *exactly* what it is!"

But the Seer simply looked away.

The North Britain boy didn't say anything more for a long while after that. San Francisco neared, less than half an hour away.

"Okay, then … what's next?" Solomon finally asked.

The Seer pointed at the jar.

As the steam train slowed and they passed beautiful scenery, and a big university in Berkeley, and then approached the eastern end of the gorgeous San Francisco Bay, they barely looked out. They were all feeling terrified. They were almost broke. Booth, Pawn, and Moseley were close on their tail, Los Angeles was still a long, paid train ride away, and Coop was heading there anyway. The Seer had spent the last fifteen minutes, right up until their arrival at the Oakland terminus, which was across the bay from the big city, frantically pacing up and down the aisle, deep in thought.

When the train stopped, he gathered his followers and pointed into the jar. That was what he always did just before they put on a show. He had been training them as a larger performing troupe ever since the wilds of the New Mexico Territory, training them for the show of their lives. They had all the firepower they needed now: eleven of them. Ten remarkably talented people and a weirdly skilled animal.

San Francisco was the great city of America's Promised Land … and they were about to give it their all.

But their pursuers would be here in a few hours. The little troupe would have to be gone by then.

The Seer veritably ran from the steam train and the rest followed. In minutes, they were out in the streets of Oakland and heading on the double for the wharves and the water. There were frequent ferries across the bay, and they got onto one quickly, using up almost all of their last coins. They fidgeted on the boat, their gorilla hidden, but still drawing looks. Up ahead, they could see the marvelous skyline of the one and only San Francisco. This wasn't the way the North Britain boy wanted to see this legendary new city, the wild place of adventurers, gamblers, and high rollers. Mark Twain had once lived here, and Solomon had read of it in the stories of the great Jack London.

He could see its remarkable buildings nearing, built on hilly terrain. Passenger balloons all the colors of rainbows were tethered to roofs. There were theaters and saloons and millionaires' mansions, but also the dens of sin of the dangerous "Barbary Coast" neighborhood where lowly entertainment took place in dance halls and parlor houses.

The second they hit land, the Seer led them to a streetcar. These conveyances amazed them. They all ran on electricity. It seemed supernatural. Up and down they went over the steep San Francisco hills, staring at the jammed-in, strikingly painted buildings, many of them made of wood, a few of stone or stuccoed. The towering San Francisco Mint went by, like a cathedral to America and its money.

They got out at Market Street, the "widest street in the world." It cut at an angle through the center of the teeming downtown. They ran up it until they got to Kearny Street. Solomon tried not to gape at the colorful scenes. San Francisco was so used to exotic people and things that few of its citizens stared back at the bizarre little group. But the poor sat or lay on the streets here too, even in this wealthy new city. They turned left onto Kearny and headed into Chinatown. There they could smell strange food cooking in the restaurants and saw the Realms of Asia Chinese in their unique garb — long shirts and caps with ponytails falling out — who walked and worked amidst white people, though few deigned to even look at them. The eleven friends raced through the rivers of pedestrians following the Seer, who seemed unimpressed by everything they encountered, as if he had seen it all before.

In moments, they came to Portsmouth Square, a green opening in the crowd of buildings, with tall theaters, oyster bars, and businesses surrounding it. Inside its black iron fence, eight walkways led to a central area with a fountain. Trees dotted the lush space. It was shortly after the noon hour, approaching one o'clock, the sun was high in the sky, and there were many people in the streets near the square.

The Seer gathered his friends. They were all breathing heavily. He held up his hands with his palms toward them to ask them to relax, to try to breathe slowly like he was doing. Then, he pointed at the jar.

Solomon was surprised at the show they did that day in Portsmouth Square in the heart of San Francisco. The Seer led them through a controlled performance, a little more spectacular than what they'd done in the Tivoli Club in Denver, to be sure, but far from what they were capable of, far from what he was grooming them to do. Nevertheless, the crowd grew to a great size by the time they were done; people seemed to come from all over the city, despite the fact that the performance was over in just ten or fifteen minutes. The show started with Ayesha sending the ravens up into the skies to call people toward the square, making all sorts of claims about what was about to be seen, then Robert Elvis's music blasted through the neighborhood, an almost alarming sound, punctuated with his mournful voice; then the gigantic Angus did his acrobatics, the human cannonball her leaps, the Simian Houdini escaped from his handcuffs and thanked the startled audience, Solomon did his jar routine, and the Seer found the smallest hat in the crowd (on the smallest child) and had Geronimo shoot a hole in it as the giant held it up in the California sky between his pinkie and second smallest finger (an entire Douglas dollar was given to the hat's awestruck little owner at the show's conclusion). But J.S. Chan wasn't asked to fight the toughest man in Frisco, Zara didn't die and come back to life, and most importantly, Napoleon (whose dangerous act worried and excited the Seer at the same time) didn't fly from the roof of any of the nearby six-story hotels.

It was obvious that they didn't have time to do their full show. That was being saved for Los Angeles. A great deal was being saved for there.

For now, they just needed fast money, not a vaultful, just enough to feed them for a while and get them quickly onto a train to the south, down to that smaller city and into a place to stay. The Seer had raced through the San Francisco crowd with his hat and soon had enough for what they needed.

Long before he had reached everyone, he began to run away, back toward the streetcars. It was a good thing too because a few city policemen had gathered to watch the show and began to confer with each other as if trying to decide what crime had been committed.

The ten others raced after their little leader. But before Solomon was out of the Square, someone grabbed him by the arm. When he turned to see who it was, he saw a woman, stunningly attired in a bright, pretty dress and bustle, a dark veil over her face.

"Take me with you," she said in a desperate voice.

"Who —"

"My name is Aida, and I am the most beautiful woman in the world."

CHAPTER TWENTY-FIVE
HOLLYWOOD

Aida Israel Mendoza came with them that day. She got onto the streetcar, crossed back over the bay on the ferry, and boarded the steam train for Los Angeles. She didn't have a Douglas dime, but the others didn't care, so remarkable was their new companion. All she had to do was lift her veil for an instant, a sort of flash that she gave them after her quick introduction, and they were sold. She had the most beautiful face Solomon had ever seen, a sort of intoxicating mix of glowing black hair that curled in hundreds of ringlets, flawless skin, and jet-black eyes that sparkled, all set on a countenance that was perfectly shaped — high cheekbones, dainty ears, and a slightly cleft chin. Her golden earrings glinted in the San Francisco sun and her makeup, expertly applied, made her face almost shine. Her red satin dress clung to her to emphasize her hourglass figure. There was something about her, though, that made the troupe feel bad too. Solomon could feel it in his heart and in his friends' expressions as she unveiled, casting her eyes downward as if she had been forced to display herself to gain their approval.

The Seer didn't appear guilty at all. He took one look at her and nodded, and then patted Solomon firmly on the arm, as if he had done something well.

She became their twelfth and final performer. Any trembling, even the movements of the train as it went in and out of stations, scared her and she often spoke of her belief that the California coast would one day suffer a gigantic earthquake attack. But most of the time, especially when she was veiled, she was happy, and her upbeat mood made her an excellent companion. It was remarkable that she was so vivacious, given that she not only hated her current stage role but had been orphaned at thirteen and soon after taken into show business, or more accurately, forced into it by poverty and rapacious showmen. She was put in the Freak Show first, then taught to sing and dance, but it was her beauty that remained her great claim to fame. In fact, when she found Solomon and his friends in San Francisco she was one of the toasts of the town, billed as "the most beautiful woman in the world." The great Coop had asked for a private audience with her. She was said to be twenty-two, but that was at least four years older than her real age. She was also said to be a native of the Caucasus area where Europe meets Asia and where, as her advertising boards touted, "*the most attractive people on earth live, the home of the purest of our Caucasian race!*" But behind the scenes, others knew she was Jewish and Latino and treated her as if she were inferior. Lately, she had been performing in a play that was drawing sold-out audiences. Throughout the show, she was dressed in an almost see-through wrap of linen wound tightly around her shape and featured in a spectacular scene where she rode "almost naked" on a mechanical horse across the stage. San Francisco could not get enough of her, the shouts of the mostly male audiences were thunderous every time she graced the boards, and there was talk of taking her to New York and London. But she had long since had enough of all of this and wanted to escape both it and her bosses, who kept a close eye on her. But then she wandered out into Portsmouth Square that fateful day and saw the Seer, Solomon Hunt, Cleopatra, the giant, and friends: all of them young, operating their own show, looking free. She latched onto them.

Solomon wondered how long it would take until she was missed, and if the little group would be pursued by her owners too. That was all they needed.

For the first hour of their train ride south, Solomon sat next to Aida and talked to her, as Napoleon, Geronimo, J.S., Zara, and Angus crowded in, equally intrigued by everything she had to say, and Cleo sat nearer to Solomon than she usually did, holding her big book, their legs touching, her hand accidentally caressing his from time to time, especially whenever he seemed particularly fascinated by their new colleague. The Seer remained deadly serious and didn't listen to their conversation at all. He sat there drawing that dangerous contraption. It looked more and more like a giant *human* catapult to Solomon and when he considered who in their party their little leader might choose to fly from it and sail through the air in a spectacular act, he worried even more. Cleo was the obvious choice. Solomon knew the Seer wanted them to do something extraordinary in Los Angeles. It was the last place on the map, and it was now clear to the boy that, one way or another, they were going to go out with a bang. He figured the Seer wanted Napoleon to finally fly, even if he wasn't ready (and he didn't appear to be), but Solomon didn't know if he could stand Cleo being put into perhaps even greater danger. The Seer had a destiny up ahead and they were being pulled along toward it with him.

It was probably not much more than forty-five minutes into this last leg of the trip, after they had swung south of Monterey Bay and Salinas, everything impossibly green and the stunning coastline of the Pacific in the distance, that Cecil Griffith reappeared.

"Ah! There you are!"

He came walking briskly up the aisle toward them like a welcoming breeze of fresh air from the ocean. But what he had to say wasn't in the least inviting.

"I have been looking for you."

"You have?" Solomon asked. "How nice." And he meant it.

"There are three men searching for you in the next car. Actually, more than three, but it's the trio who are making inquiries."

Aida's presence had made Solomon and his colleagues momentarily forget about the fact that it had taken them a few hours to get into San Francisco, do their show, get back to Oakland, eat something at the terminus, and board the train for Los Angeles. That was just enough time for Booth, Pawn, and Moseley to catch the next train to the San Francisco area from Sacramento and arrive in Oakland. They must have seen the little troupe in the Oakland station, and Solomon and his friends, glowing at Aida, hadn't noticed them. The villains were obviously immediately in pursuit again, and this time, had actually gotten onto the train they saw the twelve young performers board. And it seemed that in moments they would be in the same car! Would they try to attack their prey publicly? Solomon glanced around at his companions. Everyone was terrified. The Seer was beyond that. He had given a little cry at the news and leapt to his feet. Cleo took him by the hand and brought him to down to his seat.

Griffith stared at him. “Don’t worry, they can’t get in here, rest assured. Passengers aren’t allowed to travel between cars on this line. I take it often and I know the head porter and when I heard those nefarious-looking men asking questions about you, I asked if he would let me into your car. But he *will* stop *them*. You are safe for now.”

The Seer, whose face had turned red and looked like it might burst, let out a huge sigh of relief, though he still seemed plenty anxious.

Griffith kept regarding him.

“I know why this little man feels that way,” he said grimly.

“You do?” asked Cleo, “I’m not sure you could know exactly —”

“Oh, no, I know … You’ll recall that I thought I’d heard tell of him before. Well, I met up with an old business friend while I was eating my dinner in the station. He knows everyone in the industry. I was thinking of the conversation I had with you lot about Coop and the tiny bell that rang in the distant cobwebs of my old brain when you mentioned this little fellow’s name. So, I inquired of my friend about it.”

“What did he say?” Solomon asked, almost before Griffith had finished his sentence. “Did he know something about Coop and the Seer?”

The troupe’s leader shrunk down in his seat and pulled his jar up in front of him again.

“He sure did. He said that there had always been a rumor in the industry that Coop got his amazing ideas in a sort of secretive way, that someone or some group or some power was feeding him his groundbreaking concepts … and the word *Seer* had always been attached to that. We thought it was a kind of code word."

Silence reigned over the group. All they heard was the chugging of the train.

"And that ain't all," said Griffith. "My friend said there is word in the industry now, as Coop struggles through this artistically dry period for him, that he has lost his 'Seer' ... and is willing to pay a king's ransom to get it, or him, back. There are probably lots of insiders searching for *the Seer.*"

Solomon looked over at their leader. He wasn't looking back. He had pulled his head so far down into himself that he looked like a tortoise withdrawing its head and neck.

"A king's ransom?" Cleo asked.

"One hundred thousand dollars," said the man. Solomon thought he saw a greedy look cross over his face. Napoleon whistled out loud. That sum of money could set someone up for life. "Now, my recommendation to you is to get this little man as far away from Los Angeles as you can."

The Seer jumped up and shook his head violently.

"But Coop might grab you and harm you or worse!" cried Cleo. "Mr. Griffith is right. We need to either turn around as soon as we get to Los Angeles or keep on going past it and get as far away as we can!"

"How do you get away from Pawn?" said Angus.

But the Seer shook his head and sat down in his chair, his arms crossed. "I'm going to Los Angeles!" his attitude repeated.

Why, Solomon asked himself, does he *want* to go there? His sense was that Coop frightened the Seer even more than Pawn. Solomon looked around at his companions: a killer lad with guns, a giant of enormous strength, a lethal boy-girl with his-her fists, and a gorilla. That was when a number of things became clear.

Yes, the Seer hated Coop ... hated him so much that he would plot his death!

The little man had the weapons and the people to do it now. The whole troupe was loyal to him. Did he imagine that they would help him, first, rid himself of his pursuers by whatever means, and secondly, kill the evil Coop? The Seer wanted to get to Los Angeles because he wanted to put on a show unlike any that had ever been seen before, one controlled by him and his new recruits, not by adults, not by conniving owners, not by one race, and certainly not by Coop. It would make their reputation and fill their coffers. But what if, *at the same time*, he could do away with his mortal enemy? His competition too. What if he was protected against anyone else who tried to kidnap him? He could take the price from his own head and gain his freedom forever. He could also remove Coop as a power and influence in America — perhaps begin the destruction of a world he detested. *That*, Solomon realized, was the Seer's plan now! When the boy first freed him back in York, his new friend's hope was to just run away, take Solomon and whatever performers he could find to support their flight, and simply run, hightailing it in the least likely direction their trackers would consider they would go: out to the frontier, to the west and distant Pacific coast. But then, when he saw that advertisement in the *Denver Pioneer Post*, he had realized that somehow Coop knew where he was and was coming to get him. Insiders had been passing the word. He realized then too that Coop would *always* find him, no matter where he went. So, thinking of his growing army and the many weapons around him and betting he could free himself and his new friends for good, he had concocted a desperate scheme.

Desperate or not, Solomon was willing to help. And he knew that Cleo, after all she had been through and what her parents and her people had endured, would help too. She would be happy to eliminate the great white Coop. So would Napoleon, J.S. Chan, and Geronimo, and the others, all with grievances and a deep desire for liberty. The Seer's plan entailed getting the job done in Los Angeles. The genius fugitive had feared meeting Coop and Booth and Pawn and men like them on the road. Why, Solomon didn't know, but he would wait for the opportune moment too, for the time when the Seer gave him the signal.

Solomon looked at him. His friend gazed back. Their eyes met.

"No," the North Britain boy said, "the Seer is right."

"Right?" asked Cleo. "What do you mean, Solo?"

"We need to go to Los Angeles, do our show, and then get away. He hasn't steered us wrong yet. Let's stick to the plan, be brave, and then be gone. I need the money from our show for my family, anyway."

A slight smile spread over the Seer's lips.

"Those men," said Griffith. "I recognized them. They used to work for Coop."

They had heard their pursuers admit to that back in Buffalo, but when Solomon heard it now and connected it to the other things they had just learned, another big piece of the Seer's story fell into place.

It was apparent now that Booth and Pawn had kidnapped the Seer, taken him away from Coop in a daring operation. Coop would kill those two villains if he caught them ... and they knew it. Booth was the brains of their plan and Pawn the awe-inspiring muscle, either a henchman or a performer from the show. They had stolen Coop's sacred secret weapon, the key to his wealth and future plans. They thought they could use the Seer to make themselves rich (or more — "*control amusements and you control America*," Booth had said) and when the young genius wouldn't cooperate, they had punished him by making him do that humiliating act back in York. But the little genius hadn't given in — it had remained a tawdry show. And the day the Seer saw Solomon Hunt — just a kid too, searching for something and without an agenda — he saw an opportunity to get away and bolted and took the boy with him. Each and every performer they had then picked up on their flight was released from a sort of prison. The Seer had known about them (perhaps even been the mind behind the creation of some of their acts) and freed them just as he had always hoped someone would extricate him from Coop's iron grip.

Griffith stood up. "I wish you all luck." He gently raised Solomon by the arm and pulled him down the aisle with him. When they got to the door between the cars, he spoke softly. "Your little one has the look of someone who has been abused, badly abused." He paused. "You know, I will admit I was powerfully tempted to try to seize him and get him down the line to Mr. Coop. But that wouldn't be right, no matter how much money I'd get. There are many roles we can play in life … I have learned it is best to play a good and honorable one. Break a leg, young man, and Godspeed."

In about five hours, they'd get to Los Angeles. It would be nearing midnight and pitch dark. The minute they stepped out of their train car, all those beasts in the next one would be on them. What would those villains be willing to try in that train station? And what would the Seer be willing to do in response? What would *Solomon Hunt* do? And if the twelve friends survived, what *exactly* would they undertake next? How would they get to Coop … and finish him?

Despite having so many questions answered about the Seer, there was one that was still a mystery. *Who was he … really? Where had Coop found this secret weapon of a man?* Solomon remembered what Booth had said to Pawn back in the Showman's Hotel in York. "Maybe," he had said, "he's the son of God." The big man hadn't liked that comment, not one bit. He seemed spooked by it. *Where, in the world or outside of it, did this little fellow come from?*

Hours later, they passed through a town named Santa Barbara. If Solomon hadn't been so anxious, it would have fascinated him. He had read outlaw novels set there, but today it looked far from that: a beautiful town on the ocean, its streets lined with palm trees, obviously growing fast, likely because of the oil being pumped from the derricks they saw offshore nearby.

Not more than an hour later, the steam train pulled into a green, flat area nestled below some verdant hills. It was the last stop before Los Angeles. They were just six miles away. They heard their porter call out the little town's name.

Without warning, the Seer leapt to his feet and raced for the door. The entire troupe followed, almost stumbling over themselves to keep up. Excited to be moving, Solomon was also thinking about what they were sure to face once they got out. Their tougher companions did too — Geronimo kept his hands on his pistols and J.S. Chan's eyes were alert as they alighted in the warm southern California evening.

Once they were out, they all turned toward Booth's car. Solomon clenched his hands into fists.

But then they saw the strangest thing.

Griffith's friend, a porter, was helping two wealthy-looking older people disembark from Booth's car. He winked at the twelve friends and tilted his head back up toward the car's windows. The blinds had been drawn on every one of them! The porter called out and the steam train immediately began to pull away.

They were safe for now!

Griffith and the Seer had had the same thought: The old showman had figured that the Seer would have his group jump ship just before the final stop, in order to make a run for it. With the blinds down, no one could look out the car windows at them. Pawn, Booth, and Moseley, and whoever else was in pursuit, would get a surprise at the central Los Angeles steam train terminus.

But Solomon had the feeling that this was where the Seer had wanted to get off all along anyway. Everything he did was well planned. The North Britain boy looked up at the sign on the roof of the small station in front of them.

"HOLLYWOOD"

Why had they come here?

CHAPTER TWENTY-SIX
PREPARATIONS

They slept in a field that night, a field of lemon trees. In the morning, the Seer led them down a wide dirt road, the adjacent green hills beautiful in the early light. There was no sign of their three pursuers yet, but Solomon didn't doubt that they would see them soon.

There were maybe a dozen streets, all lined with palm trees. They saw ranches in the distance, a couple of markets setting up for the day with tables full of oranges and plums and peppers, the vendors staring at the unusual traveling troupe. There were about fifty to a hundred homes, all prosperous looking with big lawns, telephone poles along the hilly streets, and many real estate signs on open lots. It was obvious that this was a growing little suburb, a wealthy one for Los Angeles just to the southeast. When the twelve friends reached a street called Prospect and neared Highland, they saw a streetcar coming from the burgeoning city, which they heard people simply call "L.A." Right in front of them stood the most impressive building in the village by far. It was five stories high, bookended with turrets, peach-colored in the blue sky, and set back on its huge grounds. “HOTEL HOLLYWOOD” read the sign on the roof.

The Seer took them right up the palatial front steps and in the front doors. Two men sat in basket chairs on the porch, a big black moving-picture camera on the floor between them, its long-legged tripod unhitched; they stared at the new arrivals. Inside, the group found a spacious lobby. But there weren’t many folks about. It was obvious that this enterprise, a gamble built upon the idea that Hollywood would someday be a much bigger place, was less than half full.

A young woman behind the counter, attractive and blonde, and her face done up with more makeup than someone with her job usually wore, took one look at them and immediately fled through a swinging door to her left. In moments, she returned with a tall woman, nearing sixty, Solomon guessed, and wearing a white blouse done up to her chin, a long gold skirt, and sporting a monocle. She was smoking a cigarette in a holder.

“My name is Mrs. Flynn, widow of the inestimable Mr. Flynn, and I am the owner of this establishment. May I help you?” she asked gruffly.

The Seer reached up and seized her hand and shook it. She pulled it back. But before she could say anything else, he produced a drawing he had been working on all night. It featured the lady’s hotel looking grand and imposing. There was a massive crowd surrounding it, and the porch that wrapped around the first floor and all the balconies higher up were full of customers. In the midst of all of this, on the big lawn, a colorful show was taking place. It was the performance the twelve friends had been developing.

Mrs. Flynn paused and then took the drawing into her hands. As she did, the Seer motioned to Angus. He sprang up into a handstand, his feet almost touching the ceiling.

Within an hour, with Cleo and Solomon interpreting the Seer's gestures, they had an agreement with Mrs. Flynn to put on a show on the grounds of her hotel in two days. They would charge admission onto the property and keep what they made. She, in turn, would have her hotel filled to the brim. She also, reluctantly, agreed to allow all of them to stay in two rooms, though at the rear of the building. She would feed them back there too.

Then the Seer set out to create the show and advertise for it. This performance, or performances, would make them *much* more money than they had ever made before ... a veritable treasure.

That evening, they stayed in their rooms, wary that at any minute they might hear a sudden pounding on the doors and have to face their enemies. But there were no knocks that night. The Seer kept working on the show, drawing pictures of all their acts, though he lingered most upon the depiction of the catapult. J.S. Chan had fetched the *Los Angeles Times* from the lobby and was fascinated to read that the bare-fisted heavyweight champion of the world, a towering, well-built man named Jack C. Keaton, a dandy with a reputation as a lady's man, was staying in the city this very week. J.S. read the story aloud. It was the only bit of conversation to which the Seer listened and when J.S. was done, the little fellow mimed that they must invite the champ to the show.

The next morning, the Seer instructed Napoleon, Geronimo, and J.S. to stay with him, and let it be known that the rest of them were to go into Los Angeles and begin promoting the show. He arranged for the hotel to provide large sheets of paper, red paint, brushes, and glue. They had two days to get the word out.

They painted three simple words on their paper: "*SHOW!*" and "*HOLLYWOOD!*" and "*SATURDAY!*", each one on a separate sheet in big, bold letters. As the eight left that morning, the Seer appeared with tools he had obviously borrowed from Mrs. Flynn. He and Napoleon headed out to a nearby ranch that had its own sawmill, J.S. next to the leader, fists ready, and Geronimo Jones trailing them, scanning their surroundings, fingers near his guns. The little man was about to build something, and the troupe's inventor was going to help him.

Not wanting to cause a scene on a streetcar that day and interested in the scenery, the other eight walked to L.A. Moving briskly, it took them a bit more than an hour. But in less than half that time, they could see the city up ahead. It was surprisingly big but felt more relaxed than other places in the Empire, like somewhere people went to get away from things and have fun. Theatrical beggars pleaded for money, pink and yellow and baby blue passenger balloons hung in the skies. People wore lighter-colored clothing and seemed to smile more but appeared more concerned about how they looked too.

This would have been a wonderful opportunity to send money home. But the group had almost none now and were surviving on their deal with the Hotel Hollywood. Solomon would have to wait for their big show to get the money he needed.

Their giant gained the eight of them a following wherever they went in L.A. They glued their signs to posts and stores, but the Seer had instructed them to do more than that. So, finding a busy spot near two main avenues … they killed Zara Patel Chaplin. Or, at least, they had her fall down dead. A crowd formed after Ayesha and Solomon had shouted many times for help, crying out that a woman had collapsed in the street. Robert Elvis began playing a mournful tune. Zara's face went as purple as a plum, her eyes rolled up in her head, and her chest — laid bare at the top after they ripped open her blouse to make it look like they were desperate to help her breath — appeared as still as ice. She lay there for more than a minute … then suddenly came back to life! She leapt to her feet. Women screamed and men cried out. As Zara rose, Aida, at the back of the crowd, flipped off her veil, deftly removed her dress in one swoop, and wiggled forward in her bright pink undergarments, wound as tightly around her form as they would go. There was an audible gasp from the audience, almost as loud as the one that the dead girl's reincarnation had drawn. Solomon felt bad that she had to do this, but she didn't seem to care today, as if her freedom was just around the corner. Breathtakingly beautiful in the Los Angeles noon hour, she held up a sign. "SHOW!" it read; she popped up another. "HOLLYWOOD!" it said, then produced a third. "SATURDAY!" Angus plucked her into his arms and carried her high above the crowd while she displayed all three signs in the sky. Bystanders shouted their approval. As she was carried aloft, she began reciting Shakespeare, passages about how life was a performance, as if to show the crowd that she was so much more than a pretty face.

"Come to Hollywood!" cried Edgar and the other ravens as they swooped above. *"Greatest Show Ever!"* they cried. *"The Flying Man! … The Human Catapult! … Saturday! Saturday!"* They

flew off over Los Angeles, cawing out their message. Then a huge creature moved into the middle of the gathering, disguised under a blanket. Spectators stepped back. Solomon snatched the blanket off him with flair. "*Thank you!*" growled the big gorilla to screams and applause.

They enacted their drama five more times that day throughout Los Angeles. Each time, they gained a mob of a crowd. By the time they left for Hollywood in the late afternoon (remembering to leave an invitation at the heavyweight champion's hotel), they had papered the city with signs and could hear citizens talking about their show everywhere they went. The policemen, apparently as enthralled as everyone else — and loath to stop Aida when she was displaying her charms — let them go about their business.

But Booth and Pawn and Moseley didn't.

By the time the eight of them were doing their last turn, those three frightening men appeared in the crowd. Searching for their prey in Los Angeles, the villains had been drawn to the troupe's pop-up performances. Booth and Pawn, though, didn't try to seize them. The gorilla was probably a factor in their caution, but more importantly, this part of the group didn't include the Seer, so the three men simply followed them at a distance all the way home to their hotel. There was nothing the frightened friends could do. The grin on Moseley's face was lecherous. Cleo was shaking and took Solomon's hand as they walked.

But the North Britain boy wondered. As they moved, he kept thinking that the Seer had known all of this would happen — that their three pursuers would find them and their loud appearances in L.A. and tail them back to Hollywood. This was somehow part of a plan … for their enemies' destruction. At least the elimination of these first three.

Napoleon and the Seer were on the front lawn of the Hotel Hollywood when they all arrived, working on a large contraption, wooden with pulleys and springs and a gigantic lever. J.S. Chan and Geronimo Jones sat off to the sides in basket chairs, surveying the entrance to the grounds. They looked up when they saw their friends approach and stopped what they were doing when they noticed who was following them. By the time the other eight reached them, Pawn, Booth, and Moseley were nearing the iron gate at the entrance to the grounds, the latter pulling his sword from his cane. Solomon could see several other suspicious men, obviously having made the trek from L.A. as well, standing in the distance, watching.

"You gentlemen may stop right there," stated Geronimo evenly.

"Keep quiet!" growled Pawn.

"We merely want to converse with your little gentleman," drawled the short showman, putting on the most polished of his tones.

"Converse with this," said Geronimo … and shot Booth's bowler hat off his head.

His gun had come up and fired in a flash, as if out of nowhere.

For a moment, it seemed like Booth might faint.

"The next bullet goes into the big man's left eye … and the one after that into his right," said the troupe's gunslinger, blowing the smoke off his six-shooter.

The short showman grabbed Pawn's massive hand and pulled him away. He didn't look back as he marched off toward Los Angeles, his face red, his upper body held stiff, tugging on his henchman every time the big man looked back. The pumpkin head scowled at Solomon and the Seer each time it turned, but it obeyed.

The following morning, Coop's advance people arrived in Los Angeles, one day ahead of schedule. They were mostly publicity people, ready to paper the town.

But there was a group of large, tough-looking men with them too, who dressed in dark clothes and said very little.

Booth and Pawn's temporary retreat took them back to L.A. too.

Solomon, Cleo, and their friends never saw them, or Moseley, again.

Just as the Seer had likely planned, when Coop's sharks circled, these three lesser villains vanished … like severed heads floating out into the ocean. The little man had drawn them here to their death.

But what was the endgame? The Devil himself was nearing. Solomon could only imagine what might happen next.

CHAPTER TWENTY-SEVEN
THE TREASURE

The Seer rehearsed them that night and Solomon was amazed at what he was planning. It would indeed be one of the most incredible shows an audience had ever seen. But they didn't attempt their last two acts. One involved the catapult, which obviously needed some fine tuning, and the other was Napoleon's flight.

The troupe simply did all their acts in order and stopped before the finishers. But Napoleon had stood atop the roof of the Hotel Hollywood ready to fly, his knees shaking, in his beautiful and intricately designed wings, made of cattle bones and skin and gorgeous white, spreading feathers, and had surveyed the grounds below, his eyes calculating. He looked terrified and didn't make an attempt to leap. Solomon had also seen knowing looks pass between Cleo and the Seer and had caught them standing near the catapult at the end of the rehearsal, he motioning and wordlessly explaining something to her. Running up the weapon's middle was a twelve-foot piece of flexible wood strapped down by ropes with a gigantic spring underneath. Solomon pretended to retire into the hotel and then sneaked back out and discovered Cleo lying on the catapult on that twelve-foot ejector. She quickly got to her feet when she saw her friend.

"She's not doing this!" he shouted at the Seer, who wouldn't look at him.

"Solo, I am a seasoned professional," said Cleo. "If I choose to do this, then I shall and I will be safe. I know what I am doing. But … we aren't certain yet about it anyway." Her voice broke a little on the last word.

The Seer nodded. Solomon didn't find any of it convincing.

Just before bedtime, Cleo appeared in Solomon's room, took him by the hand, and led him out onto the balcony.

"We have to trust in what the Seer is planning," said Cleo. "It's worked so far, and it's helped us all."

"Not if it's going to put you in —"

"I think that somehow, deep down in his unusual way, he believes in a world of entertainment that is more than just amusement, more than diversion from what really matters, something that's the opposite of Coop, the opposite of America the way it is now. Our troupe is about respect and friendship, sharing, instead of money and acclaim. We are about flying. *All* of us flying."

"And a damn good show too, though," said Solomon. "He understands the power of entertainment, really understands it like no one else — how it can be the most powerful thing in the world! That scares me sometimes. I wonder what he'd do, how far he'd go, just for a sensation, just for his art. You've seen that look in his eye."

Cleo didn't say anything for a while. "I believe that, in the end, he will do the right thing."

"Well," said Solomon, "I guess we'll see."

Cleo took him into her arms and hugged him.

The next morning, they all did the same as the previous day. The Seer and Napoleon worked on the catapult with J.S. and Geronimo riding shotgun, and the rest went into L.A. for a final day of promotion. Their little leader assured them that Booth, Pawn, and Moseley would not bother them anymore.

As the eight left, they met a young man and woman on the front lawn not far from the catapult. He had set up a big camera on a tripod, its body about the size of a barrel and its stilt-like legs holding it up to his eye level. He was turning the film with a crank and making it work, trained on the woman, a very blonde young lady wearing a striped bathing suit, her eyebrows painted on. He introduced himself as a Mr. Senate and his actress as Miss Pickman. He ran a company called Eyescope in New York but had moved his business here, making moving pictures, from cowboy tales to slapstick comedies and romances. He said he was looking forward to their show and intended to film it.

Their second day in the city went well. They could sense the growing interest in their show and their unique way of promoting it. The only disturbing moment came when a line of big men in dark clothes watched their last turn in the front row of the crowd. They observed without applauding or saying a single word. Zara's return from the dead, even Aida's alluring presence, couldn't wipe the blank looks from their faces. Word was whispered that these were Coop's men.

Then, as the eight friends made their way home on the streetcar (the Simian Houdini disguised under his blanket), they heard a passenger whisper something to another, and it made the blood run cold in Solomon's veins.

"They say Coop himself is arriving tonight."

And so, the devil had come, half a day early, the night before their great show.

Solomon didn't tell the Seer what he had heard until after they finished supper and were in the middle of their rehearsal. The Seer had met the moving-picture maker, was intrigued by his interest in filming their show, and had asked him to get started immediately, testing things out during rehearsals. The man cranked away as they worked, the Seer letting him know exactly how he wanted it done.

They still didn't try Napoleon's act or the human catapult, though Solomon had seen watermelons smashed to smithereens lying on the ground on the other side of the hotel. These melons, there was no doubt, had been his experimental flying women. The size of human skulls, they had missed the top of the building and struck the rocks on the far edge of the back lawn.

The minute Solomon mentioned Coop's imminent arrival, the Seer's face turned grave, and he halted the rehearsal. He turned and headed into the hotel and didn't say another word all evening.

It was difficult for any of them to get to sleep that night. Solomon had given Cleo a hug before they went to bed and had actually almost kissed her. She knew how he was feeling. She hugged him back and pressed her cheek to his. "It will be all right, Solo," she said softly. "We will do the show and make the money we all need. You can send most of your part back to your family. I will be safe, I promise you. Then we will get out of here. We will get away from Coop … somehow." She seemed awfully sad and that scared him. He wondered, even if all did go well, what he would do. Would he stay with the Seer, with Cleo? Or was his place back home?

The Seer woke Solomon Hunt just past midnight. He was fully dressed. He put his finger to his lips to keep his friend quiet. Geronimo Jones, who kept a small, loaded pistol concealed in a trouser pocket for emergencies, was asleep in the other bed. As Solomon rose, he saw the Seer silently pick the pistol from the sharpshooter's sleeping form then slip it into one of his own trouser pockets. Then he motioned for Solomon to follow him.

The North Britain boy's heart was racing as the two of them walked out into the warm night, the moon full above them, the sky and air so clear that they hardly seemed to exist. Solomon couldn't imagine there had ever been even a wisp of fog in Hollywood or L.A.; only the pollution of a million motorized vehicles, or the end of the world, could ever cause that to happen. The sunshine had been spectacular ever since they arrived.

The pair headed for the city. They didn't say one word to each other all the way there. The Seer seemed to know exactly where he was going.

They walked into the downtown area and before long arrived at the beautiful steam train station, looking like a classical Greek stone edifice among all the shiny new American Empire structures. But the Seer didn't take them through the big iron front doors. Instead, they went around the building and emerged on the far side on the tracks. Out in front of them sat a train with a long line of cars, maybe thirty, all told. It was unlike the other steam trains in the yard. It was painted all the colors of the rainbow. Lions and tigers and elephants and leopards leaped across its surface — there was a strongman too and a beautiful flying trapeze artist barely wearing anything. And all along the top of every car were the words, emblazoned in pink under double-edged swords: "*LEOPOLD J. COOP, THE GREATEST SHOW IN THE UNIVERSE!*"

Now Solomon's heart was really pounding. But he didn't say anything and stuck with the Seer. The little fellow's face was grim, his eyes narrowed to slits. He shoved the tiny pistol down lower in his pocket to disguise it. How in the world were they going to do this? Could they simply march right into Coop's luxurious car and finish him? Maybe, if they were lucky, he would be asleep. Solomon couldn't believe that he was about to assist in a murder. But he also knew who they were killing — an evil man who he was sure had done terrible things to his precious friend and most probably to many others too. A man who might hold the future of America in his hands.

Coop's car was at the very end of the steam train. The sight of it scared Solomon even more than he had anticipated because all the lights were on inside. In fact, he could see a white cowboy hat in there, its brim sparkling with diamonds, and the back of a long, white-haired head above a flashy buckskin jacket. It was *him*! The wizard of entertainment, the monarch of diversions in the American Empire!

They could see other people milling about inside, three or four big men dressed in dark clothes, and a young woman, blonde and heavily madeup, scantily clad in a spangled extravaganza dress, cut low on her ample chest.

Then the Seer surprised his friend, as always.

He didn't fire his gun through the window where Coop's lizard-head was clearly visible; he didn't slide up stealthily to the door, put his fingers to his lips, and engineer some clever maneuver to get inside undetected. No, he just grimly marched up the car's steps with Solomon close on his heels, grabbed the handle, flung open the door, and stepped inside. The North Britain boy entered behind him.

The room looked like something one might see in the finest hotel in America. There was a chandelier hanging from the ceiling, beautiful oak tables and chairs, and a settee upon which Coop was lounging. It looked like it might have been made for a sheik. Next to it was a mahogany desk to suit a king, with a gold-encrusted telephone machine on top. The rest of the room was decorated in silver and purple. "*Entertainment is Everything! Diversions are Life!*" read an electrified sign over the largest of the three portraits of Coop. Solomon saw a water closet at the back ... and guessed that the toilet seat inside was made of gold too. At first, the room was filled with conversation, punctuated with curses. But then Coop saw the Seer and silence reigned.

Once again, the Seer did the unexpected. From behind his back, he slipped the Simian Houdini's extra set of handcuffs out from a back pocket where he had been concealing them. He secretly slapped one end over his wrist and the other over one of Solomon's. He dropped his head down, as if defeated.

"Uh," he said sadly.

"Well, well!" cried Coop, springing to his feet. His head was wide at the top but tapered to a knife-sharp chin, his eyes were the shape of almonds, his skin very white and dry and pasty. The bone in his skull seemed thin. His long hair, looking as if it had been combed a thousand times, backward and forward to cover bald spots, appeared orange near the top and as white as snow as it hung down below his shoulders. He had what folks in North Britain called a "heavy" American accent. In other words, a voice that was strong and loud. For a moment, he said nothing else. He simply glowed at the Seer. It was an ugly, needy look. It gave Solomon the shivers. Coop tapped his long, spidery fingers together.

"Who is it, Leo?" asked the girl in a girly voice. She looked about eighteen years old or maybe younger.

"It's HIM, boss!" shouted one of his henchmen.

"Yes, it is, indeed." The lizard-like showman turned to Solomon. "Coop has nothing but the utmost gratitude to offer you, sir, whoever you are."

"What is so important about *him?*" The girl pouted. "Why he's just a little, wee —"

"Shut up, Clara!" snapped Coop.

"I … I am Solomon Hunt."

"Coop would not have thought of a mere boy bringing in his little treasure." The showman smiled. "Coop would have thought that those imbeciles Booth and Pawn might have done the trick for us … unintentionally, that is!" He turned and grinned at a couple of his hulking men. Solomon noticed they had bloodied knuckles, freshly ripped open. And for the first time he could see holstered pistols under their black suitcoats. "We always figured that tracking *them* was the best way to retrieve our dear little boy. But they messed up in the end. They are feeding the fishies and thus cannot collect. But you, my excellent young man, you have brought our tiny thing to Coop without any fuss, saving us untold unpleasantness ..." He glowed at Solomon. It almost turned the boy's stomach. "Get out the strongbox, Two."

"I'm bored," whimpered the girl. Coop reached out and slapped her hard across the face. She fell to the floor, crying.

The biggest henchman unlocked a cupboard and brought forth a big metal box.

"Count it out."

"No," said Solomon. The Seer pulled hard on the handcuffs, hurting his friend's wrists.

"Do not be shy, Master Hunt," said Coop. "You deserve this. Coop is not sure how you, a mere child, who looks like you are not even in the profession, came to know of the ransom we were offering for my secret weapon, but you did and that is all that matters. Since Coop, who is the greatest of the great showmen, keeps his promises and has an undying sense of honor ... you shall be rewarded what you deserve. Two?"

The henchman got out a huge stack of banknotes and began counting them off, licking his fingers as he did. They were all $1,000 Douglas bills! Solomon had never seen even one before, not even in a photo-picture. The henchman plucked out one hundred ... *one hundred thousand dollars*!

"No," Solomon said again.

Another henchman approached the two friends, deftly undid the handcuffs, slammed them and the money into Solomon's hands, and roughly carried the Seer over to Coop. The famous showman ran his palm down the Seer's cheek to his lips and smiled at him. "Hello, no one," he purred. The Seer looked terrified and then resigned — his remarkable violet eyes went dead. On the wall up above, Solomon noticed a big glass jar, much like the one his little friend had carried across America for performances.

"NO!!" Solomon yelled.

But the henchman seized him.

"Boy!" cried Coop. "Do NOT give us grief. I know you are embarrassed to be receiving such a motherlode, such an honor, from the great Coop. Money will buy anything and this has bought you. Not one more word!" He turned to his henchman. "Throw him out!"

The boy was flung down the stairs of the steam train and onto the hard ground. When he leapt up to rush back, one of the men stood at the top of the stairs, his pistol trained on him. He was the oldest of Coop's goons. Solomon could see the lines in his face, the streaks of gray in his hair. He seemed a little different from the others — there was less hardness in his eyes, and he actually looked reluctant to shoot. But another bigger and younger henchman advanced past him, carrying a crowbar, coming right at the boy. His boots clanked on the iron stairs. Solomon picked himself up and ran. He felt enormous shame, but he had no choice.

The Seer had sacrificed himself for his friend, for his friend's family, and for everyone in the troupe. Solomon ran as hard as he could out of Los Angeles, tears rolling down his face, the money clutched in his hands, imagining what they were doing to his little friend.

Solomon Hunt and the Seer had come to the end of the rainbow ... and the little man had delivered what he said he would. The North Britain boy had $100,000 ... the treasure from the map.

CHAPTER TWENTY-EIGHT
THE SHOW MUST GO ON

Solomon stopped halfway to Hollywood and slumped to the ground in a daze. It was an hour or two before he rose and several more before he got to the hotel. He sat on the porch in one of the big basket chairs waiting for the sun to rise, unable to sleep. Was the Seer *really* gone? Was there any way to get him back?

There were many tears when he told the others; even big Angus wept. But J.S. and Geronimo were defiant. They started discussing a plan to free their friend. Solomon stopped them.

"Who knows where they have taken him by now?" he reasoned. "Scaring off Booth and his cohorts was one thing, penetrating Coop's inner sanctum and stealing back his prize possession is another. He is the world's most powerful showman and one of its most powerful people … he will do *anything* to keep his secret weapon!"

"But —" began Geronimo.

"He's right," said Cleo, wiping her face.

"And besides," Solomon said sadly, "this is what the Seer wanted. This was his plan ever since Denver City. And the last part of it doesn't involve any of us losing our lives on his behalf. I was in that room with Coop. I could tell what he and his people are capable of. They disposed of Booth, Pawn, and Moseley, just like that! It took them no time at all. Do you think the Seer wants Coop to do that to us?"

J.S. and Geronimo grumbled that it wasn't right, the eleven of them sitting around while their friend was held prisoner.

"Then," said Cleo, "let's not sit around."

"What do you mean?" asked Ayesha.

"Let's do the show. That's what the Seer would want. That's what he was planning. … the show must go on!"

"That's right," agreed Angus.

"Look!" shouted Napoleon. He was gazing down the hotel walkway past the gate to the street and beyond. Though the sun was barely up in the sky, the first streetcar from Los Angeles was depositing an overflow crowd of passengers. They were heading in the direction of the hotel.

By noon there must have been ten thousand people gathered around the grounds, on the porches drinking, in the restaurant eating, booking rooms so they could watch from balconies, and growing more and more excited about what they were about to see. They had walked and come by streetcar in great mobs. An entire regiment of policemen, half of the L.A. force it seemed, had made their way here too, likely as interested in seeing the performance as in keeping the peace.

And so, it began.

CHAPTER TWENTY-NINE
SHOW

Just as the Seer had insisted, they made their spectators wait until late in the day, until the sun was almost setting, creating a sort of glow on the peach-colored exterior of the hotel. The electric lights on the building and upon its grounds added to the eerie atmosphere. They kept the crowds waiting and waiting: anticipation reached a fever pitch. The people started chanting, calling for the show.

Suddenly, a blind, mixed-race boy appeared in a spotlight on the flat stretch of roof between the two turrets. This would be their elevated stage. A rooftop musical performance was an inspired idea on its own, but this was unlike any other that anyone had ever seen. Napoleon had remembered what Nikola Tesla had taught him — wires ran to a little stand in front of the performer, upon which sat a disc the size of a plate. Somehow, using electricity, he had amplified both Robert Elvis McTell's voice and guitar!

Robert crunched out chords, slashing his fingernails across the strings, playing faster than the beat of the human heart and supernaturally loud. The sound boomed off the hotel and echoed around Hollywood, drawing the first of many roars from the crowd. No one had ever heard such a sound. "Welcome to the Hotel Hollywood!" he shouted. Then he chanted lyrics to the pounding beat, short fast, rhyming words about freedom, human worth, and identity.

He stopped abruptly, his sound still reverberating around the grounds.

The lights went out on the roof.

Below him, on the grass, a dim glow lit three men, or two men and a woman — the latter's gender wasn't clear — Napoloeon, Geronimo, and J.S. — bearing spade shovels and digging in the big garden near the front entrance, no more than fifty feet from the front of the crowd pressing against the fence. The three of them looked to be excavating a grave. There was silence as they worked. Out from behind them stepped Ayesha, dressed in white, her face made up in the ghostly powder and paint Aida had applied. She looked as if she had come from another, even darker world. On her arms and shoulders sat the ravens. She whispered to them, and they ascended above the grave and out over the audience, some swooping over the packed balconies in the hotel.

Up above on the roof, Aida and Cleo unfurled half a dozen white bedsheets stitched together. On the grounds, the filmmaker switched on his projector, sending a beam of light up at the sheets. Soon an image of a countdown appeared on the homemade screen, flashing from number ten down to one. The ravens began cawing and then calling out. "*Death!*" they cried. "*She is dead!*" "*She shall never return!*"

"*SHE IS NO ONE NOW!*" "*Nevermore!*"

Both up on the screen and in the grave being dug on the ground, a body was unearthed. It was Zara Patel Chaplin, stiff and absolutely still, a frozen corpse. The three gravediggers lifted her into the air (Napoleon secretly slipping her breathing straw from her mouth) and held her aloft. She had been stripped to her undershirt. On the screen, the audience could see her stilled chest. There was no heartbeat inside.

Ayesha wailed and the ravens cried out. The audience recoiled in horror and dead silence reigned for more than a minute. *But then Zara sat bolt upright! And sprung back to life!* The others tossed her into the air, and she alighted onto her feet. Geronimo Jones turned to the roof, and as the film finished, fired bullet-hole words into the sheets.

"*LIVE!*" it read. "*BE SOMEONE!*"

The crowd erupted.

But they didn't have time to gather themselves. As the screen was dropped, an eight-foot-tall man appeared where it had been, bearing a human head inside a jar.

Aida and Cleo stepped to the side and lifted a new set of sheets between them.

Solomon did his act to the thundering beat of Robert Elvis's guitar, played on all the lower strings, his rise from inside the glass projected on the screen for all to see in gigantic size. He had never done it better and when he arose, no longer a face in a jar but a full-sized boy, and Robert shouted, "SOLOMON HUNT!" ... he felt like "*someone*" indeed!

The show kept moving.

Aida stepped to the edge of the stage, doffed her dress to reveal her tight, pink undergarments, cut low at the chest, bare legs and high-heeled boots beneath, and a roar came up from the crowd. She glared at them. The giant immediately tied her to a rope and lowered her five stories to the ground, her form caught in a spotlight.

"Ladies and gentlemen!" cried Angus up above in his huge voice. "The heavyweight champion of the world!" Aida turned and swayed her hips as she walked up to the porch where the champ was sitting in a big basket chair, reserved for him, filling it with his muscular frame, a black top hat on his head, dressed in a black suit with white shirt and cravat that almost burst from his size. His black mustache was groomed and his black eyes glowed as Aida took him by his sausage-like fingers and led him down the steps to the grounds. As she did, she sang to him, her voice somehow amplified and extraordinary. She purred and curled about him, wrapping her legs across his midsection, her arms around his shoulders, but then gently pushed him away each time he tried to hold her. She sang of a "big, strong man and a shy young lass" who "wanted a role in his life, the role of his wife." Unable to resist her charms, the great Jack C. Keaton finally succumbed — he reached out and seized her in his powerful arms. He kissed her full on the lips to the shouts of the spectators, who cried out their pleasure en masse.

The gorgeous Aida struggled to pull herself away.

But then …

John … or Joan Sullivan Chan came racing to her defense. Doing a flip off the porch, he or she landed next to the couple in her dress and boots, his long hair flowing under her bonnet … and thudded a fist on the big man's shoulder. Keaton turned, looked down at her, and laughed. The crowd laughed too. But instantly, they were silenced … because J.S. Chan slapped the champ so hard in the face that the smack resounded throughout the grounds. It was obvious that it wasn't fake. The great man, stunned at first, tried to laugh, but Chan reared up and thundered a kick to his stomach, sending him into a heap on the ground. Jack C. Keaton rose to his feet, his face turning red. A murmur went through the masses. He pulled off his coat, undid his shirt and cravat, and tore them off. He stood before the crowd bare-chested, his muscles on display, drawing more murmurs from the spectators. He raised his fists into fighting position. The champ wasn't fooling.

Up above, Robert Elvis began to play. And for the next few minutes the heavyweight champion of the world swung his meaty fists at J.S. Chan, thundering punches that had knocked cold the greatest pugilists on earth … and never once connected. Every now and then, Chan would counter, striking him cleanly with punishing blows that resounded like gunshots in the night air and made the audience gasp, amplified as they were by the speakers. At the end, when Chan fled up the porch steps and into the hotel, the champion staggered after her … or him … little spirit left for a fight, making an (unintentionally) hilarious exit that had the crowd in stitches.

Immediately, the mood changed. Up on the roof, Cleo now appeared with Angus, and then, to the sounds of Robert Elvis playing a sort of waltz, they moved up and down the side of the hotel, enacting a unique acrobatic performance that was both stunning and beautiful, the elegant young woman and the gigantic young man, who looked all of his eight feet now, a revelation to the spectators. And when it ended, Angus again lowered a figure with a rope from the roof, a figure in a straitjacket, hanging upside down. The Simian Houdini then escaped not just from the jacket, but also from the handcuffs and the chains on his hands and feet. When he was done, he was raised back to the roof, where, to great applause, his amplified voice grunted, "Thank you … thank you, very much!"

But then the moment came that Solomon had feared for so long. The catapult was lit by a spotlight at far end of the grounds and Zara and Geronimo turned it toward the hotel. The North Britain boy had been watching from the roof, enraptured by what they were doing, forgetting what came next. Cleo was suddenly on the ground, advancing toward the machine. Robert Elvis was playing an ominous beat, like the sound of a pounding funeral drum.

"No!" Solomon cried out. He had lost the Seer and now he was to going lose Cleo too. He raced from the roof and down into the hotel. Outside he could hear Zara announcing the act. "The Flying Woman will now be 'urled by this medieval weapon of war to the five-story roof of the 'otel 'ollywood!" He could hear the audience gasping.

What was the point of all of this, of each of them being free, of the Seer's sacrifice, if Cleo's life was lost? Solomon would rather live back in the north, a "no one" as his father had called him, and keep her with him there, a "no one" like him, than do these spectacular things, praised and applauded to the sky ... and have her crippled or worse.

He raced down one flight of stairs, then another, then another. How could the Seer have planned this? Solomon hated him now.

When he emerged onto the lawn, she was being strapped to the deadly machine.

"NO!" he shouted as loudly as he could.

But Cleopatra wouldn't do the act that night, nor would she ever.

Out from the crowd, the outline of his pistol evident in his little pocket and his violet eyes on fire ... strode the Seer.

CHAPTER THIRTY
FLYING

The Seer had a big smile on his face. The first one Solomon had seen there since he saw that article in the *Denver Pioneer Post.* Their leader motioned for Cleo to get down from the catapult. Thrilled to see him, almost forgetting that she was on stage, she moved to embrace him. But he stepped away from her ... and ascended the terrifying machine! The audience was buzzing.

He strapped himself in and nodded to Zara Patel Chaplin, who didn't move.

"UH!!" shouted the Seer. So ... Zara released the lever. Up the fugitive shot, straight into the air. Solomon watched his angle of ascension, holding his hands together in prayer. Up and farther up went the Seer, sailing toward the roof of the Hotel Hollywood. Way up there on the edge looking down, his arms stretched wide, stood the giant.

The audience held their breath. Silence fell over Hollywood.

The Seer hit his apex and then began to descend. It looked for an instant as if he had been shot too far, that he would be smashed liked those watermelons on the hard ground on the far side of the hotel. But Angus reached up, impossibly high, and as his friend rocketed over him, he caught him in welcoming arms.

The crowd erupted again.

But they didn't have time to breath, for another boy now appeared beside the others on the roof. He was wearing his wings. They glowed pale white in the spotlight in the night above the peach-colored hotel. Solomon could see, from where he stood below, that Napoleon's legs were shaking.

"No," said Solomon.

The crowd grew silent again. They could sense Napoleon's fear and feel that it was real. Solomon was certain that at this point someone was supposed to say … "THE FLYING MAN!!" and Robert Elvis was supposed to play ominous music.

But no one spoke and no sound was heard.

Then he leapt.

Out off the roof he went, straight out at first, wobbling … then flying! He flew as surely as the Seer's paper flying machine had flown in the Buffalo train station.

The Seer was jumping up and down and clapping his hands.

It was apparent that Napoleon was supposed to fly over the lawn and immediately descend. But once he was halfway across, the young man actually soared higher and sailed out over the audience. They stared up at him in awe as he made a steep turn, swooped over them again, and landed gently on his feet near the catapult.

The crowd began to clap and roar and just kept roaring.

It was time for their group bow, but when they looked to the Seer, they could see that he wasn't going to take even a moment for that. Solomon saw him pointing into the crowd. There, struggling to push their way through the mob to the front, were Coop and his black-coated henchmen.

The Seer turned with Angus and raced down the stairs into the hotel. The rest of the troupe left the lawn on the fly too, running toward the building, Napoleon struggling out of his wings and carrying them as he moved. They all met inside. As soon as Solomon saw the Seer, he picked him up in his arms and hugged him.

The others surrounded him, the girls and J.S. and Napoleon burying him in kisses.

"How did you get away?" Solomon asked.

The Seer took his gun from his pocket and stuck it into his friend's ribs and then held his hands up in the air like a man under arrest. Geronimo noticed that it was his stolen pistol and smiled.

"*That's* why you brought the weapon!" Solomon cried, realizing that the little fellow had never revealed it or given it up inside Coop's train car. "Not to shoot him, but to escape after?"

The Seer nodded excitedly.

"You *made* them give us the money … and then you got away too!"

He nodded again, his face resplendent.

Solomon remembered all the pacing the little man had done on their way to California, all the figuring, and he imagined him in the tight confines of Coop's apartment, his gun driven into the hideous showman's ribs at the opportune moment. The old man would have done anything, even allow his precious Seer to get away, to save his own skin. The North Britain boy recalled how fast his friend could run, especially if he had a head start. And even after Coop and his men had pursued him and gotten to the hotel grounds, they were stuck in the huge Hollywood crowd, unable to get at him while he ascended the catapult.

The Seer didn't want to linger for another second. He pointed to the back entrance, and they all rushed toward it. They *had* to move quickly. Solomon noticed that the Seer had picked up the jar and was clutching it to his little chest as he scurried forward. They didn't bother to ask Mrs. Flynn for their gate money. She could keep it all. The troupe still had their treasure — the $100,000 in Solomon's pocket!

Angus slammed the big back door shut and bolted it from the outside. Both the door and the bolt were thick, and it looked like it could hold in an elephant. The twelve friends raced into the backyard, which wasn't nearly as spacious as the front, the ravens up above. A narrow street ended at its edge. But standing there, blocking the way through the back gate, with his legs wide apart and gun pointed at their little leader, was one of Coop's henchman! Like lightning, Geronimo raised his own pistol and fired. But all they heard was a click. He had used all his bullets during the show! The Seer still had Geronimo's pistol, but he knew not to raise it against such a deadly enemy, who already had him in his sights and could then kill his friends.

"Stop right there!" shouted the man.

Then Solomon noticed who it was — it was the older henchman, the one with the lines in his face, the gray in his hair, and the slightly softer look in his eyes. He lowered his gun.

"I just want you to listen to me … then I'll let you go."

They couldn't believe their ears.

"There are things that need to be said …" He paused. "I have been with Mr. Coop for forty years. I have seen him do some terrible things, but none more horrible than what he did to Master Seer."

The little person looked up at him, tears welling in his eyes.

"He kept your friend confined from the day he was born, never let him out of his sight, and never allowed him to leave our train, our trailer, or hotel room ... except to do his job."

The Seer's chin dropped to his chest.

"All this boy ever heard, all he ever saw, and all he ever knew was show business: it wasn't just in his mind but in his soul. He had no friends, and he couldn't speak; Coop never taught him *anything*. But the Seer knew what would work on a stage, what would charm an audience, how to make any act better ... *much* better. It began when he was a baby: when he would react to things performers would do while trying to impress Coop in the master trailer. The things the little one responded to always turned out to be the magic things, the moves, the illusions, and the ideas that really thrilled our crowds. From the moment he could see, he had been watching, taking everything in. From his place in Coop's inner circle, he not only saw performers, but heard the American Empire's greatest showmen discussing talent and plotting the best way to entertain. I guess he came to understand humanity's need for amusements; to know our imagination. It became his only language. He *knew* like no one else."

The Seer silently nodded his head.

They could hear voices inside the back door now.

"I think it shocked the boss when he started to see what the child could do. Leopold J. Coop isn't a religious man, but he told me once that he thought the boy had been sent to him by God, that this was God's gift in exchange for Coop's soul. The old man continued to keep him away from others. He took him to auditions in the Big Top but kept him under a tarp, holes cut in it for his eyes. Only Coop's closest associates even knew what the boy looked like, though there were rumors in the business. He went everywhere with us — to New York, Buffalo, Chicago Town, St. Louis, New Orleans, Denver City, and even San Francisco. He saw all the acts in the Empire and by the age of seven, it was really him who was guiding Coop's show … and that show became a sensation. The company grew wealthy beyond compare. The human cannonball was the little one's idea and the five-ring extravaganza and many other things, like the creation of a giant acrobat and other acts the crowd saw tonight." The henchman paused. "God, or Satan, gave us the Seer."

"It was God," said Cleo firmly.

Now they were hearing thuds on the back door. Someone was trying to break it down!

The Seer was looking away, clutching the jar tightly. The others wanted to run. But there was something else Solomon needed to know.

"You said Coop had him from birth. Is he his father?"

"Uh!" cried the Seer with repulsion.

The man paused. "… Do you know what a punk is?"

The Seer hugged his jar.

"Yes," Solomon said quietly. He remembered the babies on display in Booth's horrible show in York.

"Most punks are fake babies … fake dead babies in formaldehyde jars."

"Uh," sobbed the Seer.

"But Coop bought one about eighteen years ago from a sideshow supplier and when he took it home … it shocked him.

"Why?"

"Because the baby inside the jar … was still alive."

Solomon couldn't help turning to his little friend, whose head was straight down.

The cracks and thuds on the door were becoming thunderous.

"Every night Coop put him back in that jar to sleep," said the henchman. "And that's where he always spent his nights, a living display, a living entertainment. I remember seeing him in there, staring out. The only thing the old man ever gave him was pens and paper, so every night he would draw. He learned to picture life like Toulouse-Lautrec himself. He drew the acts, how they were and how they might be, and spectacular new ones that never had been. Acts that have put Coop on the verge of taking the very helm of the American Empire."

Solomon looked back and saw the tip of an axe blade break through the door, followed by the business end of a big rounders bat. But he stayed riveted to his spot — he wanted to hear more.

"The boy never grew much," said the henchman sadly, regarding the Seer. "He can still fit into that jar. In fact, he slept there until six months ago when Booth and Pawn stole him away. They have paid dearly for that crime."

The door was now coming off its hinges.

"I … I am deeply sorry," said the henchman. "Coop took me on as a youth and was a father to me, so I did as he said. He never named any of us. He called us One or Two or Three. It was his inner circle who called the little one 'the Seer,' not him. And that name became a sort of code word for Coop's genius in the entertainment world, for his secret to success. But the old man always called the little one by a different name."

They could hear Coop's voice now, screaming on the other side of the door.

"What name was that?" asked Cleo.

"He called him ... *No One*."

Solomon remembered hearing Coop say that very thing to the Seer last night when he creepily took him into his arms. But it had never occurred to him that that was his name.

"That wasn't right," said the man sadly, wiping a tear from his eye. "When I looked into the little fellow's eyes last night, I felt ashamed about everything. And when I saw your show tonight, the joy you all took in it, that boy flying through the air, the smile on the Seer's face — I had never seen him like that before — I knew I had to do something. Everyone needs to be allowed to be someone. Everyone."

They could hear Coop even clearer now, through the big holes punched in the door and the space between the hinges and the walls. The entrance was about to come down,

"Then, let us go!" Solomon said crossly.

The elder henchman stepped out of the way. "Don't stay in Los Angeles. Go to the docks, get on a boat, and sail away, anywhere. Go to the Australian Continent, or to the European Empire or the Kingdom of England. I'm sure that's what the Seer is thinking anyway."

"Why would we do that?" asked Cleo. "Coop will just follow us."

"He has never left the American Empire. He knows nothing about any other place. He doesn't need to. He has never set foot on a boat, and he won't now. Who knows? He may be afraid of water."

The Seer actually grinned.

"He will be livid. If he doesn't have the Seer, I don't think he'll ever be president. It will put a dent in his world, maybe in America as we know it too."

The Seer grinned again.

"I'll tell the old man that you've fled south."

A few hours later, the twelve friends were at the Los Angeles docks. They found a ship for the Australian Continent within an hour, its departure time just an hour after that. But Solomon wasn't happy. Their troupe *had* to leave America, there was no question. Far over the water, the group could start life together, free and unpursued, gaining a good living daily with their extraordinary talents, Coop's power declining in America without his Seer. But Solomon couldn't go with them. He knew that. Cleo must have known it too, for she became quiet and stayed that way until it was time to depart.

The others boarded, walking up the plank with smiles, not noticing that Solomon didn't follow. Only Cleo, guiding Robert Elvis by the arm, and the Seer, stayed behind.

Solomon didn't want this to end. He didn't want to return to reality. During the last few months, he had lived a life like those in the adventures in his satchel. A world filled with nothing but diversions. A world filled with friendship and respect too. It had been irresistible.

"Come with me, Solo," cried Cleo suddenly, putting her arms around him. "You can send money home to your family at our first port of call. I will give you some of my share for them too."

"I can't leave," said the North Britain boy. "Not now. I can't desert them, you know that … I have to go home. But you, Miss Cleopatra, are finally free." He tried to smile.

Solomon had been imagining what their life together might be like as they waited for that boat too. A white boy and a Black girl would be treated badly in America and not much better anywhere else. Solomon would always be *just* her friend. He couldn't stand that.

Without warning, Cleo kissed him full on the lips in the middle of the crowd that was milling about on the dock. They lingered in each other's arms.

"Disgusting!" cried a white woman, glaring at them.

"Shut your mouth!" answered Robert Elvis McTell. "THAT is the way it should be!"

Then Cleo, with tears in her eyes, pulled herself away and took Robert up the plank, not daring to look back.

Only the Seer remained. He still clutched the jar. Solomon handed his friend the bundle of money, that treasure so cleverly won, which would set up the troupe forever, only keeping a single $1,000 bill. The little fellow took the thick stack and shoved it into his pocket, then set down the jar and brought out his pen and paper. He drew a picture of Solomon, appearing exceedingly handsome (much more so than he really was) and beside him a smaller boy who looked like Solomon and a little girl who was similar too; and next to them a mother … who somehow was *exactly* like the widow Mrs. Hunt. He took the money back out of his pocket, peeled off $20,000 more, enough for the North Britain boy's family and their farm to survive forever with Solomon and his mother's guidance, and handed it to his friend. When the boy tried to refuse, the little man looked angry and jammed the pile into his old companion's pocket. Then he took Solomon by both hands, squeezed them, and looked into his eyes. He opened his mouth and struggled.

The Seer was trying to speak.

His lips were forming the words "thank you" … but he couldn't make a sound. So, he looked closer into Solomon's eyes and concentrated. "*Love,*" he said clearly. Then he picked up his jar, turned around, and ran up the plank to the boat. On deck, Solomon saw him hold up his jar … and pitch it as far as he could into the ocean.

CHAPTER THIRTY-ONE
HOME

Solomon Hunt took the steam train home. He went a different way, to see the sights, traveling north through the states of Oregon and Washington and New Columbia. In the burgeoning American coastal town of Vancouver, its buildings built right out into the water, the smoke billowing in the air, passenger balloons flying in the rain, and folks not very friendly to North Britons, he switched steam trains and went east across the Rocky Mountains, through the states of Alberta and Saskatchewan and Manitoba. It was October and getting cold, the snow just over the horizon. Solomon wondered, as he traveled through this awe-inspiring land, with a sky as big as the universe but its space jam-packed full of buildings and wealth and poverty and crime and so many houses of entertainment, and news dailies bulging with red page sections, what it might have been like if North Britain had held on to this area long ago when there was a possibility that the little country might have gone from east coast to west too. But it wasn't to be. The Empire of America was all consuming.

When Solomon arrived in York, he got out and kissed the ground. The city didn't seem as big and scary as it had a few months ago. It appeared friendly and felt like home. He noticed poor folks in the street, and struggling First Inhabitants, people who hadn't been treated right, both now and in the past. His country wasn't perfect, no place was, in fact it had a long way to go to be even close … like all homes, he supposed. But when the boy reached the family farm, he got onto his knees and grasped the cold soil in his hands.

In the kitchen, he clutched his mother and brother and sister in his arms and wouldn't let them go. They all held tight to each other until everyone felt weak.

And then Solomon handed his mother his treasure, the Seer's treasure. The joy on her face was the greatest applause Solomon Hunt had ever heard. His father had been wrong. He was, finally, *someone.*

And so, he began to play the role that was destined for him.

But often, when he should have been tending to the fields, he would instead go upstairs and read his adventure books, imagine what could be, and then look out the window, southward toward the city and America and beyond. At those moments, he thought of Cleo; of Napoleon and Angus and Geronimo and J.S. Chan and Ayesha and the ravens; of Aida and Robert Elvis McTell and Zara Patel Chaplin and even the Simian Houdini. And of course, he thought of the Seer.

Every day, he thought of the Seer.

ACKNOWLEDGEMENTS

I conceived the idea for this novel more than a decade ago, and yet, somehow, it seems to fit our world now. Time, it appears, doesn't change much about human beings, nor about certain countries. What is topical now seems to have been so a decade ago, even a century ago, and even in an imagined world. One hopes for a community where everyone is accepted for who they are, and money and power and the amusement of ourselves are not gods; a place where true art and kindness are valued. We can only keep hoping.

First and foremost, I want to thank DCB Young Readers and especially Barry Jowett, who supported this sometimes daring and tricky story from the beginning and guided it through the initial editing. Gillian Rogerson then gave it an excellent copy-edit. Thanks also to Sarah Jensen, Marc Côté, Fei Dong, Marijke Friesen, and Sarah Cooper at Cormorant/DCB.

I also want to thank my agent, Pamela Paul, who has been so supportive of my work over the years. I will miss my ally in literature and business, though I still have her as a friend. This seems a fitting novel for us to end the business part of our work together.

And (almost) finally I want to thank The Great Farini, William Hunt, likely not the greatest personality in Canadian history, but undoubtedly the most amazing. The years I spent at the beginning of my writing career researching and writing the story of his extraordinary life in the circus and allied arts helped me gain the knowledge I needed to write this novel. It allowed me to understand a fascinating world.

Thanks also, of course, to my wife Sophie, and our whole family: Johanna, Hadley, Sam, Mac and Ash for their support and input.

The author respectfully acknowledges that this novel was written while he was living on land located in the traditional and treaty territory of the Michi Saagiig (Mississauga) and Chippewa Nations, collectively known as the Williams Treaties First Nations, which include Curve Lake, Hiawatha, Alderville, Scugog Island, Rama, Beausoleil, and Georgina Islands First Nations.

SHANE PEACOCK is an author, playwright, journalist, and screenwriter, published in twenty languages in eighteen countries. He has won seven Junior Library Guild of America Selection honors, two Arthur Ellis Awards, the Libris Award, the Geoffrey Bilson Award, and has been short-listed for the Governor General's Award. His young adult novels include *The Book of Us*, the acclaimed Boy Sherlock Holmes series, the Dylan Maples Adventures, and *The Dark Missions of Edgar Brim* trilogy. He is also the author of *As We Forgive Others*, the first novel in the Northern Gothic Mysteries, for adult readers. He lives in Cobourg, Ontario, with his wife, journalist Sophie Kneisel.

We acknowledge the sacred land on which Cormorant Books operates. It has been a site of human activity for 15,000 years. This land is the territory of the Huron-Wendat and Petun First Nations, the Seneca, and most recently, the Mississaugas of the Credit River. The territory was the subject of the Dish With One Spoon Wampum Belt Covenant, an agreement between the Iroquois Confederacy and Confederacy of the Ojibway and allied nations to peaceably share and steward the resources around the Great Lakes. Today, the meeting place of Toronto is still home to many Indigenous people from across Turtle Island. We are grateful to have the opportunity to work in the community, on this territory.

We are also mindful of broken covenants and the need to strive to make right with all our relations.